The Perfect Buddha's Head

Maya & Karma from 1969

THINK MORE BOOKS
Beverly Hills

The Perfect Buddha's Head

Maya & Karma
from 1969

a novel by

Anthony Lojac

THINK MORE BOOKS
Beverly Hills

This is a work of fiction. Names, characters, places and incidents either are products of the author's imagination or are used fictitiously. Any resemblance to actual events or locales or persons, living or dead is entirely coincidental.

This is a work of parody, as defined by the Fair Use Doctrine. Any similarities, without satirical intent, to copyrighted characters, or individuals living or dead, are purely coincidental.

This work is intended for adults only. Some of the content of this fiction is graphically violent and/or sexual. It is intended for readers age eighteen or over.

Publisher's Cataloging-In-Publication Data
(Prepared by The Donohue Group, Inc.)

Lojac, Anthony.
The perfect Buddha's head : Maya & Karma from 1969 / Anthony Lojac.

p. ; cm.

ISBN-13: 978-0-9818604-2-8
ISBN-10: 0-9818604-2-7

1. Young men--Fiction. 2. Love--Fiction. 3. Cults--California--Los Angeles--Fiction. 4. Philosophy, Comparative--Fiction. I. Title.

PS3562.O512 P47 2009
813/.54 2009928849

THINK MORE BOOKS
269 S. Beverly Drive #1400
Beverly Hills, CA 90212 USA
www.thinkmorebooks.com
editor@thinkmorebooks.com

My gratitude and awe go to
the ancient Greeks and Egyptians.

The people and their deities.

Their mysterious religions.

Their belief in an afterlife,
rebirth,
and redemption.

Their knowledge that love is
more powerful than death.

"All things are born of Being.
Being is born of Non-Being."

Tao

"The last enemy that shall be destroyed is death"

I Corinthians 15:26

"I know LSD; I don't need to take it anymore."

Albert Hoffman 1906-2008

Contents

1. NEW YORK CITY 13
2. BURROUGHS, BUGS, AND GUNS 22
3. WAKING UP IN 1969 29
4. LOS ANGELES 31
5. WHY ME HERE AND NOW 37
6. THE FINAL LAST SUPPER 39
7. WAI YU IN LOS ANGELES 50
8. WILLIE WALK LIKE AN EGYPTIAN 58
9. ONE MORE CITY FULL OF ANGELS 61
10. BANGKOK 82

11. ON A DARK AND NARROW PATH 93
12. ALLISON'S WONDERLAND 102
13. THE HOLY CONMAN 111
14. THE LIZARD LADY 116
15. SERIOUS GENETIC DAMAGE 130
16. WE ARE ALL PRE-PROGRAMMED TO FORGET 137
17. I AM AS I AM IN TOKYO 156
18. FROM THE UNREAL TO THE REAL 166
19. SAYAKO IN HIGH SCHOOL 181
20. SLACK AT WORK 191

21. DRESSED FOR SUCCESS 198
22. THE WAR AS IT IS 205
23. EVIL AND DESTRUCTIVE FORCES 215
24. THE DREAMER'S NIGHTMARE 221
25. SOMEONE'S INTUITION, BUT NOT MINE 234
26. MORTAL EXISTENCE 237
27. THE WHOLE TRUTH 246
28. AND NOTHING BUT THE TRUTH 253
29. TRYING TO SURVIVE MAYA 260
30. TRYING TO SURVIVE KARMA 265

31. MR. PRESIDENT 269
32. WHAT IS IT? 272
33. NOTHING HAPPENS BY CHANCE 274
34. VCK VERSUS CIA 281
35. THE BIRTH OF EVIL 285
36. THE FINAL WARNING 287
37. THE PERFECT BUDDHA'S HEAD 290
38. SOMEWHERE ONLY YOU CAN FIND ME 294
39. BORN AGAIN AND AGAIN 296

Preface

The Perfect Buddha's Head is a metaphysical story about birth, death, and re-birth, in a secret world full of mysterious and destructive forces.

It is about our Existence and our sense of Identity.

It is about our Fear and Creativity.

It is about Love.

And, it is about Time.

We need a new God, now.

09/09/09

The Perfect Buddha's Head

Maya & Karma
from 1969

1. NEW YORK CITY

An album is spinning on a turntable. There is Sitar music blasting from two massive speakers in the corners of a small dark room. One speck of light shines like a star on the tip of incense burning on a makeshift altar. A young man is sitting on a cushion, at a low table, covered with books. He is facing the altar, meditating.

The incense smoke lingers in the air and slowly weaves its way across the room.

The whispering, screaming, crying, laughing music finally climbs to a crescendo.

The young man is where he wants to be now.

He has forgotten about his possessions. The table, the cushion, the mattress. His books, albums, and a pile of clothes.

He is a hippie freak, in a typical hippie freak's room. He owns almost nothing. All he wants is the freedom of the young, and the wisdom of the old. And he is blissfully unaware of any contradiction that might entail.

He gets up and lights a few colorful handmade candles on the altar.

He picks up the album cover, *West Meets East*, and sits back down on his cushion. He stares at Ravi Shankar and Yehudi Menuhin, each sitting cross-legged, one holding a Sitar, and the other a Violin.

He looks up from the album cover to a kaleidoscopic Mandala above the altar, between his other psychedelic rock and roll posters.

His eyes are wide and getting wider.

Everything is vibrating. Everything is alive.

He understands. Energy is contained inside every single thing.

He sees himself sitting there in front of the Mandala.

He sees me.

I am that young man.

That is who I am.

I look, and I see myself living inside that Mandala.

I am warm, peaceful, exhilarated. Ready to tell you what happened.

I will tell you everything, including some things you may not want to know. But you should listen to me, because I will not lie to you. I have nothing to hide anymore.

* * *

I look back down at an open book on the table. I pick up my blue Bic medium ballpoint pen and scribble a note in the margin. Then I underline one passage and read out loud, "Don't cling to the visions. Don't flee from the wrathful deities."

I close the book slowly, staring at the title, *The Tibetan Book of the Dead.* I hold it in my right hand, and stare at the mysterious clay mountain on the cover.

I lift a purple cloth sack off the floor, and carefully slide the book down to the bottom of my shoulder bag. I pick through the other books around my table, grab Allen Ginsberg's *Planet News* and stuff that and my Bic ballpoint into the sack too.

Then I dig out some wrinkled dollar bills from my jeans pocket, and make sure they are all still there.

I get up, throw the purple sack over my shoulder, and go out. Tripping through the East Village, in the crisp autumn air, with the books on my back.

I pass by the fountain in Washington Square, and see friends hanging out, listening to the electric echoes of Bob Dylan seeming to come from every direction, just for us.

I keep walking east on West 4th heading toward MacDougal Street, singing in my best Dylan voice, "I'm ready to go anywhere, I'm ready for to fade, into my own parade, cast your dancing spell my way, I promise to go under it."

I slip nimbly through the usual crowd of winos, panhandlers, and all the other sidewalk freaks.

There is a tall, slender Black man, wearing outrageous clothes, like a pimp, or a whore, it is hard to tell the difference. He is animated and euphoric for no apparent reason. He raises his right hand to slap me a perfectly timed and graceful five as I walk by, as he squeals out at me, "*Hey, free man.*"

I slap him back five and say, "Hey Willie, what's happening?"

My bills were gone and there was a pink pill in my hand, just like magic.

Willie announces his favorite weather report, "Gonna be colder than the nipple on a witch's tit tonight bay-bee."

I ask him, "This is pure, right? No speed or anything?"

He sings like Sly Stone, "Gonna take you higher, duh duh duh duh duh duh duh duh, gonna take you higher."

"No speed or anything?"

"You ain't never gonna come down."

I take the pill, and Willie gives me a swig of his wine in a brown paper bag to wash it down.

"I'm going to the Bodhi Tree."

Willie looks at the purple sack. "Free man, you the only guy I know, takes books to the book store."

I smile. "Willie, I'm the only guy you know who *goes* to a book store."

He keeps talking, "Why don't you have any honey wit' you anyway?"

"Why don't you?" I ask back.

"I *am* the honey bay-bee, you know that. Sweeter than sugar, and that's for sure."

"This stuff is really pure right?"

Willie smiles, "You ain't never gonna come down."

I nod, shake his hand and start walking.

He says, "You be just like me from now on *free man*. High all the damn time."

I smile again, and keep walking.

I want to find the Bodhi Tree Bookstore before it gets all dark and cold outside. I walk faster, thinking of the fragrant and free, warm herbal tea. I think how good it will feel to peak out there with all the books on philosophy, metaphysics, cosmology, and the other stuff I like.

I walk a few minutes.

Then, out of nowhere, there is a hot-looking, young girl standing in my way, trying to give me a pink piece of paper.

I know it is for me because she says, "Here, this is for you," as she reaches out and lays the paper on top of my open palm.

My hand is near the end of her long blond hair. My fingers start to float up to touch her. I can almost feel the straight yellow strands of hair slide lightly across my palm.

"Wanna come to a lecture?" she asks as if we are old friends.

I am searching her eyes for any sign of earthling-type humanity, but I find none at all that I can recognize.

"Yeah. Sure, I'll go to a lecture."

"My name is Allison," she says, and asks my name.

"Genetic Freeman," I tell her.

She says she likes my big brown eyes.

I follow her down the street, into a red brick entrance, and up a flight of worn wooden stairs, to a surprisingly large and modern interior. I see neatly dressed people hurrying through the halls. Then she leads me straight into a windowless room and leaves me sitting in the front row.

A little guy drawing diagrams on the white-board turns around and starts talking. He acts like he is speaking to a full room, but I'm not sure other people are in the room behind me or not.

He explains that he will give a lecture about life, reincarnation, and immortality. But first he shows a twenty-minute film. Then he makes me look at a lot of charts and diagrams. Then, the little guy points up at the poster hanging on the wall. He deepens his voice and lengthens each syllable until he sounds like a clunky old reel-to-reel tape recorder on half-speed playback, "This, ladies and gentlemen, is...
The O-ri-gi-na-tor."

I still didn't know if there were any other ladies or gentlemen actually in the room with me. And that poster, or picture, or whatever it is, I am specifically trying to ignore that giant face. It is way too creepy for my over-sensitized nerves right now. It is freaking me out the more I have to look at it.

It is some kind of ordinary-looking White guy in a white shirt that developed all these diagrams and charts and stuff. And he is smiling, because he is king of the world in here. And now he is looking down at me like I am a subject in his world too.

Allison is waiting for me after the lecture. She escorts me into a tiny cubicle just wide enough for the two of us to sit face-to-face, with a dark wooden table between us. She smiles as we sit.

It feels good to be with her again. She smells as beautiful as she looks too. Shalimar. Man, I sure love that stuff.

But I don't know what she is going to do.

She is staring at me through dime-size black holes centered in two balls of electromagnetic white gel.

I just sit, and smile, and look at her.

"Well Genetic, did you like the lecture?"

I tell her the little guy talked about the big guy in that picture too much.

She frowns.

I feel myself perspiring.

"Ah, but it was really good" I think I hear myself say out loud. Then I just kind of stare back and listen to her talk, because I know I sound like an idiot.

She lives in the Village, by New York University. She says she came here for a party a couple of months ago with some people she met up at Woodstock.

I notice her skin is pale white and sprinkled with small silent freckles.

She says she got a handout, just like the pink one she gave me. Then she heard the lecture about Psytron and never looked back at what she was before.

Allison carefully and patiently explains what I already heard in the lecture. "Psytron means the psychology of electrons."

"Psytron Theological Technology is based on the manipulation of the electro-magnetic structure of the human aura, the physical manifestation of our humanoid souls."

"Psytron is the only way for us to get fully-conscious, personal immortality on this planet at this time."

"The Originator, through years of hard work, courage, and commitment, has not only given us immortality right here and now in our own humanoid lifetimes, but he has also identified and located the Holy Conman who has dominated Earth and plagued our universe since the beginning of time."

I am still staring. I see her cheeks are finely curved, so delicate, and ready to yield to the gentlest touch.

She says she could never be the same again. "That's what it's all about, isn't it? Spiritual transformation. For real. For yourself. And forever."

Yeah. Absolutely. I agree with her all the way.

Sure, it is expensive, she tells me. Psytron is not for the losers. It is for the elite, the dedicated, and the capable.

I giggle about those words, but she is serious.

She has money from a trust fund. She can pay for it all. But she still works for Psytron because she wants to help other people. It is our responsibility to help others. She says I can work here too and help people like she does. Psytron trainers never get paid any more than necessary for bare survival. But I can get trained for less money if I pledge to work ten years, one hundred years, or even one thousand years. I think she says that. And I can work here, like she does. I can earn my training courses while I help other people transform themselves too.

I really don't know what she is talking about anymore. I can't believe my ears. I have no idea what the psychology of electrons even means. So I am quiet. I just sit there, trying not to reveal my hallucinations, but they are growing too strong and too fast.

I miss something else she says. Maybe it is important.

Then I hear her ask, "Really, where does it all begin?"

Somehow, the conversation continues, but I am not sure I am the one talking or listening at any particular time.

I feel my destiny, or something like my destiny, trying to coexist with something like my free will, but they get all tangled up like the dusty mess of wires behind my stereo system.

I am thinking to myself, human lives can be so very much alike, yet different; each individual life filled with so many ordinary events and decisions, interesting and fateful only to that one individual.

I think I am thinking to myself, but I am not sure anymore.

I need help, and I know it. I need a guide, like in *The Tibetan Book of the Dead.* I need a guide who can teach me to maintain my spiritual balance.

I clutch the book in my purple sack under the table. I remember what it says.

Don't cling to the visions. Don't flee from the wrathful deities.

It is only in your head.

It is just in your head.

It is all, just in your head.

I feel myself being seduced by Allison's melodious voice. I am carried away, looking into her brilliant eyes and feeling more and more as if I have finally found someone who can understand me. Someone who has the power to forgive me.

"Forgive you? *Forgive you for what?*" She asks.

"I do not really know. But I need help. I think you can absolve my guilt. Make me fresh again, like a newborn baby."

So I confess.

I tell her I am crazy.

"I will not, and cannot, hide the truth from you any longer with my psychedelic disguise. I cannot afford to be cool anymore. I cannot afford to care whether people think I am good or bad.

I tell her the secret. "I'll be eighteen December six. Something bad is going to happen. Some kind of psychic malignancy is going to explode and infect everyone, everywhere, and we are too late to stop it."

She isn't even surprised. She says, "My birthday is December six too. And I'm going to be eighteen too. We were born on the same day."

I can't believe she knows about it. "You don't really know do you?" I am shaking all over. "Please, I don't want to get you involved in this. I am already damaged beyond repair. I am already doomed, like Cain, in the Bible, to be scorned and despised by all who see me. Let that be my problem Allison, not yours. You should stay pure, beautiful, and unsoiled."

Her pale cheeks flush precociously. Her eyes lower for the first time.

I feel an ink-like cloud settle around my shoulders and coalesce into a thick cover around my eyes, ears, nose, and mouth. It is too late. It is already too late.

I can't see her face anymore. Maybe I only have one more chance to speak. I think I say, "I love you."

I think I say, "I need you. Please help me."

Then I pass out.

2. BURROUGHS, BUGS, AND GUNS

September 6, 1951, Thursday evening:

In Cincinnati, at the first such presentation ever made to a professional organization in the United States, Dr. Mark Pincus reported to the American Psychiatric Association convention that by using LSD he was able to induce states remarkably similar to schizophrenia and psychosis.

And in Mexico City, William Burroughs shot his twenty seven year old common-law wife, Joan, through the head, and killed her. He was using a small and cheap .380 automatic pistol, trying to shoot an apple, which she had voluntarily placed on top of her head.

* * *

She, like many other women in the 1950's, had had obsessive fears of post-atomic radiation.

He, like many other men in the 1950's, had been possessed by evil spirits.

* * *

In the other, secret world, of which William Burroughs so often spoke, the demons observed these earthly events with wicked intellectual detachment.

"This is Joan. It is her time, but she is afraid to be a girl again."

"Burroughs and his buddies theorized the male/female dichotomy was the most dangerous malignancy in our universe."

"Didn't he say language is a virus from outer space, first infecting us and then using the fabric of our own minds to replicate and perpetuate itself?"

Joan answered, "Yes, I think he said something like that. But I can't recall anymore exactly what he said. I can't recall his words. I can't even recall his language."

"Yes. Well, that's really too bad Joan."

"We understand."

"He just shot you in the head and killed you, didn't he?"

"Well, you know, accidents *will* happen Joan. But life does have to go on, I mean, even after you're dead, of course, if you know what I mean."

Joan cried out, "I'm too scared to be a girl again."

One demon said, "So now what should we do with you?"

A second demon said, "But you were brave enough to let Bill shoot an apple off your head, weren't you?"

And another demon said, "You have three months to get ready dear."

* * *

She couldn't think straight for a long time. She had too many problems all mixed up.

In the other world, nothing is ever forgotten or forgiven.

Her problems and his problems were all the same now.

* * *

Bill's giant cockroaches, with mouths like viscous garbage disposals, are running all over the place, attacking the town and devouring the inhabitants. They are ugly murderous insects with psychic powers to terrorize their human prey.

Me? I am caught in this dark and mysterious war, through no fault of my own.

That is to say, it is through no fault of my own, as much as it is possible for a human to be free of personal fault.

I am hiding here, crouched in a black corner of occupied territory, holding on tight to a tiny little handgun. It is supposed to be a .380 automatic, which would be barley big enough to do the job anyway, but the barrel diameter of this particular gun is even less than that of a .22 caliber. And although it is supposed to be short, this weapon is absurd. The gun barrel is barely long enough to hold the full length of a single bullet as it explodes out of the chamber.

I try to forget I know the gun will be utterly ineffective. It is all I have to defend myself against the roaches and their two-legged allies.

Yes. They do have allies. Sickly white zombies. At times they seem translucent like termites. At other times they appear more opaque and glutinous, like fermenting corpses. All I know is, they surely are not human. They may be something from Earth's deep past, long before the flood. Or they may be another kind of sub-human from somewhere else altogether.

The cockroaches and their zombie allies both share a fear of the light. But on this black moonless night, they hunt with no fear at all.

I suspect somewhere along the line, these zombies, or whatever they are, managed to crossbreed with their cockroach friends and they are all carrying a little insect blood in them now. That makes their inter-species communication much easier. They have the right exopheromones to send urgent chemical messages back and forth to each other.

They all seem so comfortable in the dark. Searching for me, confident in themselves, each walking with a relaxed gait and a self-assured posture. Not at all the way you'd expect half-dead creatures of the night to carry themselves.

They know I am afraid. They can smell it for sure.

I try to think of myself as strong enough to be a worthy opponent, but I am not even good enough to be their enemy. I am not dangerous enough. I cannot harm them. I am simply their prey.

I hold the tiny gun up now as I crawl along this dark gutter, constantly banging my shoulders against sharp metallic objects. I hope to God I can shove the gun into someone's face and see him back down and leave me alone. But I cannot dissolve the fear that I am just a tempting morsel, and the little gun is a mere distraction.

I reach a secure place. There are cement walls all around me, so I can huddle in the corner. I switch the gun from my right hand to my left.

Why didn't my superiors train me for this? Why didn't they give me the weapons to fit the mission? Why the hell did they send me in here alone?

I bite down on the tip of my right forefinger pulling at a loose piece of dead fingernail between my teeth. When the sliver of fingernail holds tight at the very edge where the nail grows out of my flesh, I pull harder.

Now I am pulling straight out with the quarter-inch snippet of nail stretched taut between my teeth. One more jerk and it pulls loose, ripping some flesh away with it.

I let the nail fall out from between my teeth and see it dangle from the fingertip. It is still hanging on a stubborn strip of tissue.

A drop of blood forms at the seam where my flesh clings to the nail.

I hold the gun so the thumb and forefinger of my left hand are free to grab the nail in a pincer hold, and quickly rip back the other way to get the increasingly troublesome mess off my finger. It works, but I tore open my skin all along the underside of my nail. There is a bright red line. My fingertip is pushing out one drop of blood after another, to each beat of my pounding heart.

I can't think about this. I've got to get out of here.

Leaves rustle above and to my right. Old mildewed boards are lifted up and thrown carelessly aside. The dirt shifts above my head, slides down, and settles in new piles by my feet. First I am hit with a wave of insect regurgitation. Then a sickly man-in-the-moon face appears inches above mine.

He has a relaxed friendly smile, for a zombie.

He's happy to see dinner.

I raise the gun awkwardly in my left hand, bringing up my right hand to get a double-grip, but trying to conceal my bleeding forefinger.

It was more than embarrassing. The bloody fingertip was a disgrace. It dishonored the warrior image I was trying to convey.

The moon-faced intruder didn't change his expression at all, at the sight of my little gun or my bleeding finger. He was simply delighted to find me here.

He slides in gracefully, stands right in front of me and looks down into my eyes. He is way over six feet, maybe two hundred fifty pounds.

I have to move real fast now.

I push the gun straight into his face. Stick it into his mouth. Shove it between his lips, past his teeth, and fire two rounds fast. Then I scramble behind him and kick at the back of his knees to knock him down. I jump up on his shoulders to get enough height for a handhold on the wall so I can climb out onto the level street.

I run and run, without looking back.

Now, I am careful to remind myself, I have to watch for roaches in front of me, or attacking from the sides. They aren't fast enough to catch a running human from behind, but if I lost my footing, or if I were cut off by a band of marauders in a frontal assault, they could easily catch me, and eat me alive.

I know the shots didn't kill that guy. My dinky gun could only cause temporary confusion even when the bullets were popped right into his mouth.

I imagine he swallowed some blood, and by now he is maneuvering the bullets in his mouth, pushing them forward with the back of his tongue so they don't get sucked down his throat. Then he rolls his tongue, sliding the bullets toward the front of his mouth so he can spit them out, just like I spit out my own fingernail.

That only buys me about fifteen seconds, maybe twenty.

Fortunately, I use the time wisely, to escape from being his dinner, to run through this cockroach hell.

They know my scent now. They got a taste of me. They know my blood type. They know my gene sequence. They will never give up the chase. They will hunt me down, until they find me again somehow, somewhere, and get what they want.

But I swear I'll never be caught as defenseless as that ever again.

* * *

Exactly three months later, on December 6, 1951, on Long Island, New York:

In a corner-room suite on the third floor of Mount Sinai Hospital, in Forest Hills, Allison came out first. Her twin brother, Abraham, came out a few minutes later. Their mother was naturally relieved and full of joy they were born healthy. But there was also a deep loneliness showing in her damp eyes and at the edges of her tight lips. Her husband was away on a secret mission in Korea. He would be gone a full year, and would not likely be able to communicate with his wife during all of that time. So she couldn't even tell him she just gave birth to a beautiful baby boy and girl.

And in not-too-distant Far Rockaway, at Saint Joseph's Hospital, a nine and a half pound baby boy was born. He had fine brown hair, full lips, and skin that seemed to want to be the color of tea. His mother, in her medicated daze, could already see him being Baptized, then receiving his first Holy Communion, being Confirmed, serving as an altar boy, and someday, maybe a priest.

The baby boy's father was in the waiting room, smoking an unfiltered Camel and spitting a stubborn piece of tobacco off the tip of his tongue just when the nurse came to tell him he finally had a son.

* * *

And exactly eighteen years after that, on December 6, 1969, up in Northern California:

It was the culmination of the Rolling Stones 1969 tour with a free concert at Altamont Speedway near San Francisco.

Mick Jagger was singing about the sweet satisfaction of being Satan, while an eighteen-year-old Black man was getting beat to death by the Hells Angels, with pool cues, there, at the concert, in front of the stage.

Three other people died at that concert. Many other people were beaten.

And the Woodstock generation quietly crawled into its own deathbed just four months after it was born.

3. WAKING UP IN 1969

The stages of sleep, taken one at a time to fulfillment, can be deeply comforting.

I see myself in my dream and I am assured of my own being.

I am a lucid dreamer, a conscious observer of my own mind as I gently float back up to the surface from the sometimes murky, sometimes hyper-colorful depths of dreamland.

I feel a sudden jolt from the surprise of seeing a blond-haired girl suspended in space just outside my bedroom window. Her long hair is blowing in the gentle breeze. I extend myself, fly by to inspect her, and run my fingers through her hair.

She seems too good to be true. The energy and material of her being are surreal and disturbing. Her electromagnetic vibrations are pulsing too fast. Or are those my own vibrations? I'm confused. I am overcome by the need to immediately verify my own time and place. I must ascertain my own identity.

Right, I think, this is my bedroom, I tell myself. It is early morning, and I'm still dreaming. Okay. Now, I should just relax back into a more smooth and gradual wake-up mode.

So I do that.

Then, a while later, I wake fully. I get up, and walk into the next room.

There she is. The blond-haired girl is sitting in a soft armchair I have never seen before, in a room I have never known.

She says, “All that we see or seem is but a dream within a dream.”

I feel claws tear at the fabric of my universe.

She continues, “Beautiful words aren’t they. But Edgar Allan Poe was wrong.”

My universe is made of a fabric with a conscious need to mend itself.

She smiles, “I’m so happy to see you again.”

4. LOS ANGELES

Back on the East Coast, the Punks were thriving in Greenwich Village. They were growing like clusters of plastic and chrome mushrooms at the bottom of all the dark grooves the Hippies had left behind.

Sure, New York was cool, but Allison needed to be at the center of her own universe, and that was out west now.

In the 1970's, New Yorkers had a certain kind of mental clarity and a sense of reality we didn't find as compelling in Los Angeles. We cultivated a greater sense of freedom on the west coast, and we were rather proud of our mental flexibility.

California was Hippie Heaven.

New Yorkers were proud of the clarity of their reality, and we were proud of the flexibility of our dreams.

And although we each thought the other was kind of silly, no one was surprised at all when the Originator built his base here in L.A.

After all, we were giving birth to all kinds of unique ideas, impossible ideals, and strange new worlds in the warm, welcoming womb of the west. Of course, we could accommodate one more theological oddity.

The Originator had his headquarters and his home located on a secure compound in an exclusive section of the Hollywood Hills. The other offices and academies of Psytron were spread out on a dozen prime pieces of property in various Los Angeles neighborhoods. The Psytron Secret Security Contingent, the SSC, occupied a stucco and brick, one-level complex of what had been medical offices, just off Hollywood Boulevard, below the rolling hills of Griffith Park.

Inconspicuousness was their first line of defense. Then there were concrete reinforced walls, bars on the windows, and alarm systems. Finally, there were armed, round-the-clock, SSC guards, who would fight to the death and fire on their own humanoid mothers if they were told they should.

The SSC had a weekly review every Friday evening at 9:45 in a secure section of a damp and drafty underground parking structure filled with folding chairs, tables, and a dinky loudspeaker system.

A steely-eyed lady, whose jaw sometimes made cracking sounds when she spoke, was squeezing the microphone with her right hand.

"Let us review the basics.

"Psytron means the psychology of electrons.

"Psytron Theological Technology is based on the manipulation of the electro-magnetic structure of the human aura, the physical manifestation of our humanoid souls.

"Psytron, in case you don't know or don't remember, is the only way for you to get fully-conscious, personal immortality on this planet at this time. The Originator, through years of hard work, courage, and commitment, has not only given you immortality right here and now in your own humanoid lifetime, but he has also identified and located the Holy Conman who has dominated Earth and plagued our universe since the beginning of time."

Elizabeth, the Originator's third wife, and head of the Secret Security Contingent worldwide, concluded after a dramatic pause, "Now, what have you done for the Originator today?"

Elizabeth was relentless. She shot her words out like bullets, right into Allison's brain. Allison didn't know how people stood there and listened to her like this. She didn't know how long she could take it.

Then, finally, a blue-and-white-uniformed minion scurried up to the microphone to announce, "Daily reports are due in every senior's in-box by hand delivery at 23:30 hours."

And another blue-and-white minion came over, tapping Allison on her shoulder.

Elizabeth wanted to see her now.

Allison followed a step behind the fast-walking young man and made a conscious effort to continue breathing slowly and deeply.

* * *

This was Allison's first day in the elite SSC uniform. She had expected more. Something better than this poly-cotton blend. This was the worst material she had ever worn.

Allison was sensitive. She was sensitive in general, and especially sensitive to fabrics. Cotton didn't do much for her unless it was thin and tight. She preferred to wear silk, satin, or fine lace. Materials that sharpen stimulation, rather than buffer it like cotton. Then she would feel her nipples tingle from just the right kind of friction.

Often, on the train, back in New York, when men were leering at her, she had wondered, could they see how hot she was? They were looking so hard, and she knew they liked what they saw. But could they actually see the heat spreading from her breast up to her head and down between her legs, making her want to moan just from the feeling of her own blouse on her breasts?

Did they have any clue about her power? Her energy?

Could they actually see how she felt?

She had wondered often.

* * *

"Allison, come in. The Originator has told me all about you."

She had never been this close before.

Her eyes locked on the eyes of Elizabeth, whose eyes had already locked on her own.

"Knowledge of your own immortality brings you into a select group Allison. Now you have more responsibility to help."

She replied as expected, "Yes. Anything I can do."

"I knew I could count on you. I've heard about your dedication, and I've heard you are, what shall I say, *eager to please.*"

Allison blushed. Like any other Psytron she was happy to help the Originator, but this was his wife talking. Or was she just the head of the SSC now?

"It is too soon for you to wander far from home. We have yet to finish the most vital work to do on Earth. That is why the Originator himself is still here. Is it not?"

"Yes. I mean, I understand." She was trying to respond as correctly and as clearly as possible but she felt increasingly self-conscious about the hollow sounds of her own voice.

"With immortality, there are dangers worse than death. There are pains that can last longer than a lifetime. As you know, the Holy Conman seems to have ceased direct interference in ordinary humanoid affairs. Earthly concerns have simply become too boring and predictable for him. The Holy Conman has become the victim of the totality of his own control."

Allison nodded agreement. This is all as she had been taught. As she had been drilled and tested repeatedly.

"Of course, it is not as simple as that, and we know a plan of apocalyptic proportions has already been prepared for execution early in the next century."

Elizabeth slid back in her dark leather executive chair.

"However, as far as you are concerned right now, once you become a consciously immortal Psytron, you are sure to attract more attention. The Holy Conman will surely become intrigued with the possibilities for increased punishment."

"Increased punishment?" Allison asked, "For what?"

"Well, of course, in your case, for being a woman."

* * *

Allison felt sick to her stomach now.

It sounded utterly nonsensical. It was silly beyond belief. Stupid. Yet, she felt the impact of Elizabeth's words resonate deep inside as she struggled to accept a truth as true as any she had ever known.

Jesus wanted to use His divine power to give Mary Magdalene a male soul, *to fix her*, repair her spiritual flaw, so she could be redeemed as a male.

Now Allison relied on her training, on the drills, to regain her own equilibrium.

I ate the same apple again and again, and gave it to Adam again and again and again, she thought. "Time does not exist here. The problem is always the same," she said as expected.

Evil does not do away with its victim, she recalled. It needs the victim to define itself. Whenever you turn to face it, Evil is all around you. Evil is everywhere. And it is always familiar. In all the timeless encounters and endless battles with no resolution, Evil is always the same.

Eve ate the forbidden fruit and then gave some to Adam.

The eyes of both of them were opened, and they discovered that they were naked.

God said, "Behold, the man has become as one of us, to Know Good and Evil."

God is *plural*, speaking for all of us.

The man is a singular *one*.

GOD IS PLURAL! Do you see? The words are specific and significant. GOD IS NOT SINGULAR.

And the sequence is equally important. The woman has already given the man Knowledge of Good and Evil, and God continues talking. God says, "Now, lest he put forth his hand and take also of the Tree of Life and eat and live forever, let us send him forth from the Garden of Eden."

Again, God is plural and speaking for *us*, but the man is a singular and separate *one*.

Then to the East of the Garden, God stationed the Cherubim with a sword whirling and flashing to guard the way to the Tree of Life.

We've had Knowledge of Good and Evil for a long time.

All of us. Men, women, and children. We have known Good and Evil for a long, long time.

However, we haven't had Eternal Life until now.

God prevented woman from enticing man to Eternal Life.

Allison couldn't avoid the questions in her own mind. What did I say? What did God do? Why is woman so bad? Or is God bad?

What does it even mean to ask if God is good or bad? Singular or plural? One or many? She did all the drills exactly as she had been instructed, but she still wasn't clear on those points. She still didn't know what to think. And she still thought it was crazy to think about it too much. But she knew there was only one question she was allowed to ask right now.

* * *

"What can I do?" Allison asked, "I mean, about God?"

* * *

She told me later, it was a question she did not live long enough to really have time to regret adequately.

5. WHY ME HERE AND NOW

My name, by the way, the name I use now, since I changed it back again, is Genetic Freeman. That was my psychedelic alias up to the day I met Allison. My last day as a humanoid.

No one in Psytron, except Allison, knew about it. So I reclaimed it when they expelled me from Psytron.

Unfortunately, that is how they dealt with me in the SSC. Elizabeth interviewed me herself and released her findings upon consultation with the Originator. Elizabeth says I'm insane and dangerous, because I'm *anti-Psytronic*. I've been infested and infected by psychic germs, or maybe I myself am the germ. I'm not sure. There is no such thing as a request for clarification, or any other avenue of appeal, either in Psytron or out. I'm not just an ignorant, ineffective humanoid any more, now I'm anti-Psytronic.

I am aware these current conditions are much more dangerous to all parties involved, especially me.

That is just the way it is.

They monitor my actions and thoughts now. If I do anything, or show any intent to harm Psytron or the Originator, I will be neutralized by any means necessary.

This is classic amorality. Simple expediency for the sake of the number one priority. Actually, they only have *one* priority. Protect and propagate the theology of Psytron, and don't let anyone get in the way.

So I have to deal with these people as best I can.

I'm studying the hidden history of religious organizations and the formation of cults and secret societies. I know the complicated and convoluted stories of self-preservation. I know the unimaginably amoral acts of amateur and professional spies, agent provocateurs, occult assassins, and other evildoers and black magicians.

I know the logic of evil.

Most important of all, I know help from the outside world is never there when you need it. Not now. Not here. Ordinary people simply cannot comprehend. There is no way anyone from the outside world could ever penetrate the veil of incomprehensibility. When you are alone in the secret dark world of the occult, you are alone forever.

But I don't show what I know.

I can easily live with their scorn and their pious false pity; but I couldn't live if they feared me. If they feared me they would destroy me. And there is no power on Earth to stop them.

So I plan to outsmart them. I will stay alive by convincing them they are right, I am in fact hopelessly confused, probably insane, and at best, utterly ineffectual.

Then, if I am lucky, they will leave me alone.

If I am lucky, they will leave me alone until I can find Allison.

No matter she is dead.

I'll find her no matter what I have to do.

No matter who gets in my way.

6. THE FINAL LAST SUPPER

After Hiroshima and Nagasaki, the Originator knew there would not likely be another world war. Yes, of course, geography and natural resources were crucial, but the human mind was, and always had been, the real target of governmental greed and control.

Over the next few decades the war would be fought on the newer scientific battlefields of Microbiology, Neurochemistry, and Genetics.

The Originator also knew that Timothy Leary knew the same things.

The Originator had a lot of troubles in the sixties. He saw the whole Hippie phenomenon as one big juvenile prank by the Holy Conman.

"We are all one. Let your ego dissolve as you merge into the light of universal love. *Float downstream, you are not dying....*" And all that other psychedelic crap. Straight from the Holy Conman, he thought, as he continued to scan the spaces between the stars for his Allison.

Of course, the problems of the sixties had mostly grown from the rotten seeds of the fifties. But the Beatniks had been easy to deal with. There were actually only a few important individuals involved. And, as far as the Originator was concerned, they were generally weak and degenerate individuals anyway. All he had to do was focus on the leading players, and manipulate their actions at crucial junctions.

Truth is, Kerouac hated Ginsberg anyway. Most important thing for the Originator to do was keep Burroughs and Ginsberg as far away from each other as possible, for as long as possible. So Burroughs, who the Originator believed could easily be seduced into anything, was lured away to Tangier, a seaport city on the North African coast. He was isolated in Tangier, and allowed to create nightmares of his own choosing, until the Originator needed to use him again.

It didn't take much work. One way or another the Beatniks self-destructed right in the midst of all the prosperity and capitalism they had rejected.

And then in the sixties, Kerouac grew to despise the Hippies that idolized him and built their lives on his ideals.

But in fact, the Hippies were different. They had divine assistance to become more creatively insane.

He located Allison in the other world now. He held her in a way that defied detection with a gentle but secure psychic touch. He had immeasurable things to teach her.

"*He is one and I am one and you are one and we are all together....*" Yeah, nothing but puppets for the Holy Conman. Great. Who could fall for such a story if they weren't fueled by LSD?

Well, that's the heart of the problem.

There were a great many things Allison didn't know yet. Things no one else knew either, so he couldn't really blame her. He had to teach her. He had to train her to do the job with the tools and resources he made available to her.

First, in the forties, the Office of Strategic Services, the forerunner to the CIA, developed the science of Personality Assessment to help select more effective agents and operatives. One of the operatives was a brilliant, straight, and establishment-oriented young psychologist named Timothy Leary. And Professor Leary, just like all the rest of them, eagerly fed the government's insatiable appetite for authoritarian control. The psychologists and the spies made perfect bedfellows.

The Originator knew his own thoughts were complicated, but after all her training, he expected her to absorb them like a sponge.

Then in the fifties, after being shaken up by the Communist brainwashing of U.S. POWs in Korea, the CIA developed the MK-ULTRA mind-control program. It was unacceptable for the U.S. to lag behind the communist countries in the development and application of mind-control techniques. Surely if we applied ourselves, we could produce whatever defensive and offensive tools we needed to deal with our less legally restrained godless communist enemies.

The National Institute of Mental Health was just one of the bigger front groups financing psychedelics in academia to ascertain the utility of LSD, then widely believed to be the most powerful drug known to man.

Needless to emphasize, things got way out of hand in the next decade.

On October 12, 1964, a lady named Mary Morris was shot and killed in Washington D.C. in an as yet unsolved murder case. Of course that is not so unusual.

She was one of President John F. Kennedy's lovers. And neither is that so unusual.

But she was also a CIA operative and the *de facto* executive liaison to Professor Leary, who by that time had become the most prominent of the psychedelic gurus.

The born-again Leary and his friends said *The Tibetan Book of the Dead* was in fact an esoteric metaphor in a rite of pre-mortem death and rebirth, rather than an actual guide for the dead and dying. The big secret was not death, he claimed, but ego-loss while still alive.

The Originator found it amusing that the best minds of the western world could do no better than describe their own psychedelic experience in terms of an ancient Tibetan model.

But that's the way it was.

LSD would inevitably wreak havoc on American society before any of the professors could figure it out any better than that, or before anyone else could do anything at all about it.

There were many colorful goons marching in the guru parade, but none of them knew or could explain what was happening any more.

The CIA Director, Admiral Stansfield Turner, needed to know if any of his own agents or operatives had been using LSD. There was, unquestionably, only one man he could trust to distinguish hallucination from reality in this new and nebulous chemical war zone.

In the spring of 1967, Leary was arrested during a raid on his International Foundation for Internal Freedom, at Millbrook, New York. There was a handpicked team of forty specially trained narcotics agents to ensure the job was done right. That would seem like more than enough gun-wielding agents to apprehend a house-full of academicians. But there was still one more man on the scene. One man the director deemed indispensable to a successful operation. This man had personally selected each of those forty agents, and he alone was responsible for the content of their training. Yet, they knew him only by the whispered rumor of his initials: VCK.

He had been the original instigator of extra-academic LSD research in the United States. He answered only to the Director. And, VCK said only as much as he wanted to say.

The Originator continued directing his thoughts along a smoothly curving line, like the string on a psychic kite riding along on an interplanetary current, directly to the disembodied Allison.

From that point on, it was easy enough for us to keep a tight reign on Leary via the SSC network of agents and operatives. It was a simple thing to get that fool arrested whenever it served our purposes. We put him in jail when we wanted to confine him, and then we took him out again when we wanted him free.

But he wasn't the same man anymore.

Leary learned how to survive in jail. He learned from Charlie Manson: *fear equals awareness.*

So I wonder, did the Harvard professor finally become more aware from using primal fear, like street-smart Manson, than from using LSD?

When he was free, it was easy enough to keep Leary on the run. It was easy to keep all the rest of the so-called radical underground gagging on its own paranoia too.

We convinced the Black Panthers that Leary was led to Algiers by the Weather Underground as a CIA operative to spy on their revolutionary organization. We convinced Leary that his host in Algiers, Eldridge Cleaver, had put him under house arrest because the Panthers were planning to kill him.

The Originator begins thinking just to himself, reminiscing about his own army of one, Vinney Cold Killer.

What happened when you tried to dissolve *his* ego Leary? Float downstream with VCK for a while, and then tell me you're not dying. What did VCK tell you about your own wife's suicide Leary? Maybe something you didn't know before? Or you didn't want to know?

Like a bad trip from the CIA brand Orange Sunshine that turned the ubiquitous vibrations of universal love into a malignant murderous maelstrom starting December 6, 1969, at Altamont.

Goodbye Twiggy, hello Sharon Tate.

Okay, back to the lecture Allison.

Of course, the seventies were even worse than the sixties.

The Satanic Bible, Process Church of The Final Judgment, Peoples Temple, and all that other garbage. Those neat-looking fascists from Korea. 3PK and the Disciples from Hell. Nobody, and I mean nobody, but VCK, tangles with them.

Son of Sam gets his throat slit at Attica. Good job. Fifty-six stitches kept him quiet.

You had to be either murderously evil or suicidally insane in the seventies. You had to be. You were a cannibal, or you were somebody's dinner.

You cannot fight the morality or the immorality of your own time and place. You cannot change it. You can only hope to see it, to understand it. It is an inescapable rule, like the Heisenberg uncertainty principle of morality.

It makes me laugh to think of all those hip psychologists and cool physicists with their psychedelic post-grad degrees spending all their time writing and speaking to the intellectually impaired. Today, they still don't know what really happened.

VCK was the only brain behind the CIA mind-control program. He was the only one who should have graduated with a real Ph.D. in MK-ULTRA.

So, he concluded rhetorically, what do we do? We put him to good use. We make him the enforcer, the Luca Brazzi of the Aquarian Age. Vinney Cold Killer.

Now, don't forget who and what you are Allison. You are a liaison. You are my liaison. Find VCK for me now. Talk to him for me.

* * *

Today his head is filled with old pictures, all crumbling and dusty. The soundtrack is scratchy like sand on glass. Back on September 6, 1951, Vinney was on his way to Seoul, Korea. It was one year after the war started. He was in the Special Forces, Psychological Unit. His wife was pregnant. He had to leave her back in the Long Island suburbs. He'd miss the birth of their first child. Might even be twins, she kept telling him before he left. She was colossal.

They were both fresh and youthful, expecting only the best.

He was not yet known as Vinney Cold Killer. But he was one of the West's up-and-coming greatest commie fighters of all time. On the first of many solo missions. Steeped in plausible deniability.

But he knew why he was killing people in those days. He recognized his enemies just as quickly as he recognized his own face in the mirror.

Now what was he doing? He didn't really know.

Returning to Korea. First time since the war. He thinks he is dreaming. Seeing apocalyptic visions of race wars. Black men in uniforms. They are as hard as iron bars. Beating soft White men, women, and children.

The politicians are speaking all day long, selling everything, like a Seven Eleven, all day long, for immediate consumption.

Koreans are in the streets with guns.

Dead red Indians and brown Indian mystics are on the run.

Black people are killing Black people in Africa.

Could history really have begun there, and end in hunger and warfare?

He is caught in the nightmare, narrating his own story for an unconcerned posterity.

* * *

The sharp repetitive pain.

I'm getting stabbed repeatedly with an ice pick.

Quickly in and out, and in and out again. In my thigh and hip. In my stomach. In my chest.

I want to die so the pain will end.

I saw it coming. I knew it had to happen. That was the most fearful time. It was a partial relief once it began. Now I just want it to end the only way it can.

I don't know why I am here to begin with. I don't know why I left the Agency.

Someone dragged me into this dark and evil affair without my consent, before I could retreat or escape. Sure, I've got a mission. Sure, I follow orders. But this? This is beyond the call. It's not even natural.

Black people in jail in Korea!

What does that have to do with me?

Nothing. Except, it would be the cause of my death.

* * *

We were moving down the road, becoming increasingly obvious targets. We entered the no man's land and ran from one burned-out car, to another smoldering remnant, to another dark passageway, to even deeper and deeper hiding places.

I don't even remember what he was after that was so vital to his operations that he had to drag me down this far. And now, there is no time to think about it anymore. I can't think about anything but the immediate danger.

We were allowed to reach this destination, to infiltrate to this depth, only because that ensured we could never escape or be rescued anymore.

There were police here, but only those who had been abandoned by their own kind like lepers. All they could do was stay put and wait for their time. The prisoners couldn't kill everyone at once, but they could kill each one in his own time.

They were escaped Black prisoners in Korea. Locked up like animals for decades. Bred and crossbred. Experimented upon. Observed.

Now, they were a breed of their own. A community, of sorts, with hope for nothing but violent revenge.

No one cares whose side I am on. There are no good sides here anymore. We are all doomed to die violent deaths. We all kill and get killed in return.

The world outside is just waiting for the last of us to stand alone and slit his own throat.

Killer and killed. Nothing separates us anymore. Just a thin porous membrane. Identity seeps through. Time and reality change when you don't expect it. I'm not myself anymore. I'm outside, somewhere else, talking about someone I see. And I see myself.

* * *

I dream.

I sit down at my own Last Supper.

I fall in love with a gray stone statue that transmutates into a live demon. It has the face of a woman on the body of a sea serpent like a mermaid.

The legs fall from the table and start hissing as they slither away. Dark demented serpents with bright red eyes. I wake up to find myself on a black marble floor. It's a big room, with old friends at one table and dead friends at another.

I rush over to a table of strangers to which I am beckoned. I'm surrounded by models and other beautiful people, who are hungry for someone significantly less beautiful than they are, to show themselves to. They see me looking at them, and they know exactly what I think of myself because such measurements are the precious currency of their trade.

Elsewhere, naked babies are lying on the cold floor, crying. Face-to-face with death, self, and each other.

The difference between self and others is too clear, and too many others are dead.

Those thought to be weaker than the others are alone at their respective tables.

Tall, slender Willie is the resplendent guest of honor, sitting at the head of the table for homosexuals and drug addicts.

There is a tense table full of liars, thieves and other petty criminals. There is a rather quiet table of intellectual frauds and failures. But for those addicted to fame and wealth there is a large raucous banquet at the front of the room.

And then, there you are, or no, I think it might be me.

There he is, Mr. Jones, sitting all alone in the corner, as always. Pointing his broken finger straight at me now. Talking about me. Blaming me personally for all the tables, and the labels, all the words and the damage done.

I'm sitting, staring at the difference between what I see and all that I have been shown.

Don't blame me. Don't blame me for what is or what is not. I don't call the shots here. I'm just looking at what I see.

The Heisenberg uncertainty principle. In the physics of subatomic particles it is a crucial fact that we cannot know both the position and the momentum of a particle.

The wave-particle duality of light.

The wave-particle duality of matter.

We alter the experience by our act of viewing it. My vision got in the way of my vision.

The universal primary phenomenon is not a wave and is not a particle.

Energy equals mass times the square of the speed of light. I could have known that too.

Time is the fourth dimension.

The fifth dimension is Good and Evil. I should have known that.

This is my birthright. I should know these things.

My brain has a hundred billion neurons, each as complete as a mainframe computer. Each connected to ten thousand other neurons.

Norepinephrine is a prehistoric chemical found in the nerve-like cells of the crab, spider, and worm. It is also found in the otherwise empty spaces of our own embryonic skull cavities. There, it attracts cells from our earliest lizard-like brain formation, causing them to float up and organize into complex hierarchies, settle down, and produce axons to weave into the fabric of our higher cortex.

The Holy Qur'an says Allah gave mankind the ability to know all things in the universe.

Electron excitation.
The formation of electrical molecular bonds.
The breaking of such bonds.

Photosynthesis is the production of energy by the excitation of electrons by photons, and the use of that energy, as the basic means of bonding and building biological structures.

Bioluminescence is the reverse process whereby energy is transferred to an excited electron, resulting in the emission of a photon.

DNA holograms.
Patterns of radiant energy.
Electromagnetic formation of the processes and objects of reality.
Beneath the molecular level, biology disappears and there is only physics.

I see new designer plants and designer insects beckon to each other and dance in endless symbiotic trance.

I think about my *self*, who I was, who I am, and who I am not. And I wonder what it means when I can distinguish my self from others, and when I cannot. And what does it mean to do violence to others, or do violence to self, or to not.

7. WAI YU IN LOS ANGELES

Freckle-face redneck told me about jail down south. Told me about his brother, "Shot through the head by them niggers." He pulled my face close, kept his hand tight on the back of my neck, and kissed me on the cheek. Said he knows who his enemies are.

I don't know what that was all about, but I figure it meant something special in jail. To grab a guy tight like that, and kiss his cheek.

He called me late at night, drunk; told me about the faggot he just beat up in the men's room of a bar. Stuck his head in the toilet and held him down, forcing the faggot to suck up toilet water as he choked for air.

I wonder, what did he say to the faggot in the men's room before he stuck his face in the toilet? Was he testing him? Did the faggot give the wrong answer?

Freckle-face redneck is always testing me too. I know he is, but what can I do about it? He probably thinks I'm a fag too. Maybe a lot of people think I'm a fag. What am I supposed to do about it?

This guy thinks I'm stupid because I don't hate Black people like he does. I know how his mind works.

I think it is better to let people think whatever they want. I don't care.

Anyway, I never knew what Red was going to talk about next, and the only thing he ever told me about more than once was Elvis. Red loved the King. When he got drunk and talked about Elvis, he'd lose control of himself until all he could do was slobber and cry about how great the King was and how tragic it was when the King died.

I don't care about Elvis. I don't care about the King. I don't care about this freckle-face redneck either. But I'm really starting to worry about myself. I can't live in this world anymore. It is too ugly and too depressing here for me. I'm too sensitive. Or too weak.

There is too much hate.

People are too violent.

I just can't stay here anymore.

* * *

I wear a tight brown leather jacket zipped over a yellow T-shirt from the Bodhi Tree Bookstore. Riding gloves and a full-face helmet, brown hair messy out the back. Always the same jeans. Belt with Indian-head nickels, handcrafted thick silver "GF" buckle. High-top Converse on my feet.

I feel my tire kiss the curb, and whisper, "Hey babe, I'm still alive."

I'm slow to cut the engine and dismount.

I nod to a new friend.

Wai Yu is standing at his window watching me.

He is frail and gentle. Pale. Almost albino. Wrapped in saffron.

I want to yell at everyone in the world, "WHY DON'T WE ALL BE LIKE HIM?"

Wai Yu invites me into his room. Front corner of a late 1940's Hollywood home. Big porch. Heavy front doors. Half-walls and columns define the hallway. Lots of dark brown wood painted over in most places. Bright red, pink, orange, yellow, gold, and purple. Colors the Good Ghosts and Hippies prefer.

I live across the street in the Kwan Yin House of Compassion and Mercy, on the back porch, with nothing but screen windows for walls. Ten yards from the temple bell built up with ornate red tile roof, reaching higher and higher to a sharp peak, sloping down to calmly focus on four deities. One god for each corner. Rebuilt with patience and compassion after the neighbors burned it down.

I leave my sneakers by his sandals outside the door. The wood planks squeak faintly as we step and slide across the hallway floor. I bend low and follow him into a dark, incense-filled room, which at first glance is familiar and easy to understand. There are books, a bed, and a table. I sit on a cushion when it is offered. I drink the tea he pours.

His eyes caress me like a mystic lover as he asks about my life.

Patti Smith screams, "*...i am an american artist and i have no guilt....*" She is my made-for-the-plague phantom lover in 1978.

In *The Rolling Thunder Revue*, Bob Dylan is in makeup with a cool powder-white face, squirming, squealing, and twisting his lips.

Leary is out of jail, speaking at USC about space migration and immortality. He is looking at me, just looking at me.

There are indigestible remnants and cold leftovers still on the table from Burroughs's *Naked Lunch*. Jack Kerouac is dead, but he is still there in clear Colorado air, at the School for Disembodied Poetics. Closer to home, Charles Bukowski sweats and ejaculates poems at Hollywood and Western.

The gentle monk has me stand.

I never mention Psytron.

Wai Yu prostrates himself in front of me, face down to my feet.

He kisses them.

My socks feel damp and steamy.

I wish my feet were clean.

He kisses my feet again.

He bends his neck way back, looks up and says, "This is what it is like to be me."

I wish I knew what he was going to do next.

He has me sit again, and listen, as he begins a story.

He says he escaped from Vietnam disguised as a Buddhist nun, a female, smuggled out with a group of other nuns. He was sent to Thailand, to work in the service of a unique master carver, an incomprehensibly old Tibetan monk living in the slums of Bangkok.

The old monk's escape from Tibet to Thailand was even more unusual.

By special request of the Dali Lama to President Truman, the CIA sent in an undercover agent to help transplant the old monk to Bangkok during the Chinese invasion of Tibet. Twelve Chinese soldiers died in the process. One double-crossing Thai monk killed himself with a rusty can at the feet of the angry American agent.

The old monk got a new home, and no one ever bothered him again.

He was trying to carve a perfect image of Buddha's head from a sacred block of Yew. The wood came from specific trees grown in the forests of eastern Tibet, and was delivered to him through a route as reliable as it was unknowable.

It was believed that if this particular monk could accomplish this particular act of perfect creation, he himself would be transformed into one of the infinite and immortal faces of Buddha, perhaps even becoming Maitreya, the future and final Buddha. And in that form he would have the power to transform the entire world. More than the historical Buddha had done. More than Jesus had done. More than Mohammed had done.

Now, a boy was needed to care for the old monk.

Wai Yu had been asked several years earlier but had refused.

He couldn't accept endless years of sweat and stench in a Bangkok slum all alone with that ancient, undying monk. He thought of his own life and believed this old monk had nothing to do with him.

Wai Yu says his father was French. His mother was mixed, Vietnamese and Hong Kong Chinese. He was clever, multilingual, and not afraid to live on his own. So he ran away from his village and headed for the big city, Saigon.

Soon enough, he found work on a U.S. military base, cleaning and running errands. Trivial stuff, but he was stoic about life, and he did every job as well as he could.

Then one day, a young American officer, a doctor, with short blond hair and a friendly smile, told Wai Yu his natural intelligence and linguistic skills could be put to better use as a medical aid. Wai Yu was surprised of course, but mostly, he was grateful. He wanted to learn, and he wanted to help. He studied diligently, trained hard, and was eventually allowed to work as a medical aid.

He followed along as the doctor examined the casualties, separating the hopeful from the hopeless, while they tried to avoid the incoming shells.

He was baffled beyond admiration at the doctor's courage and optimism under the most adverse circumstances. He was honored to help him save other men's lives and help lessen, however slightly, the staggering pain and agony of the war. Wai Yu didn't know that the doctor himself was statistically projected to die during his tour of duty in Vietnam.

At night, Wai Yu began to dream of his wide-eyed mentor. And in his dreams, Wai Yu became the doctor himself. He was a doctor with short blond hair. He had been born in the U.S.A.

Then, when they became secret but passionate lovers, Wai Yu finally came to understand what the American doctor had been telling him all along, "Destiny, Wai Yu, this is your destiny."

Wai Yu was caught in a whirlpool of desire and fear. He wanted to satisfy his lover, yet he felt the unbearable pressure of thunderous waves crashing down on him. It was an ocean of relentless passion, and each wave was larger and stronger than the one before it.

Wai Yu was deeply perplexed at his own existence. Ill at ease, he felt like a stranger in his own skin.

But then, other times, there were silent moments, with warm water gently lapping at white sand.

Wai Yu knew nothing but joy and peace then.

For a while, he could forget the wounded and dying men crying out all around him, afraid to leave the world of blood and guts, but equally afraid to remain.

Then, late one night just like any other night, the two of them were trying to close a nasty stomach wound on one of the many young soldiers carried into the base hospital earlier that evening. A Vietnamese sniper who actually lived inside a tunnel under the center of the base opened his camouflage cover and quickly lobbed three homemade hand grenades at crucial targets, including the base hospital, for the great demoralizing effect such attacks could have.

The doctor was hit by flying metal fragments and his stomach was ripped right open.

Wai Yu moved forward, but his hands froze in mid-air as his lover fell into his arms. He held onto him as best he could, but the insides kept sliding out. He panicked, thinking, something is missing, something is missing. He looked around the room in shock, but couldn't identify any missing pieces. One pile of goo looked the same as any other.

Wai Yu's own stomach functioned perfectly, reacting violently, causing him to double-up in pain and heave spasmodically at the feet of his dying lover. But he didn't let go of his grip. He didn't let his mentor, his hero, and his lover fall. He held him up as best he could, but he couldn't stop the wounded doctor's insides from coming out.

He brought his face close, so they could look into each other's eyes one more time. And the doctor let his last breath escape directly into Wai Yu's tortured lips.

All Wai Yu could think was, “I don’t belong here anymore. I’m not a soldier. I’m not a doctor. I’m a monk. *That* is my destiny. My Karma.”

* * *

Shortly thereafter, Wai Yu arrived in Bangkok, ready for service to the old master carver.

For five years he ministered to every need of that crazy old man who never completed a carving. Wai Yu saw him successively burn twenty-three heads in various stages of completion because they were somehow imperfect.

It was unendurable for Wai Yu. His own sense of destiny was nothing but an illusion. His own Karma was nothing but insubstantial Maya phenomena. He couldn’t take it anymore. He won't be fooled again. He ran away. He escaped, all the way to America, here to Hollywood, where the heart of Buddhism has been transplanted to the dying body of Los Angeles.

He will stay here now, to help Buddhism, Los Angeles, and America all survive in a fragile, dangerous symbiotic stasis.

But, he told me, “If I were you, I would go to Bangkok, and see just how far that old master carver has progressed on the perfection of the Buddha’s Head.”

* * *

Clearly, if it was not Wai Yu’s destiny, someone else’s destiny was at stake now.

Clearly, Wai Yu had figured something out.

Clearly, Wai Yu knew something I didn’t know about Maya and Karma.

* * *

Vinney Cold Killer confronted the attacker correctly, with no weakness showing and not one instant of hesitation.

There was only the slightest movement of his right wrist: a subtle tightening of muscular threads lifting the palm backward, turning the tubular wooden handle one-quarter around, placing the needle-sharp point on the attacker's left eyelid with just enough pressure to produce a slight indentation in skin, then a barely perceptible flick, down and across, and a liquid red X appears in the middle of the eyelid.

And the needle-sharp point came down again, to rest ever so lightly, right in the center of the red X.

Without a blink, Vinney said, "If you can't figure out instantly, that despite your expectations, it is not you, but I who am in control, then you will die."

The freckle face redneck's bowels exploded with such violence that his head jolted forward and his left eye was skewered on the ice pick.

8. WILLIE WALK LIKE AN EGYPTIAN

When you are trying hard to figure out the meaning of your life, you know some things are of crucial importance, but you still cannot remember what they are. Some other things may not be important at all, but you cannot forget them.

When you are young, you can never figure anything out anyway. You only think you can.

In junior high school, the first openly homosexual guy I know asks me to jerk off in a cup and bring it to school. He says he'll drink it.

I almost gag.

He can't be serious.

He must be trying to gross me out on purpose.

Black Willie. Tall and thin. Walks like an Egyptian.

Willie is a good guy, but why is he so sure I like to jerk off that much? I never told him anything about it. I thought it was a secret thing I did alone and no one ever saw me.

But here is Willie, right in front of me, talking for four minutes between two classes I already forgot about before they even happened. Willie's face and hands both say the same thing. He talks with a facial expression and hand movements I can never forget the rest of my life. Willie knows what he is talking about. He is slender and graceful. You can't even begin to disagree with him. Just his posture and manner are sufficient to deny anything you can think of before you even say it. Yes, Willie certainly knows what he is talking about.

Walk li-i-ike an E-gyp-tian.

I remember reading Margaret Mead. She said something about the intricate biological pattern of the female becoming a model for the artist, the mystic, and the saint.

I think there is an unspoken deal: You don't act like a queer, and we don't beat you up too much.

I don't know what that has to do with me. But I'm losing it again. I can't keep a grip on my own identity. I can grab my own dick for sure, Willie was right about that, but I can't grab a hold of my own self.

Walk li-i-ike an E-gyp-tian.

Today, I fear, uncontrollable screams will keep me awake all night long.

It's time to tell my tale.

All success must finally fail.

Nothing is as easy as it seems.

White gowns and indelible red bloodstains are not as ugly as it could ever be, with all the disgusting juices and gels warm beneath our skins.

Car noise and hard edges keep me moving from one room to another, one decade to the next, thinking my skin will thicken into a nice protective hide, but it never does, and whatever is hidden inside keeps breaking out to terrorize me whenever I am alone. So I finally accept that I cannot ever be alone.

My responsibilities are growing like vines. All around. Always underfoot.

Tears from the tough guy, you, who wanted me to be, who?

There have been too many words and faces. Millions of faces in all the big cities. And more words. And faces on country roads, in towns, passing car windows. Frowns mostly.

On days off, I don't know what I'm doing wrong. But they can see me better than I can see myself. They think. I don't know. So I go on hiding until I'm sure.

I'm good at what I do.

What do I do?

I don't know.

I'm running from the man who wants to kill me for ruining his life.

The men. The women.

All the people whose lives are ruined so damn easily for so many reasons.

Why didn't they ruin their own doomed lives before they met me?

Why did they wait so long? And who is really ruining whom anyway?

Go away from my window bitch!

Don't blame me.

* * *

I try to leave myself alone for a while before I ruin me too.

I need more time.

I just need more time to work it all out.

I think there is a fatal flaw in my personality. I'm too permeable. I absorb poison. I can't understand it. I can't identify or distinguish myself in the world among other people. I'm not sure where my edges are. I don't know what the correct form or shape is for my own being.

* * *

I don't know what motivates Willie, but I still admire him for being so passionate about what he does.

Walk li-i-ike an E-gyp-tian.

9. ONE MORE CITY FULL OF ANGELS

I learned all I needed to know from Wai Yu.

I sold my trusted old Harley Davidson Sportster for a good buck and bought a one-way ticket to *Krung Thep*, the mysteriously steamy, almost semi-liquid City of Angels, Bangkok, Thailand. I believed in my own ability to tame and conquer all the demons that would be fighting for my soul there.

Also, I felt I'd be escaping from the U.S. just in time. Things were only going to get worse here.

* * *

My departure date was December 5, 1980. I thought maybe I could miss my own twenty-ninth birthday by the shrewd exploitation of a fortuitous geographical irregularity, if I could just lose one day as I flew over the International Date Line somewhere west of Honolulu.

I talked about that with a guy I met at Honolulu Airport while I was waiting for my next plane.

He told me to be careful. I was flying west into the evil spirit of the East, and it was already reaching out to get me.

I said, "What?"

* * *

He gets real close and says, "Now listen good: What one equals one?"

I say, "You mean like nothing from nothing leaves nothing?"

He says, "You think life means nothing?"

I say, "No man, I mean the way you said it, like it sounds like one and one and one is three, or something like that, you know?"

He says, "I say it the way it is, that's the way I say it."

So I think hard and fast as I can, look straight back into his eyes and say, "Hey, one equals one."

He smiles, grabs my shoulder, pulls me even closer and says, "Hey? Hey to you! Listen up Cracker Jack, there is a lot more to life than one equals one."

* * *

He left his Japanese-American wife crying at home.

He courted her years earlier, and successfully seduced her away from her Buddhist upbringing and her various acquired occult tendencies into a world of born-again Christianity. Then they lived together, happy for a while, until all these imaginary beings he called *little people* came to live with them.

As the biblically authorized male head of the household, he insisted he could effectively govern the whole group of these little people as long as he prayed to God for guidance and continued to study the Holy Scriptures.

His wife loved him. And she believed him.

She couldn't see the little people herself. She didn't know what they were really like. But she did believe the Bible could solve any problems in life, even a problem with imaginary little people invading your husband's body and mind. So she trusted him, and followed his directions as well as she could.

She didn't know why or what he was doing, but just before he left for the airport, he carried his Bible into the bedroom alone, took off his clothes, and sat down on the floor naked.

He was exposing himself to all the unseen eyes of the otherwise unknown entities from the other world. He was violating the word of God in a purposeful, evil, narcissistic orgy. Desecrating all that his wife thought he believed. Sacrificing himself. Draining himself all over the Bible in a series of ecstatic spasms, giving himself to the demons, praying for the evil power to kill what he could not understand.

All the little people were happy now. They eagerly reciprocated the young man's sexual passion.

It was exhilarating. It felt better than he had imagined it would.

He fell back, exhausted, satisfied with himself, satisfied with all his demonic lovers, and satisfied with evil.

He rose, as he knew he would, utterly refreshed, invigorated, and empowered.

Now he was prepared to unleash himself, to face his own future, and fulfill his own fate.

It was not his problem that the rest of the world wasn't ready to deal with his peculiar but powerful Karma.

Mark David Chapman got up, got dressed, kissed his wife goodbye, went to the Honolulu airport, got on his plane, and flew east to the nerve center of the West.

Then and there, across all those time zones, thousands of miles away from home, the little people answered the young man's degenerate prayer.

Mark David Chapman blasted five hollow point bullets from a Charter Arms .38 revolver on December 8, 1980, in New York City, and shot John Lennon dead.

* * *

I took an open-back three-wheel taxi from Bangkok International Airport through more traffic, haze, dust, and smog than I ever could have imagined, even in L.A. There were ten million people in Bangkok, and by my first impression, there was not enough space for half of them. The streets were flooded with two- and three-wheeled bikes, buses, cars, taxis, *tom-toms*, carts, dogs, and pedestrians. On many streets, I saw the multiform traffic overflow onto the sidewalk, right up to the edge of the buildings. I passed many foul-smelling canals that carried even more traffic floating in all directions.

I sweated in the intense humidity, and soon collected a visible coating of particulate filth and perspiration all over my skin.

The traffic barely moved. I was blacking out during the ride. Finally, I tumbled out of the taxi at the Wat Mahathat Temple near the Grand Palace in the center of the city. I gave the first monk I met all my cash, and I offered to work for food, shelter, and a chance to study Buddhism. He led me to another monk, who led me to another, who finally gave me my own mat for sleeping and my own bowl for eating.

I respected my elders.

I minded my manners.

Every day at the crack of dawn we paraded slowly along the street, collecting alms from the local people, who lined up to earn blessings and merits.

Meditation, yoga, study, work, bathing, eating, and begging for alms. Those were the rituals from which our temple lives were fabricated.

I spent as much of my time as possible in silent meditation on the hard floor of the Royal Chapel, at Wat Phrakaeo, inside the Grand Palace, where the Emerald Buddha resides. I wore no shoes and was careful to keep the soles of my feet facing away from the Buddha.

The Emerald Buddha was in the Chapel, on the grounds of the walled-in Palace compound, but it was open to the public every day from 8:00 a.m. to 4:00 p.m., as long as the Royal Family was not using the Chapel.

The Buddha image itself was scarcely two meters tall, and it was actually carved from a single piece of lustrous green jade, not emerald. Its origins were unknown, other than that it was found up north in Chiang Mai over five hundred years ago.

Yet, not to be outdone by the royal extravagance found throughout the Grand Palace, the Buddha's throne was surrounded by hundreds of other Buddhas, Bodhisattvas, guardians, holy statues, and other divine images, some bigger and some smaller than the Buddha himself.

There were many mysterious creatures, forever holding their hands above their heads, which supported the multiple layers of phenomenal reality on which the Buddha sat.

People came with prayer wheels, beads, incense, contributions, gifts, offerings, and mementos of their deceased loved ones.

The King of Thailand came to change the Buddha's priceless jackets of gold and diamonds to properly match the season.

Everyone from local Thai peasants to overfed tourists and sybaritic expatriate businessmen, we all bowed our heads to the floor with humility and hope.

That was where I'd sit, aspiring for enlightenment, before the most sacred and beautiful image in all of Thai Buddhism.

* * *

The years passed quickly, and I was surprised how irrelevant and unnecessary the supporting structures of American life had become.

There was an odd but thriving society of transplanted Americans, and other foreigners, living in Bangkok. It was pretty much as portrayed in the martial arts films and a certain genre of grade-B post-Vietnam war movies.

There was an *anything goes* mentality, like in that timely FM Radio hit, *One night in Bangkok*. Sex, drugs, and rock-and-roll twenty-four hours a day. Anything that wasn't actually legal was still pleasantly provided. And there was always a place to share a holiday dinner with your countrymen if you tended to feel nostalgic.

* * *

As for Buddhism, I grew to think it might involve the fulfillment of destiny between the Orient and the Occident in a cycle spanning all of recorded history. America's most important cultural function, other than the delivery of rock-and-roll, MTV, and Hollywood movies, may be as the final receptacle for world Buddhism, or even as the birthplace of Maitreya, the final Buddha.

Or America may be the cradle of Earth's final insanity.

And the Bible may even hold the answer in code.

* * *

Many great people and many scoundrels have had parts as colorful bit-players in this pre-destined drama. It is common knowledge that George Washington and most of our founding fathers were Freemasons who believed in ancient Egyptian magical teachings.

That is why American dollar bills are imprinted with the pyramid of Khufu. The Eye of Horus is shown in a missing capstone that has been buried by an ancient priesthood, and will not be seen again until the New Age of spiritual awakening has arrived. The Latin motto under the pyramid, *Novus Ordo Seclorum*, announces just that, A New Order of the Ages.

That is what America is all about.

We are at the apex of an ancient Secret Pyramid.

That is our place in the drama of world history. And all the players know their parts. Once you have been initiated into the cult you never doubt the purpose.

In the 1700's, the Native Americans had been subdued and all the major earth-related spirits focused their attention on the New World.

Thus commenced the occult struggle for control of America.

The most influential figure from the eighteenth century was the intellectually gifted, extraordinarily prolific Emmanuel Swedenborg. In the early 1740's, when was about 55, he had a series of visions that enabled him to talk to dead people, and to angels, and to God, with perfect visual clarity. He learned of a "Lost Word" that "...existed in Asia before the Israelitish Word..." And *the Word* was used to communicate directly with God. And *the Word* had the magical power to transform the user into a higher level of spiritual being.

People were mutable electromagnetic fields.

Swedenborg also discovered that Heaven and Hell are not future states of being but permanent and present realities that we can enter whenever we choose. If we developed our intuition and imagination, which are our spiritual organs of perception, we could reverse the Fall of Man and experience Paradise here and now.

Johnny Appleseed was a believer. He wandered the American frontier, in love with all life, planting apple trees and leaving pamphlets in cabins everywhere he went. The pamphlets were about Swedenborg, and his words were the seeds of American spiritualism.

Franz Anton Mezmer, an Austrian Doctor, discovered that our bodies are surrounded and suffused with a magnetic force that can be manipulated for therapeutic purposes. His followers discovered that animal magnetism could be passed from one person to another through manipulation of our electromagnetic fields. The universe itself seemed susceptible to, perhaps even constructed of, the mere vibrations of thought. And people possessed the power to manipulate and transform those universal vibrations.

Phineas P. Quimby was a healer influenced by both Swedenborg and Mezmer, who taught that matter comes from the mind of God and physical disease comes from a false idea in the mind of the individual. After he healed a seriously ailing Mary Baker Eddy through hypnotism, she developed Christian Science based on the idea that the mind of God is all there is.

In 1848, Katherine and Margaret Fox began receiving spirit messages in the form of knocking and rapping sounds in their family's home in upstate New York. People had ethereal, electromagnetic bodies that survived physical death. We were spiritual beings. We were ghosts. The teenage girls became celebrities. Séances became fashionable. Spiritualism flourished in America.

Also in New England at this time, a group of spiritually inclined intellectuals known as the Transcendentalists rebelled against Western religious orthodoxy and began a literary movement looking to Mother Nature and Eastern Philosophy for wisdom and enlightenment. Henry David Thoreau, the most well known Transcendentalist, published *Walden* in 1854. And almost a hundred years later, Jack Kerouac first learned about Indian Philosophy and Oriental Religion from reading *Walden*. And the message was passed along from the Beat generation, to the Hippie counterculture, to the New Age, and the next age.

* * *

In the nineteenth-century, an unfrocked Roman Catholic priest named Eliphas Levi, a.k.a. Alphonse Louis Constant, caused an occult revival in France that spread throughout the Western world. Levi was a master of the Rosicrucian interpretation of the medieval

Jewish Kabbalah, which is a pillar of modern Western magic equaled in importance only by the ancient Egyptian Hermetica.

The Kabbalah explains how the entire phenomenal universe comes from a hidden and infinite energy that has no qualities or attributes of any kind.

God is an Unformed Nothing.

The Kabbalah uses a "tree of life" to show the ten stages through which the infinite gradually becomes finite. Occultists use the tree of life to show the ten levels of consciousness people can use to retrace a path from the finite and mundane world we live in, all the way up to the infinite world of the Supreme Godhead.

Levi was also well versed in Eastern Philosophy, especially the Hindu scriptures. He taught the existence of a secret doctrine that unites all magical and religious systems. And, he says, immortal teachers with magical powers transmit the secret doctrine to worthy individuals at the proper time.

Levi is constantly studied and quoted by mystics, magicians, and occultists up to this day.

A close friend of Levi's, Edward Bulwer-Lytton, wrote occult novels about immortality, dreams, and the spiritual world. He relied on the earlier work of Swedenborg and Mesmer as well as on the help of Eliphas Levi. And Edward Bulwer-Lytton also wrote about the Rosicrucians, the source of the Secret Brotherhood.

The Secret Brotherhood of the Rosy Cross was created in seventeenth-century Germany by a group of Lutheran mystics, and named after a non-existent fourteenth-century knight, Christian Rosenkreutz. The Brotherhood possessed occult, alchemical, and Kabbalistic knowledge brought back from Egypt. They wanted to build a unified system of all knowledge to prepare humanity for the Final Judgment.

So the Freemasons borrowed from the Rosicrucians. The Rosicrucians borrowed from the Kabbalists. The Kabbalists borrowed from the ancient

Egyptians. And all the ancient Egyptian magical traditions were collected by Hermes Trismegistus into the Hermetica, a series of forty-two books that were stored in the Library of Alexandra. Those books are the bedrock of all Western magic. They are believed to be the oldest accessible human wisdom.

Hermes Trismegistus means *thrice great Hermes*, and that is the Greek name for the Egyptian god Thoth. He ruled as the most powerful philosopher-priest-magician-king that ever lived. And he lived for 3,226 years. And *his* books give us the greatest of all occult maxims.

As it is above so it is below.

If you understand that, surely, you can understand anything at all.

* * *

Then, one of Edward Bulwer-Lytton's loyal female readers would use his stories and ideas about western esoteric cosmology in conjunction with eastern polytheism to create a spiritual revolution that would indelibly influence the course of American culture.

Madame Helena Petrovna Blavatsky was one of the most colorful and significant characters to tramp across our American stage. She was born into an aristocratic Russian family in 1831. At the age of twenty, in 1851, she met her first occult teacher, a disembodied "Master from the East" with a white turban wrapped around his head. She soon began to amaze her family and friends with her newly acquired psychic powers. Then she disappeared for more than twenty years, allegedly traveling through Greece, Egypt, and Tibet.

And no one knew anything else about her.

Then she came to America in 1874, a stout and powerful old lady with light brown hair, piercing gray-blue eyes, and a broad, massive face. She was exotic and profane. She wore loose, badly fitting clothes. She rolled her own cigarettes with tobacco she carried in a furry animal-head pouch worn around her neck.

She said she had lived in Tibet seven years for initiation into a secret esoteric order headed by the "Lord of the World." She had been personally tutored by "Master Morya," one of the supernatural teachers linking humans with the *secret chiefs* in the ruling hierarchy of divine beings. And she rose to the highest level of enlightenment and occult power permitted to human beings at that time.

The most profound secrets were illuminated to Madame Blavatsky because she was adept at reading from the Akashic Records. These were vibrations in an electromagnetic field spread throughout the entire universe, pulsing at the same frequency as our own brain waves, on which all knowledge is recorded.

She was also mistress to a group of elemental spirits she called *diaki.* They were little people, with no real physical body like humans. They were somewhat inferior spiritual beings, of a lesser order than humans. And they liked to play jokes on Madame Blavatsky. But she had a sense of humor too, and they all got along just splendidly with each other. She was easy-going, and completely untroubled in the supernatural world.

She met Colonel Henry Steel Olcott, a successful scientist and lawyer interested in spiritualism, and they founded the Theosophical Society in 1875.

In 1877 she published *Isis Unveiled*, a 1200-page tome on Science and Theology that has never been out of print to this day. She often wrote through a process of astral dictation, exactly as her divine teachers wanted her to. She had direct supernatural access to scientific laws of nature unknown to ordinary people, that were still just as scientific as the other more demonstrable laws that govern the physical universe. She fulminated against Christianity, and explained how Buddhism was better because it could be used to dissolve apparent contradictions between science and religion and give us a perfectly unified system of knowledge. And, she said Darwin was wrong. He was narrow-minded. Human evolution from apes was just one step on our path back to divine consciousness because we were first of all descended from higher spiritual beings.

In 1888 she wrote *The Secret Doctrine* to elucidate how both the individual person and the entire planet move through stages of initiation to higher levels of personal and cosmic consciousness with help from the Masters. Moving up the ladder from one rung to another is the fundamental purpose of existence.

She influenced many well-known people in the intellectual and artistic circles of and after her day, including W. B. Yeats and Frank Lloyd Wright, and later, Aldous Huxley.

Several of her early students became gurus with considerable followings of their own. There was Gurdjieff, and Ouspensky, and then Krishnamurti, who many believed to be the manifestation of Lord Maitreya, the new Messiah.

Although the Theosophical Society and its numerous offspring still survive today, long after her death in 1891, it appears Madame Blavatsky and her followers tended to prevaricate, and misrepresent various things. Her enduring and prototypical legacy is one of scandal, fraud, and charlatanism. However, fraud and charlatanism are inextricably entwined with her bona fide insights into Eastern religious philosophies and Western magical techniques. It seems as if she had to be the scandalous kind of character she was to be able to understand and teach us as much as she did.

* * *

In the twentieth century, among all the mystic gurus and occult teachers that followed Madame Blavatsky's path and fit her pattern, some were more flamboyant and some were more obscure; but no one came close to the formidable nature, far-reaching influence, and sheer eccentricity of *The Great Beast 666.*

Aleister Crowley first pursued relatively orthodox training in the mystical and magical arts of the Hermetic Order of the Golden Dawn. But he was fiercely competitive and he could not rest until he became "the wickedest man who ever lived."

His own notoriety began in 1904, when he proclaimed himself the *Anti-Christ.* He performed a magical ceremony in a hotel room near the Boulak Museum in Cairo, and he received messages, not personally, but via his wife, from the Egyptian god Horus. He had tapped into the highest spiritual power in the universe. He had been chosen to perform sacred sexual acts and create a new *god-child* to usher humanity into the next phase of evolution.

He formed his own occult order called *Argentinum Astrum,* or Silver Star, and he wrote *The Book of the Law,* which rationalized his need to practice sexual magic rather than ceremonial magic. He stressed that his sexual practices were used exclusively for the purpose of obtaining higher magical powers.

His wife, Rose, eventually went insane, and so he unceremoniously discarded and divorced her.

Then he practiced his magic on a succession of mistresses he referred to as the *Scarlet Whores of Babylon.*

He died in 1947, apparently unable to incarnate the god-child because he never found the right Scarlet Whore of Babylon. They say an American team of occult operatives sabotaged Crowley's final project.

But The Great Beast was really just living his own Karma, trapped in Maya, no more and no less than anyone else.

Aleister Crowley was in fact an accomplished artist, and a prolific writer. His works are widely read and his teachings are widely followed to this day.

* * *

There were so many secret temples, lodges, magicians, witches, Rosicrucians, Masons, alchemists, spiritualists, people working alone and in groups, doing whatever had to be done to keep the wheels turning and maintain the necessary balance in the world.

* * *

Then, here on our own soil, the Beatniks became the first native American-born Dharma Bums. They appropriated wisdom from all times and places, instinctively desperate to fertilize what they saw as an increasingly barren and plastic postwar America.

They crafted and enacted an original vision of on-the-road homegrown American Buddhist philosophy.

Kerouac, Ginsberg, and Burroughs met in New York City in 1944 and began a documented literary and spiritual quest for God. They were a Catholic, a Jew, and a Protestant; but they could not find God in the temples and churches of America.

The message came from the books of all who had gone before them: Wisdom was in the East. They got the message, and studied all the Hindu and Buddhist writings they could find: the Bhagavad Gita, the Vedas, Lao-tsu, Confucius, and the Lotus Sutra. They strove forward. They struggled on, like true American pioneers. They taught us about Maya and Karma as they narrated their journey in their own stories and poems.

Alan Ginsberg reached Satori in 1954. And the Beat Generation took center stage on October 13, 1955, at the Six Gallery in San Francisco, when Ginsberg offered “free Satori” to listeners at his first public reading of *Howl.*

Kerouac published *The Dharma Bums* in 1958, and the first Zen lunatic mystics appeared soon enough, wandering the country with backpacks, looking, of course, for God.

Today, you can still hear recordings of Jack Kerouac reading his freewheeling American Haiku collection, *Mexican City Blues,* with jazz saxophone accompaniment. The essential Beat soundtrack was very cool American jazz, but the unambiguous message was always written in books.

William Burroughs ingested yage and felt himself change into a Black female, "a Nigress," convulsing with lust for a bucking Black man. He was seeking clues to the secret of the universe, and he looked wherever he might find them: Tibetan magic, Eliphas Levi, the Golden Dawn, and drugs.

And he fought daily against the external forces trying to inhabit his body, his mind, and his soul.

Burroughs was constantly under siege by devils he was hopeless to appease.

He published *Naked Lunch* in 1959.

* * *

Aldous Huxley came to America in 1937 after publishing *Brave New World.* He was an intrepid spiritual adventurer, a mystic with an extraordinary intellect, a discerning eye, and a deeply compassionate heart. He searched everywhere for unifying wisdom underlying theological doctrine that could be put into practice to better the human condition.

He studied yoga with the Indian guru, Swami Prabhavananda, who taught the doctrines of Vedanta. This is the foundation of Indian religion and philosophy, which aims for *moksha,* liberation from suffering, and teaches that Maya appearances are illusory and true reality is accessible only by direct intuition.

Huxley was also a great friend and supporter of the Theosophist and fellow pacifist, Krishnamurti.

However, even though both Krishnamurti and Prabhavananda opposed the use of drugs on the path to enlightenment, that is where Huxley followed a different sense of direction.

On May 4, 1953, a psychiatrist friend, Humphrey Osmond, gave Aldous Huxley mescaline crystals dissolved in a glass of water.

Somewhere in Heaven, Huxley found the doorway to Hell.

In 1954 he gave us an eloquent chronicle of his experience in two companion volumes *The Doors of Perception* and *Heaven and Hell.*

He elucidates the most important decision for each of us to make. And he carefully explains that if we begin with fear and hate, then our inevitable end will be uncontrollable madness and Hell.

Huxley's reputation suffered irreparable damage in the straight and normal world. But in the vanguard of psychedelic exploration he will be enshrined for all time as the most sagacious and well-grounded of all the visionary pioneers.

Amen.

* * *

By the mid-sixties, the Ph.D. team from Harvard University, Timothy Leary, Ralph Metzner, and Richard Alpert (a.k.a. Baba Ram Das) had published *The Psychedelic Experience, a manual based on the Tibetan Book of the Dead*, and dedicated it to Aldous Huxley.

Once the widespread use of psychedelics had fully revealed the utility of Tibetan Buddhism and other ancient Hindu, Taoist, yogic, and shamanistic techniques, the East-West floodgates were blown away altogether.

Dylan turned on the Beatles.

The Beatles went to India.

They put the message in the music like never before.

The *Magical Mystery Tour* took off on schedule.

And the curtain was raised for the final act in the modern world.

* * *

As for me, I really don't know. I'm just biding my time during the daylight hours. I do my own work at night, under cover of darkness.

So, yes, I'm here to find an old monk carving the perfect head of Buddha. But, first of all, I'm here to get the power and the magic I need to help reach my lover in the other world.

She wasn't supposed to be taken from me. Or, maybe she was? But I know I'm supposed to find her now, and help her, take her back.

We belong together. It is our destiny, like all the other immortal lovers before us, neither of us is complete without the other, neither of us can forget the other.

And I have enough faith in my own destiny to believe I can do whatever I have to do.

It is only a matter of magic.

It is only a question of implementing my will, imposing myself on the universe at large, regardless of the consequences.

Magic has many names. But it doesn't matter what you call it. Everything from ancient pre-Egyptian Necromancy to postmodern Chaos Magick is, to me, nothing but a disguise, nothing but a tool.

It is not Maya, it is Karma.

No matter what route I could have taken. I would have arrived at no other location than this one.

Even before the Greeks, since long before the days of Isis and Osiris, all the gods have wondered at this feat of separation and reunion, of one spirit into two, and two spirits into one.

There is no other drama more impossible, yet more essential, to the human condition.

However, unlike in the old tales, there is no myth here in my own story. I am not fabricating allegory or parable for your instruction. This is not a fable about the cycles of nature. I am not praying for a good harvest. I am not trying to appease the sun god so he will rise again tomorrow after passing through the underworld at night. I am not wasting your time with an esoteric weather report.

This is the real thing.

Life will conquer death for the sake of eternal love between a man and a woman. But, I'm truly sorry; it is not a pretty story.

Hold on to your stomach.

I cannot offer you much else to hold on to.

* * *

I followed the roots of esoteric Buddhist and Hindu philosophy all the way back to ancient Egypt, over ten thousand years ago. I went earlier than the Tower of Babel, and I spit in the face of the Hebrew God that tried to confuse me.

Jesus ushered in the Age of Pisces. That is a modern historical fact. It takes about 26,000 years for precession of the equinoxes, when the Earth makes a gradual shift in the orientation of its rotation. And the ages change again and again.

Jesus was the solar deity of the Gnostics. There is Astronomy and Astrology in the Bible. Jesus had 12 disciples, one for each sign in the zodiac.

The Egyptian Book of the Dead contains the root of all Judeo-Christian theology. Jesus' story is recorded in Egyptian hieroglyphics over 1,500 years before Jesus is born. The virgin birth. The resurrection. It is all so simple to see, the older comes before the newer.

Jews say YHWH is the Lord that did not exist before in the time of Egypt, until He announced His name and His presence to the Hebrew people after the Exodus. He is a new God, never known before.

I don't care. I don't believe anything. I just have to go back to the beginning. I need the truth.

I walked through African grasslands, where I could stand on the original pillars of Hindu thought.

I went back over twelve thousand years ago to the Garden of Eden in the Tassili-n-Ajjer Plateau in the Sahara Desert of Southern Algeria.

I swam in the watery chaos of the Babylonian Tiamat with the half-formed and underdeveloped souls.

Then I went even further, through the smoke of Atlantis, to the Ancient Mother of all magic on Earth. Back more than fifteen thousand years. Back before the flood.

Back thirty thousand years ago in the Americas.

Back fifty thousand years ago in Australia.

Back one hundred thousand years ago on the African continent.

Back to the Churning of the Sea of Milk when the world was created in an epic tug of war between Good and Evil. When the gods and demons pulled on opposite sides of a multi-headed snake, twisting around the mountains and churning up the sea. Milking out the elixir of life. That is the magic potion over which the gods and demons will duel forever and ever. That is the elixir of immortality extracted from the center of the universe at the birth of creation.

* * *

Time is not linear anymore.

I traveled through time to the point where all things are present.

Now, I cultivate all my connections.

I adjust my own soul to other densities and learn to cope with all the vibrational variations.

I cooperate with disembodied agents of all kinds, and I try to avoid conflict whenever possible. I try to create new life in these other dimensions more than the amount of death I must leave behind.

Sometimes I feel like I am making a whole new world all by myself.

And yet, I am still haunted by my dreams from that night many, many years ago, as if on automatic playback.

Allison's mother is yelling in my face.

"I thought there was a primary directive in Psytron: Do not kill, and do not die. So what happened to my daughter? Why did Allison kill herself? Isn't that against the rules?"

Of course, I didn't know.

"I'll tell you why she killed herself. Because of you, and you didn't even know about it."

"No, I was on a mission. I was at a retreat. I..."

"Retreat from this you worthless piece of garbage."

I jumped backwards off the cool gray slate steps as she slammed the door on my head.

"I'll get her back," I said, crying, stumbling through the rose bushes, and flailing my arms as one thorn after another pricked my freshly tanned skin.

But it didn't really happen like that.

An old crone comes screaming in my face, "You're the devil. You're the devil." She starts clawing at my skin; forcing her fingers into my mouth and trying to rip my cheeks open with her thumbnails.

Her own face is covered with that clammy old-lady sweat and it's dripping down the valleys of her fat wrinkled neck.

Lightening is flashing left and right of her.

No matter how hard I try, I cannot talk. I can't make any words come out of my mouth. I have no way to defend myself from this murderous witch.

But it didn't really happen like that.

Allison is with a CIA operative who has been pre-programmed as a sleeper to attack the President. She gives him a new biological weapon that auto-activates upon a preset proximity to the target, but the sleeper is shot dead by a psychic agent before he gets close enough to the President. Vinney Cold Killer, Allison's own father, kills the sleeper.

Allison's failure leaves a troublesome live link back to the SSC, up to Elizabeth, and to the Originator.

After a thorough reorganization, each operative is given a Bunsen burner and an unidentified specimen to cultivate in a Petri dish as part of a new experiment. A natural form of life from another dimension where evolution didn't proceed on the physical plane but only on the mental plane. The physical body remained deceptively simple. A perfectly normal thing, with abnormal powers.

How can they be so dangerous?

It is the birth of a new form of evil. Able to defy physical reality, as we know it. Bloodsucking slugs with the power to crawl across dimensions and wreak havoc, with psychic powers evolved beyond anything else on Earth.

Now, finally, everyone walks off the stage and all goes black.

Allison is dead.

There is nothing but one ill-defined lump left all alone and in the dark.

And that is what I believe to be closest to the truth.

10. BANGKOK

I wasn't as surprised as I might have been. I had suspected I might be attracting his attention recently.

Now here he was. Old, yes, but stronger, not weaker. Big as ever. Thick black hair pushed straight back. Dark eyes that sometimes didn't move at all when you expected they would.

I knew his body wasn't really there in my room with me. He was using Psytron telepathy to externalize his *psychic being* here, and talk to me just as if we were meeting face-to-face.

He told me he was worried about the perpetuation and application of Psytronic Theological Technology after his death. He had done his best to prepare for one final expansive organizational thrust during his life.

It had all come down to the interaction of Eastern Thought and Western Technology. It was no accident he developed Psytron in the fertility and luxury of post-world-war-two America.

Earlier, Count Alfred Korzybski's 1933 publication of *Science and Sanity* introduced General Semantics as a kind of neuro-linguistic, neuro-semantic system for understanding errors in human thought. Korzybski claimed that rigid dualistic Aristotelian logic distorts our perception of reality and actually causes us to go insane when we fail to differentiate real phenomena from the words we use as labels for those phenomena. A few decades later, Korzybski's remark, "the map is not the territory" would become a popular cliché.

Then during the post-war Cybernetic craze, there was a widespread academic and scientific shift of focus: from matter and energy, to form and pattern. The most pressing scholarly question changed from, "What is it?" to, "What does it do?" And this pragmatic analytical approach spread through Epistemology and Neurophysiology, seemingly on its own quest to understand the workings of the human brain.

The Originator entered the scene in 1951, when he was barely twenty-six years old. His first best seller was called *Binary Procedures*, a practical workbook on the technology of psychic balance.

The book included exercises and guided meditations structured to help you simultaneously envision two contradictory extremes to the point where you gained freedom and comfort in the middle.

Balance. That is where it all begins.

Then he followed with *Cybernetics, The Logic Of Thought*; *Brain Maps/Brain Traps*; *The Morality Of Immortality*; *Primary Principles Of Existence*; *How Many Minds/How Many Bodies*, more than a dozen other major titles, and a seemingly incalculable number of articles, tapes, and lectures.

He made passing reference to various theological scriptures and an odd selection of literary and philosophical classics from around the world, but he strove for as much originality as possible. And he much preferred inventing new words to learning old ones.

Now, finally, he has brought his ideas and techniques to a level of sophistication that requires the use of semiconductors to comprehend and apply. The urgency of his mission requires the capacity and speed of digital transmission to reach the critical mass of people before it is too late.

And he needs me to go underground again for a crucial mission here in the Orient. He says it is something only I could do.

No matter what Elizabeth and the SSC think of me, this is the Originator himself confiding in me. Of course, I listen carefully to what he wants.

He says, "Don't worry about Elizabeth anymore, your peculiar mental condition will actually be an asset to us now. You will be able to do what other people can't do, because they are too absorbed in their own identities. As if their identities really mattered. But you don't have that particular problem, do you Mr. Freeman?"

He tells me to join a Japanese cult called Iam Asiam, *I-Am As-I-Am*, and follow its leader back to Tokyo. The Dreamer, as he was called, was passing through Thailand on his return from India and Nepal. He made a grand display of himself visiting shrines and temples throughout Asia's Buddhist and Hindu communities.

The Dreamer has tremendous financial assets derived from his disciples in Japan.

The Originator continued briefing me on the Dreamer's terribly bizarre background. "He fancies himself a reincarnated female witch, burned at the stake in Avignon, France, in the 1600's. Then, after a few more colorful lifetimes, he was eventually re-born into a Japanese male body after the end of the Second World War. His father died in the bombing of Nagasaki. That's where he lived with his mother until he entered the prestigious Faculty of Psychology at Tokyo University in the mid-sixties.

"Then on March 3, 1971, after religiously following all the Manson-family Tate-LaBianca murder trial news, he went to Los Angeles, on his own initiative and at his own expense, to study Satanism and Witchcraft. He was only twenty-five years old at the time.

"A couple years earlier, Manson had been roaming Death Valley with his brainwashed followers. They were trying to incite and prepare for the *Helter Skelter* race wars that would destroy modern civilization, just as predicted by the Beatles' song. Manson was going to hide underground, in a tunnel, and then emerge as leader of the New World Order. But he was eventually arrested hiding in his cabin after the 1969 murder rampage.

"Something about Manson and his followers fascinated the Dreamer. I'm sure he envied his powers of mind-control. And he probably wanted to learn from Charlie's mistakes too.

"So the Dreamer moved in with a coven of sadistic lesbian witches headed by one very old Hollywood hag calling herself Sister Claire. He believed Sister Claire had been his lover in an earlier lifetime when they were both female witches, in France. But it all ended so horribly and she had to watch, helpless, as the Dreamer was burned at the stake for witchcraft. The entire incident seems to have caused them both to suffer irreparable damage."

The Originator continued, "Yes, I know all about Sister Claire and her coven too. But, in L.A., for some reason, she developed into an extremely anti-Psytronic personality. And unfortunately, she eventually had to be neutralized by the SSC in a rather complicated, but unrelated, incident. So she is of no concern to us anymore.

"Anyway, in the beginning, they all got along well. Sister Clair and her coven taught the Dreamer everything he wanted to know. All the things he had known as a female witch but had forgotten when he reincarnated as a man.

"He learned how to conjure up a demon by first drawing a circle with a nine-foot radius. Then a six-sided star, a hexagram, must be drawn inside the circle, so the witch can stand with genitals at the exact center, and feet and arms precisely three-feet apart.

"This is all based on the most powerful occult sequence: 0-3-6-9. Errors in measurement or execution enable the demonic powers to escape the circle and attack the witch.

"But, apparently, the Dreamer was not too good with measurements. As the story goes, some evil force of one kind of another broke lose and invaded the Dreamer's soul, through all his bodily orifices of course, and turned him into, what they call, a *white zombie*.

"The coven reacted, perhaps first out of genuine fear and the survival instinct, to quickly rebuild the magic circle and contain the demonically possessed Dreamer. And then, perhaps simply to be sure he was adequately secured, they used chains and shackles to keep him properly centered. But what happened after that was just plain ugly and evil.

"He was confined and tortured like that for more than a year. And Sister Claire encouraged all the other witches to exercise their imaginative abilities and to entertain any sadistic urge they might fancy.

"I don't know all the details of what happened during his confinement, but despite his claims of multi-lifetime friendship and passionate intimacy with Sister Claire, the Dreamer was surely subjected to brutal torment and humiliation at the hands of that filthy coven. And he never quite recovered.

"Back in Tokyo, in 1978, he was still working on rebuilding a new identity for himself. Perhaps still trying to integrate the knowledge that he was now a Japanese male, he used to be a French lesbian, and somehow despite all his occult knowledge, he just got his head stuck up his own ass in Hollywood. Anyway, he composed a collection of poems, in Japanese and English."

The Originator handed me a piece of paper and said, "I want you to read this one now."

WHICH WITCH

In the end my friend you'll see
(I can talk to you when you are not here)

Which witch you say doth speak now here
Now hear I say to have no fear
For me or what I'd do to thee
For 'twill be true as always is
To tamper not beyond the bound
Of what one thinks be as the ground.

So listen not you'll hear no sound
Till as you want to be 'tis free.
Such as without the round of men,
Such as without the round.

Yea, burn me not, I beg of thee.
Yea, burn me not I beg.
For fear's still felt from darker days
When fire lit the night
And eyes did watch and eyes did see
The eyes of me melt out for thee
Had fires set and flames I'd get
Did burn and scorch the skin off me
And boiled blisters bursting out
Could not that fire not 'er put out.

So watch I did and scream and shout
From pain within and pain without.

Yet a curse would I cast
And a one would not show.
Henceforth, you see just what your eyes to you show.
And today still not more does your mind ever know.

By Hajime Nakamura

I finished reading, looked up, and the Originator continued the briefing.

"I think Sister Claire must have helped him write that one. But anyway, he signed it Hajime Nakamura because that was his real name before he became the Dreamer.

"He thought up the basics of his I-Am As-I-Am scheme and started proselytizing with his own private satellite TV station, beaming out *healing psychic powers* to paid subscribers all over Japan. The money kept rolling in. He adapted a variety of Indian yoga and meditation techniques to produce a constant flow of new information for a gullible public.

"Then, following the usual psychotic logic, he explained how society was violating the will of God. Society was evil. The Government was evil. The Apocalypse was coming, ancient Mayan cycles, *blah blah blah.*

"You know how it goes. Sounds like a comic book about a Doomsday Cult. The Dreamer is the reincarnation of Jesus. Only He can save humanity. And of course before He can save it, He will have to destroy it. Especially, because of all the materialism in American and Japanese societies.

"But his actual plan is to dominate the entire world by military force. Listen to me now, he is well on his way to assembling a fearsome arsenal of biological, chemical, and nuclear weaponry. Of course, governments on both sides of the Pacific are somehow blind to everything this madman does. No one appears situated to stop him."

"So you came to me?" I ask.

"He'll be at your temple tomorrow."

The Originator knew everything about me, and everything I had been doing over the years since I had become anti-Psytronic. He asked me to use the special abilities I had acquired through my occult studies to observe and learn all I could about the Dreamer's use of magic and psychic manipulation. I was ordered to submit myself to his mind-control techniques, especially those involving his development and use of new psychedelic compounds.

I was to determine if he could be useful in fighting the Holy Conman. Then enlist his help or manipulate him into useful service. Finally, I would destroy his Iam Asiam cult by sabotage at the appropriate time.

Even though I was alone, I would be able to outmaneuver and overpower the Dreamer. The Originator himself would be my psychic contact on this mission. And, I was reminded, Psytronic powers are far superior to those of other occult practitioners in any other discipline.

No one else would know about this assignment. Not even his wife, Elizabeth, my former commanding officer, and still chief of worldwide security.

He said, as if in a dream, "I know all about your attempts to reach Allison using pre-Egyptian esoteric technology, but it won't work. All the ancient magical traditions on Earth are illusory and misleading. No infusion of modern terminology, no matter how elaborate and detailed, can add any substance to the essential vacuum of these old traditions.

I thought, How could he know that? If he knows that, then he knows more about me than I know about myself.

He continued, "You shouldn't feel bad about the years you've wasted. We've all wasted thousands of years on Earth. The history of humanity is nothing but the continuing story of men and women in lifetimes of fruitless pursuit of the knowledge and power to realize their dreams."

The Originator explained how he himself had to climb the same merciless mountain of human ignorance, failure, and desperation as I had. And no one had ever reached the summit alive before him, though many people thought they had.

"Illusory success is the most common form of failure," he said.

He was able to discover and develop Psytronic Theological Technology only after utilizing special karmic techniques to personally absorb the mass and weight of all prior moral and theological human failures, just the way Jesus had personally absorbed the sins of all men.

"However," he concluded, most importantly to me, "you are right about one thing. You and Allison. It *is* your destiny to be together again.

"And now that you are back on the Psytron team, I will personally take care of that for you as soon as your mission is complete."

* * *

I was up early getting ready for my mission. This will be easy, I thought. First, I listen to his lecture. Then, I let him know I believe whatever he says, and I become his follower. A simple two-step process. No trouble at all if you just give people what they want. Gurus were just people. They want to be loved and appreciated the same as everyone else.

The Dreamer appeared amidst a gaggle of pink-robed female assistants. He himself was wrapped in a royal maroon robe opened over layers of white silk covering his chubby torso. His eyes were half-closed slits. His facial expression looked too dreamy, like he was oblivious. But I saw a different problem. He had too much hair. His hairline reached down too low, encroaching on his forehead. It made him look simian.

He was carrying a solid gold staff, taller than he was, and wearing a gold handcrafted combination cross, ankh, and mystic star around his neck. The Funkadellic Pope, with his own groupies, I thought very quietly to myself.

He presented our old and revered Buddhist Abbot with a fresh peach sliced open on a silver platter.

It was moist and shiny, pinkish where the pit had been removed, fragrant, and almost seductive. The Abbot was clearly perplexed. What was he supposed to do with the peach? What did it mean?

A younger monk quickly relieved the older man of the confusingly vulgar gift at the first opportunity.

The Dreamer spoke to the assembled monks in Japanese while several translators chattered away in different corners, in various languages and dialects.

He explained that red and white were the Shinto colors of male and female, which combined to give us pink, his favorite color of all.

Then he said, "I appear to you as just another fat man. But I was born of the most important *Fatman* ever: the ten thousand pound Fatman nuclear bomb shot from the B-29 named Bockscar, 9600 meters above Shiroyama, Nagasaki, on August 9, 1945.

"Like my father, exploding, unforgiving and untouchable, far above the Earth: I am born to change the world.

"I too have cracked the primordial Egg of Chaos. I too have scrambled our yin and yang like the first Fatman did in a blazing red and black sky over Nagasaki. I too will change the world.

"Now I can tell you, Iam Asiam takes you into the heart of Oriental and Occidental magical traditions and gives you the power to transform the entire world even more than nuclear power ever could.

"The nature of the Tao is chaotic and uncontrollable complexity.

"But one single certainty is all that is required.

"That, right there, is Iam Asiam."

I didn't know what the hell he was talking about.

He warned any would-be followers, "Do not come with me unless you are *already* like a deity, needing nothing for yourself, and ready to sacrifice all you have in this world for me and Iam Asiam.

"My will is the way. I am the light. I am eternal.

"I am, as I am. That is all you need to know."

The eyes of his female followers were sparkling with admiration and awe.

"Now, let me see through your eyes, that I may delight in the pleasure of seeing myself.

"I am, as I am."

* * *

No one understood what he was saying. The other monks didn't care anymore. But I had to stick with him no matter what.

The orange-robbed Buddhist monks, young and old, weak and strong, on any path, from Thailand, China, and Tibet, practicing the lesser way, Hinayana, or the greater way, Mahayana, were unanimous in one belief: The translators must all be joking.

There was no way to comprehend the nerve and blasphemy of this over-fed, scraggly-bearded, middle-aged Japanese man. His financial contribution to their temple was sizable, and greatly appreciated, but he had already used up his welcome. If I was going to follow this funky psycho guru, I had better do it fast before they run him out of town.

I heard the next stop on the Dreamer's itinerary called for him and his entourage to appear at the Wat Traimit, Golden Buddha, later this afternoon before hosting a banquet at the Oriental Hotel this evening for some local politicians.

Wat Traimit was a simple temple that held the largest solid gold Buddha in the world. The Buddha was five tons of solid gold, over seven hundred years old. But the fact that it was made of gold wasn't discovered until 1955, when, during a moving accident, the plaster skin was cracked and the hidden body of gold was seen for the first time. The temple was south of Chinatown on Traimit Road. Just a five-minute walk from Hualumpong train station. I was sure he'd go by car, but I could get there faster by train.

I'd be there waiting for him when he got there.

11. ON A DARK AND NARROW PATH

I waited until closing time at 5:00 p.m., but there was no entourage at the Golden Buddha that afternoon. Also, as I would soon find out, no politicians or any other guests were expected at the Oriental Hotel later that evening either.

The Dreamer showed up alone just after five and walked directly to me, where I was standing before the gates.

"You like images of the Buddha don't you Mr. Freeman?"

"Oh. Yes sir," I answered, thinking how did he know my name?

"The Golden Buddha, the Emerald Buddha, do you think we can learn anything looking at these lifeless statues, day after day, month after month, and year after year?"

"I...."

He didn't wait for an answer.

"Do you want redemption for your sins?"

"Ah...."

"Or do you want redemption from your own being?"

"You know I'm not sure what you...."

Mr. Freeman," he snapped, "The universe, you know, is a machine for making deities."

"I, ah, I...."

"Do you know who said that?"

"Ah, you?"

"Yes, of course me, but before me, a Frenchman, Henri Bergson. Don't you read French Mr. Freeman?"

"No, Sir. Sorry, I don't."

"Well then, let me make this quick and clear. It is *I* who have been waiting for *you* for quite a long while now.

"You can hide your identity and your activities from the minds of these silly monks easily enough, but I know who you really are. I know you have been initiated into the Black Arts. The blackest of all occult practices. And I know everything you've done in the dark."

Okay, I thought, one more guru guy who knows more about me than I know about myself.

"Now," he said, "we must go and take what is ours. Neither the universe nor the deities should be kept waiting any longer."

He explained, "We need a Magic Triangle. Our own Holy Trinity. Three spiritual entities synchronized like a single pair of eyes to see and understand the specific and essential nature of Maya reality, independent of any other extraneous aspects of reality, subjective or objective."

"Ah, okay," I said.

He and I were two of those entities.

He would introduce me to the third entity shortly.

He spun around on his heels and propelled forward.

I followed in his wake.

We walked and walked through a maze of Bangkok streets, with no further conversation, before turning off the last paved road over forty-five minutes later. Then we started walking along a braid of narrow dirt paths, some with boards and some with stepping-stones to keep our shoes out of the sludge and stagnant waste.

The sun had set a long while ago and the scarcity of electric lighting prevented me from seeing the ground clearly. I could barely distinguish shapes sufficient to place each foot down without abnormal anxiety.

There were small wooden buildings on both sides of us, so close they blocked out the sky except for a ribbon of moist, black air directly above our heads.

Over the years, I had seen many eerie and distressing sights in this part of the world. I learned, as an American living in the so-called Third World, you had to focus carefully and selectively or you could get deeply depressed here.

Tonight, I was comforted by the sight of other people, especially children, scurrying between buildings and through spaces even narrower and darker than our own path.

There were old ladies outside their homes, passing time, taking in the evening air. They ignored us even though we had to brush right by them.

I could see inside many dimly lit rooms. One bony old man was sitting before a black-and-white television, with his shirt off, waving a paper fan. I saw a baby crying alone on a dirt floor. What else is there? What else could I expect to fill all these rooms?

Occasionally, as I walked along, trying not to lose sight of the Dreamer's back, the smell of someone's dinner cooking would give me a reprieve from the smell of the garbage and waste.

Then, finally, we reach the dead-end of a seldom-used, weed-filled path.

There is a latch on a wooden shutter right in front of me.

The Dreamer points. I lift the latch and pull open the shutter to see in the open window. There is a frail, ancient monk dressed in faded orange robes, working alone at a low table by the light of a few well-placed candles.

There are carving and polishing tools laid out on the table.

There is another monk sitting in a dark corner. He seems thin, pale, and young.

I start stammering something about who I am and why I'm there.

The ancient monk lifts up a wooden Buddha's head that he has been holding under a soft cream-colored polishing cloth.

He motions for us to enter the room through the door next to the window. We go in and sit on the dusty floor just inside the doorway.

The room seems barely big enough for the two of them to lie down and sleep on the floor.

I get close enough to see the face of the young monk.

"Wai Yu?"

He doesn't answer, but I'm sure it is Wai Yu, exactly as he was in Los Angeles.

"Wai Yu?" I ask again.

"Why not you?" he replies.

"What? I thought you were going to stay in L.A. to help Buddhism and America."

"Fuck America man. I went to L.A. for you."

The old carver starts talking.

He speaks softly, but he cannot be ignored.

I try to forget about Wai Yu for now.

The old monk explains how he carved the Perfect Buddha's Head from a single piece of sacred Yew, how he painted it and now how he is decorating it. He says he has been doing this for more years than he can count, never achieving the desired result. But this time he believes it is exactly as it should be.

"Jesus was crucified on a cross of Yew," the Dreamer mumbles almost to himself.

The old monk says, "Now, do you know why you are here?"

I'm speechless. I don't really know.

Wai Yu laughs, and mumbles, "Karma."

The Dreamer says, "We are here for the head."

I can't believe he said that, he announced it really, like it was a command.

"You like the head?" the ancient monk asked the Dreamer.

"I like what you put into it."

"I put everything into it."

"I know, I can feel it."

"No, not yet," the monk said as he reached for the cream colored cloth he had been using, and continued polishing the red dye on the front underside of the head.

My heart sunk to my stomach as the face of the head was turned away from me, and I felt my eyes start to burn.

"Why?" I said aloud to anyone.

I felt the air thicken around me as the old monk continued to massage the front of the head.

His face fell lifeless. Utterly depleted of energy.

Wai Yu was not laughing anymore.

I knew what had happened. It was obvious in an instant. He had entered into the head, literally inside the head. When the head turned around it would be animate, *alive*. I was going to see *real* magic. Not just a work of art. A truly *living* work of art.

The head turned and saw me sitting there, gross and oafish. Scarred by my past and scared of my future. Unsure of myself in the present. Tired beyond my own recognition. Older than I thought. Different than I thought.

I couldn't remember who I had been before that instant, but now I was looking at myself with cleared vision, through eyes more powerful than my own.

No one else knew what the Buddha's Head knew. The Perfect Buddha's Head knew everything in this world and in all the other worlds too.

"I am ONE. All that is Real. All that is Unreal. All that is and is not. I am undivided. I am the known and the unknown."

I didn't know who was speaking.

"This is who I am. This is what I know."

The ancient monk was undisturbed and lifeless.

The Dreamer was wide-eyed and radiant. He reached into his robe and pulled out a folded piece of dark silk, which, as he spread it open on the floor, began to look increasingly like a stained glass window, reflecting an undetectable source of light through its multicolored panels.

He reached for the head, lifted it slowly, and placed it gently in the center of the silk stained glass window. Then he deftly pulled the four corners tight, tied it up, and said, “Let’s go.”

Wai Yu sat staring into space as I got up after the Dreamer and walked out the door of that tiny room.

We started to walk the narrow paths in-line, just as we had come. The Dreamer was leading and I followed in back. But now everything was different. The trail was too steep. The ground was slippery. The angles were too sharp.

We were turning too many corners. I couldn’t see the children anymore. The old ladies were gone. I wanted to see that old guy with the bony ribcage watching black and white television. I was desperate to see him again, for a reason I could not understand, but knew I never would.

I couldn’t smell anyone’s dinner. Even the familiar, inescapable stench of human waste would have been a comfort, but it was gone. All I could smell was my own fear-flavored skin.

I had given up trying to figure out when and where these paths were ever going to end when a thick wall of moss-covered, crumbling old bricks with no apparent exit blocked our way.

The Dreamer bent down in front of me to push some weeds aside and then pulled on a squeaky, rusty metal handle. A slab of corroded iron opened out toward us making a space barely wide enough for a man to squeeze through.

The Dreamer stuck his head in first, then pushed and pulled his fat torso through the opening. And I followed him through to the other side of the wall.

I felt as if I were seeing Bangkok for the first time, even though the city had long ago become a familiar refuge for me.

I was standing at the mouth of a wounded monster, still breathing, unaware of its own approaching death.

Half-bodies sat on damp sidewalks with hands outstretched, asking for money. Bodies with no hands or feet shove tin cans and pans around to collect contributions, and then use whatever stumps they have to guard their assets.

There are simply too many people everywhere I look.

I could swear I see a head without a face pass through the crowd as we walk.

Then I see a dark rush of worms and slugs wiggling through the air in symmetry like a school of fish swimming through water all around me.

They scared me. I looked down.

The ground was dark but shiny and wet.

Somehow, the simple recognition of solid earth was a comfort to my crippled mind. But the dampness on the ground, I wonder, what is it? Is the city salivating? Is it ready to swallow something, some unseen morsel, or a mouthful of thick indigestible goo?

I see cockroaches chewing on human limbs. They have huge pincers and vicious hyena mouths. I look away, unable to find respite in anything else my environment can offer. I try to walk seeing nothing at all, knowing as little as possible.

Young boys come up to me again and again harassing me with menus they stick in front of my face. Sexual acts were listed for selection. All categories of boys, girls, and shemales were doing all acts imaginable, in any dream or nightmare you could care to choose.

It was all too bizarre.

I see Thai soldiers standing proud and tough, armed for battle. Prepared for any problems, any violations of any rules. But what could the rules in this place possibly be? How does anyone know what people are supposed to do, or not do here? I surely don't know.

I worry I might be tested and punished at any minute. But the satisfaction on a young soldier's face tells me everything is as it should be here. Everything is under control, just as *they* want it to be. Who are *they*? I don't know.

Nervous tension increases the air pressure all around my body. I am being warned: I must be careful. Fine lines are being drawn by unseen hands. I must be more careful. I try not to step on the lines. I walk like I'm a little boy again, skipping over cracks in the sidewalk by my home on Long Island.

I skip as carefully as possible over a dying man's thigh, chewed off at the knee, to follow the Dreamer as quickly as I can.

We reach the Chao Phraya River. We hop on a waterbus. We ride upstream past the Wat Arum Temple of Dawn and get off a short while later. We take a longboat taxi up one of the klongs that run through Bangkok like blood vessels, supplying the essentials of life, and slowly, very slowly, carrying away the inevitable waste. We go from one to another klong, until we finally get off at some point in the forest indistinguishable from anything else I've ever seen in the forest, and walk until we find a clearing.

The Dreamer says, "This is the place."

He bends to balance the wrapped-up head on a mound of grass.

We sit in meditative poses on either side of the head.

Our surroundings are illuminated with a beautifully multicolored Inner Light radiating through the silk wrapping.

The wrapping unties itself and slides down to a neat pile at the base of the Buddha's Perfect Head.

The Dreamer says, "You get whatever you want here," and then he closes his eyes and lays his hands gently, palms up, stretched out on top of his knees.

* * *

Whatever the Dreamer wants is up to him.
I want Allison. I've got to find her now.

12. ALLISON'S WONDERLAND

She called me. I heard her. It wasn't her usual sweet and melodious voice, but I still knew it was Allison.

"Where are you?" I yelled into the darkness. "I'm not really crazy you know. We should be together again. It is our destiny, our Karma. Even the Originator told me so."

I heard her say, "I'm sorry. I'm dead now. It was all a terrible mistake."

"No!" I said, "What was a mistake?"

She said, "All I can do, is tell you my story. I have no other power. I'm allowed no other freedom. Please, just listen while you have the chance."

And she began her story...

"After you die, existence will be more complicated than when you were alive. It certainly has been for me.

"It is surprising, but when you die, you don't learn much about death in general. All you learn is about your own specific death.

"And who you are, can vary greatly from who you think you have been."

She told me, "The first thing I remember, I was in The Hall of Welcoming Committees. There were tables. Ordinary, wooden-topped, steel-legged six-foot-long folding tables were lined up left and right of me.

"People were standing shoulder-to-shoulder several rows deep behind the tables. They were all clamoring for my attention, like at a carnival sideshow.

Too many people hooting and howling at the same time. Calling me by name, as if they knew me. Saying other things I couldn't understand, but I'd repeatedly catch the phrase, *come here, come here Allison.*"

As she spoke, the images first began passing in front of my eyes like a phantasmagoric movie, then, soon, the images enveloped my body and mind like a 3-D hallucination.

She says, "The tables were arranged like this for over a hundred yards. Lined up on ten-foot-wide granite slab steps. It was part of a huge stairway leading up to the entrance of a building, bigger than an auditorium, more like a convention center complex. I looked, but I couldn't see to the end on either side. And I couldn't see to the top.

"I felt my attention being pulled back to the rising cacophony around me. There was an increasing urgency to the voices. The characters reached the edge of panic as I returned my gaze.

"Their eyes were wider. Their faces were stretching out further, propped at the end of taut spines.

"The tension eased a bit as I resumed my slow walk up the stairway. I felt as if I knew a certain panic had been avoided, but I didn't know whose panic it was, or why, or what it was about.

"I tried to look more closely and separate one face from the others. Yet, I couldn't clearly distinguish individual faces and I couldn't match any one face with any one particular voice.

"I was walking instinctively now, just like I'd walk on the streets of Manhattan, with apparent purpose and determination, thinking that would make me a less desirable target somehow. If I stopped, the predators would be more likely to attack.

"I was still trying to focus more clearly. I was seeing the faces in flashes, more like caricatures than actual human faces. The voices were still jumbled.

"I looked down at my feet. I didn't have on any shoes. No clothes. Nothing. I was naked.

"I went into a semi-crouch to hide my pubic hair with my hands and keep my thighs locked.

"I searched for protection or shelter, but there was nothing. Just the tables, and the steps, and the faces.

"I started laughing at myself, thinking of my New York City pace and my self-defense posture.

"These faces, whatever, whoever they were, they didn't care if I was naked or not; and now I couldn't afford to care either. It didn't matter anymore.

"I resumed my ascent with a forced sense of abandon.

"The faces seemed to get closer and clearer. I saw shiny brown skin that strained at the cheekbones and stretched so tight it was brittle. I saw teeth that were constantly exposed and chattering like a dummy's wooden teeth, with lips drawn back in a fixed smile. They all looked the same, but I knew that somehow they weren't. They were different from each other just like ordinary people were different from each other.

"I started moving more to the right, trying again to selectively focus on one face and one voice.

"It was a girl.

"She had delicate hair like mine, blond and straight, absolutely alluring. I imagined it would smell so good too.

"I saw her wide dark eyes.

" 'Come here, come here Allison,' she called.

"Her voice was clearer, and becoming distinguishable from all the others.

" 'It's me. It's me Allison,' she said.

"I could hear her even more clearly now. Her words made a melody resonant and seductive."

Yes. Yes. It's me Allison.

"I was very close now. I saw her lips were fuller and more human than I first thought. Her skin pale and soft, almost like a baby's.

"She pushed up against her side of the table.

"I saw her milky-white breasts, just like my own. Her softly rounded stomach. Her bigger-than-average shoulders."

It's me Allison. It's me Allison.

"We were face-to-face. I couldn't hear anything but her voice. Everything but her face was a blur."

It's me Allison. It's me Allison.

"We were so close she only had to whisper.

"Then, I could even hear her breathing. She wasn't talking at all anymore, just breathing. I could feel her breath. It was the mirror image of my own.

"She was sucking the air from my mouth into her own.

"I felt my facial skin tighten, pulling my lips all the way back, exposing all my teeth. I saw her full red lips open, hungrily sucking in all the air. It was my air! She was swallowing it like an elixir. Exhaling with a voice eerily like my own."

It's me Allison. It's me. I'm Allison.

"My breathing had stopped."

Yes. I'm Allison. It's me....

"Her spoken words had been reduced to the underlying flow of rhythmical but indistinguishable sound."

Buh dum, buh dum, buh dum.

"I collapsed as the scene in my head went black. Black, but pulsing to that evil rhythm."

Buh dum, buh dum, buh dum.

"There was nowhere else to go."

Buh dum, buh dum, buh dum.

"The rhythm was all I knew."

Buh dum, buh dum, buh dum.

"I had to claw my way back up to the top of the blackness.

"My breath! I felt a resurgence of panic, Am I breathing?

"Yes! I'm breathing and the rhythm of life is flowing through me like a river, I thought for a second.

"Then I heard comprehensible speech again."

Sorry, I can't let you go that far. I can let you feel the rhythm, but it is not yours anymore. You are dead, you know, after all.

"And then there was silence. No rhythmic pulse. Nothing.

"I was still there collapsed on the stairway, in front of one of those ordinary six-foot-long folding tables.

"I raised my head to look around.

"There was no one but me. Just the tables, the stairway, and now I could see an immense but obscure entrance all the way up at the top.

"I still had my memory. I could remember the rhythm of my beating heart and the flow of my breath. But now both were gone.

"Yes, but I still exist, I thought, fighting to survive. I think, therefore I am, right?

"And don't forget the stairway. The Stairway to Heaven. I thank God, Led Zeppelin, and everybody else, because now I've got it right here in front of me.

"Yeah, I've got no heartbeat, and no breath, but I've still got *attitude*. Dead or not, I'm still from New York. And if there is nothing else to do, I'll just exude attitude as I trek up these stairs.

"I began walking, but the doubts were right at my heels.

"It won't work. Who am I even trying to fool? Myself, of course.

"*Myself?*

"That's a heavy concept.

"I'm so confused, I feel like I'm talking to myself out of character.

"I continue walking; trying not to doubt myself, or double guess myself. But it is not easy.

"There is too much silence, too much emptiness, and too much time.

"When I think about it, forever seems way too long.

"I had already been walking for minutes, days, or years. There was no way to measure.

"I looked at the next step and saw a limitless world. I remembered: *A universe in a grain of sand.*

"I was confounded by my own regret at having to leave the infinite intrigue of one step's surface to climb up to the next. It took effort to understand that yet another infinite universe was surely waiting for me on the next step.

"Before, in life, I had used the English word 'infinity' like other people, because it was a convenient and ordinary word, without worrying I didn't really know what it meant.

"Here and now I eventually came to understand a *multitude* of infinities.

"So I could bound from one step to the next, like a god, hopping from universe to universe across the infinite, infinite cosmos.

"Then, I was there, at the entrance, astonished at the vast depth and breath of it.

"I thought I heard a hum.

"Or was I feeling a pulse again?

"It was coming from the fathomless interior of the building. It was a profound rhythm. The building had its own unique vibration. It was subtle, yet deep and inexpressibly comforting. The building was serene, secure, and sure of itself. It was conscious. I sensed it, and it set me at ease.

"I entered with calm and contentment.

"An ambient light let me see wherever I looked.

"I felt the light too was a living extension of the building. It was all the same energy, changing its form according to its function. Different harmonics of the same living essence, producing the phenomena of matter and energy right before my eyes. Living energy."

No.

"I heard that voice again...."

Not alive, but beyond life and death. It exists here and now, and that is all you need to know. You do, after all, have a more pressing problem to solve.

"A wall of light self-illuminated into fluctuating waves of pink and powder-blue. It shot off to the right through a hallway I hadn't seen before, seeming to perfectly fill the narrow space, floor to ceiling and wall to wall.

"Particles were falling to the floor, then disappearing, like incandescent snowflakes, leaving a path made of fairy dust, too magical to ignore.

"On my first step, I found it warm and dry, but slippery, like a powdery lubricant. As I brought my other foot down, I was whooshed away, propelled by the powdery path itself, at roller-coaster speed.

"I was carried around one long bend to the left, out into the middle of a vast open cavern. I could see no walls, ceiling, or floor, other than the path of particulate light that had carried me here.

"Out there, far away, where the light ended, I was surrounded by darkness; three hundred and sixty degrees of darkness all around.

"I'm gonna be really, really lonely here, I thought to myself."

Wrong again.

"What?"

You forgot about me. You can feel me coming closer now, can't you?

"Yes. Who are you? Where are you?"

Buh dum, buh dum, buh dum.

"I could feel the rhythm again too."

Buh dum, buh dum, buh dum.

"I heard it again clearly now."

I am the only one who can save you from eternal silence after yet another and another eternal silence.

"God? Is that you?"

Here and now, I am Allison.

Now, where and who are you?

"I curled into a fetal position and found myself floating at my own bosom, instinctively sucking for my own life."

Yes, my little baby, think about it.

"The voice was coming directly from my own mouth, my own face, looking right back at me.

"I can think, but I don't believe....

"I can think, therefore, I can doubt that I am."

Good. You leave Descartes in the dust.

* * *

Do you see? You are a discarded shell. You have lost the delusion that you are at the center of your own existence. In fact, you are barely even a participant in your own existence anymore.

You are a shadow of dead skin, a fragile form without substance, waiting for me to blow you away to formless dust.

Yet, perhaps I shall keep you as a trinket.

My interest in you is the only energy that enables you to maintain your present form.

If I so much as ignore you, you would crumble to absolute and utter nothingness.

Do you understand?

Is that what you want?

Is that why you killed yourself? To become part of the undifferentiated energy randomly dispersed throughout the infinite cosmos?

Shall I leave you now, floating here like a shadow, ready to disappear?

Or perhaps, your value as an amusing trifle is equal to the scintilla of energy I use to maintain your curious form, your rather pretty feminine shape?

"I could not talk. I could not even make a sound in my own head."

Your silence serves you well.

The world does not wait for the dead.

Come along now my little Tinker Bell.

* * *

"What are you doing?" I screamed, "Who are you?"

"Somebody's got her, somebody stole her damn soul!"

13. THE HOLY CONMAN

Hidden among the stars of the Milky Way, at the center of what we think of as our own galaxy, 27,000 light years away, there is a gravity-bending mass greater than 4 million of our suns. It is a super-massive black hole of such tremendous power that it gobbles up anything and everything coming near. Scientists study it, analyze it, name it and try to describe it.

The Holy Conman made it all by himself, and he simply calls it *home*.

The Holy Conman does whatever he wants there, and everywhere else too. Whatever, wherever, whenever. There are no other rules.

There is nothing else to consider.

Tonight, the Holy Conman will forsake the comforts of his home, because something about this particular place on Earth, and this particular point in time, has attracted his attention. He wants to look through human eyes again, right here, and right now.

He does not doubt himself.

He never questions his own motivations or desires.

He is equally careless of any god, demon, or human, whether living or dead.

But of course, he does not want to actually *become* human. He would silently smirk at the thought, recalling the Jesus fiasco. It was fun for a while, and certainly worth the trouble for all the souls acquired, but not something he'd want to do again.

Yet, sometimes he wants to restrict himself to a certain extent, for example, to see only what a human could see. So he would borrow a human body again, and look through human eyes.

His crew of experienced and dedicated operators would perform all the details of the task for him. His billions of loyal legions were there to give form to his image, and to realize his will. Billions of operators, servile as they may be to him, were each a demonic wizard and master of impossible magic by earth standards.

His own body is a perfect Astronomical Map of the cosmos, and each speck of cosmic dust or point of light was an entire world full of Cities of Angels.

He is the Holy Conman, the Holy Ghost, and the Great Spirit that permeates all of life. He may be someone or something other than God or Satan, yet, he is inseparable and essential to both. He is perhaps somehow more male than female. But he is the entity whose identity is unknowable. So everything he is, he is to the degree that identity and differentiation, in human terms, become meaningless.

We cannot even say if he is only one, or one of many.

* * *

Soundwaves blasted into the brain of Genetic Freeman as if he were surrounded by stadium loudspeakers. It was a message of attack, and a warning to surrender.

“YOUR BODY IS THE TEMPLE OF THE HOLY GHOST, WHICH IS IN YOU, WHICH YE HAVE OF GOD, AND YE ARE NOT YOUR OWN.”

Again and again and again. He felt his eardrums beginning to bleed.

The advance legions of operators began to fill the body being used by Genetic Freeman. They would leave room for his spirit to coexist, or they would exclude him from his own body if he interfered with any of their finely tuned procedures.

Usually, human beings made no attempt at all to resist the Holy Conman or interfere with his operators.

Humans were more likely to feel unlimited confusion and paralysis than the urge to fight back.

All routine procedures were being followed and nothing was out of the ordinary during the incursion into the entity identified as *Genetic Freeman*. The human mind was entrusted to an elite corps of operators, as always, with a one-to-one cellular ratio strictly observed.

The world started to look different as impurities were dissolved, cellular imperfections corrected, and all bodily systems maximized.

A universe in a grain of sand.

Even when looking through ordinary human eyes, the Holy Conman saw a world far more radiant and more nearly perfect than any human could ever see.

He saw the original living complex of shapes and patterns. Energy pulsating. Flux. Infinite yet distinguishable gradations of material, form, and energy. The light spectrum made to dazzle the gods. Sounds in a vibratory system reaching throughout all possible realms in conscious search of their own divine dissolution.

The human olfactory sense was the most peculiar sense of all. Mother Nature and Humanity seemed in constant conflict to provide Earth with a surprisingly wide range of both malodorous and fragrant smells.

The Holy Conman was pleased.

He felt human emotions again. He felt human ignorance. The utter inability of humans to understand what gods did or what gods wanted.

The Holy Conman knew what it felt like to be human on planet Earth. To be human was to be unsatisfied. To be human was to feel desire and fear.

He detected the familiar human feeling of insufficient control over his environment. He felt the potential for anger, and the urge toward violence.

Yes, it was just a small task to take over a human body like this, but there was pleasure in a job perfectly well done.

The Holy Conman was hungry now.

And of course, he wanted sex too, a lot of sex.

But then, suddenly, fireballs of electricity pounded into the ground around him. The lines in his field of electromagnetic force were jerked out in all directions at once.

Someone was attacking the Holy Conman!

The operators tried to avoid damage by contracting the Holy Conman's electrical field, but for all their speed, even they weren't quick enough. The Holy Conman was pinned and stretched out like a butterfly on display.

Hundreds and thousands of operators were disintegrating each second in a firestorm of relentless electrical attack.

The Holy Conman tried to see beyond the force of the containment shield. There was a crackling noise that quickened into a fearsome urgent roar. Some operators tried to fly through to launch a counter attack.

They burned up like moths in a volcanic flume.

* * *

Genetic Freeman was seeing stars.

He was dreaming of fiber cables stretching across space like an uncountable number of crazy intersecting spider webs. Bright, pulsing, multidimensional fiber cables.

He passed out in his own dream overwhelmed by the complexities of light. He sought the refuge of darkness.

He felt a razor slash through the blackness, and he felt a cut open to nowhere. He felt the immensity of the time he would spend there.

Distance was the same as time.

Self was nothing more than static interference in the melody of existence.

There was dust on the lens of perception. Dust. Lots of little tiny specks of dust.

Then, a wave rose in the distance, rolling in his direction.

He thought someone didn't like him looking at those fiber cables.

The open cut to nowhere healed itself, and space closed up black as it was before.

The lights were contained again, wrapped up inside the cables, rushing from source to destination.

There was no time or place for self.

There was nothing but blackness.

Someone wondered why all this was happening, and where all the light was going.

At the same time, someone else seemed to be wondering, who wondered about it all anyway, and why did they even care?

14. THE LIZARD LADY

My vision is clarifying somewhat. Physically, I feel like I've suffered a powerful blow to the head. Mentally, I feel like I am in déjà vu all over again for the final time.

I remember seeing Allison, and talking to her too. But that was somewhere else. I feel certain of her absence in this place.

I am more self-conscious and feel more attention focused on me than I ever imagined possible. I wonder if I've been drugged. Or if I haven't woken up at all from whatever it was that took me out.

I realize I am walking past full-length mirrors to my immediate right, but I am too scared to actually look and see.

In my peripheral vision I see an amorphous white mass and I can't help thinking it has somehow become attached to my body, making me look like a hunchback.

I think I can feel the increased mass and weight.

I am careful to do nothing but walk slowly ahead.

I have only one desire; just one single certainty is dominating my thoughts: *I do not want to provoke them.*

Who are they? I have no idea.

But there are so many of them, they are numberless. They are doing something to me. Treating me for some disease. Punishing me for some violation.

That is all I know.

My consciousness, my identity, has been reduced to the size of a small pea, just above and right behind my eyes.

First, I think I am walking, because that is what it looks like from the progression of scenery in my field of vision, but thinking again, I cannot be sure if my feet are actually moving, or if I even have feet any more.

I just don't know. My nervous system, if it is still connected at all, doesn't work the way it used to.

I swallow. I think I swallow. I look down.

I'm moving along on a conveyor belt, but I can't see it so clearly. The light is weak and irregular. I seem to be on an assembly line in a large enclosed space, like an airplane hangar. I hear metal-on-metal noises, humming engines, and spinning wheels.

Conversation? Maybe. I'm not sure.

I look ahead. I'm approaching the end of the line about twenty yards away where it exits through a hole in the wall.

Something is waiting for me.

Someone is moving.

I close my eyes and think. I try to formulate a plan. I have one choice. To show myself, or not. I can assert my existence and at least let them know I'm alive, but I don't know whether they *want* me to do that or not.

The line stops.

My eyes open.

I see dozens of small clouds of luminous kaleidoscopic gas flying through silver-tinted air. I see tongues of fire. I hear whooshing and whooping sounds as the clouds pass by and seem to coalesce at destinations around the room.

I feel something behind me touching the white mass on my back.

I try to turn, but I can't do it.

Seconds pass. A minute. Maybe more. I hear a sharp crackle and feel a release of pressure from behind.

I turn and see.... *A nurse? A lizard?* It's a caricature of a female with green-and-black scaly hide, and a voluptuous bosom stuffed into a big white bra; and she is dressed in an all-white nurses' uniform!

I think she is looking at my eyes, or maybe she is looking at that little pea-size self behind my eyes. I feel her probing, or programming, my brain.

Things are moving too fast now, like I am being sucked along in a dangerous current.

I have to regain control of my own body again.

What is she doing to my brain?

I have to do something, anything, fast.

I reach out, and shove my hand inside the V-top of her uniform and under her bra. I find instant comfort in the familiarity of my own lust and the feel of her breast. Yes, I *can* feel it, I think to myself, and I am reassured somehow, about something, by the fact that I acted of my own accord.

My other hand makes a quick grab for her other breast.

I look up and see a smug grin on her reptilian face.

It's a trap. I've taken the bait and fallen for some kind of trick. My hands fall away, limp and empty.

I never decided I wanted to feel anything at all. Someone else decided for me.

She is smiling as the conveyor belt resumes and I move along toward the wall.

I am pulled through the final Hall of Mirrors.

I sense inside myself that I have been trained in psychic warfare. Now I am being challenged. I am being threatened by familiar and unfamiliar entities as I enter the Surrealistic Carnival of Total Demonic Control.

I try to turn away, and I find myself inexplicably working in a Psytron office in Los Angeles with people I don't really know, but I am pretending to know. There is an office boy, a half-wit do-nothing on a ten-year contract soon to expire. The office manager, in sarcastic response to one of the boy's continual mistakes, says, "What are we ever going to do without you Charles?"

I turn around and say, "I'll replace him, but I won't work as hard and I won't work as well. Is it a deal?"

"No deal," they all say.

Then, Kevin, a kid I beat up in a fair fight in Catholic school, walks into the office. He is escorting a shuffling old Japanese guy, who is holding a thin measuring stick, with a full set of false teeth balanced on top, and a string hanging down from the bottom jaw. Kevin pushes the guy toward me and says, "Here, I got him for you. Caught him playing practical jokes on another gaijin over on the Yamanote Line."

Something is wrong.

I'm in Los Angeles.

A gaijin is a foreigner in Japan. The Yamanote Line is a train in central Tokyo.

And I don't know how I know that.

I hear myself say, "Hey, he's cool. He's one of the good ones. He's a funny guy too. I like him."

The old guy is visibly relieved. He is standing up straight in his shabby, pink, pre-war clown suit, as I get thrown out on the street, like garbage, in the middle of Tokyo.

I approach a group of American sailors trying to talk to some young Japanese girls in a crowded intersection. I tell them I'm a special agent sent by the President to ascertain the mental health of American citizens in Japan.

Everyone vanishes before my eyes.

I'm walking all alone through an empty train station.

I see slim figures in the shadows at the distant end of the platform, leaning up against the wall.

I walk to the end of the platform to join them. I find three Japanese transvestites, or Shemales, or *New Halves*, as they are called here. They are wearing cheap slit skirts. Standing there. Not waiting for the train, but waiting for something else that I don't know anything about. And I can't figure it out, because nothing else comes here but the train.

I walk up the stairs and out of the station.

It is the end of the night, and the bar hostesses are getting off work. A drunken salaryman is throwing up in the gutter. A friend is patting him on the back.

A half-naked old lady comes running up the street, animated and noisy, but incoherent.

She runs straight over to me.

Does she know me?

Her skin is wrinkled and sagging. Her face is turning red, and her eyes are wide open.

She starts pulling on her own nipples. They are too long, and she is pulling too hard, left and right, on her exhausted old tits.

My face turns pale white.

I try to look away.

I see a crowd has formed around us.

A young hostess steps forward, gets down on one knee, opens her blouse and shows everyone her raw leathery nipples are even bigger and longer than the old lady's.

She starts to stroke and squeeze them until she forces out a stream of rust-colored liquid that squirts out to collect in a puddle on the already damp ground in front of the silent crowd.

I can't tell anymore if she has nipples or dicks in her hands.

I can't tell what the liquid is. Is it milk? Is it sperm? Is it blood? What the hell is it?

She squeezes it out in continuing spasms for one full minute without comment from anyone.

Then, finally, as she stops, she lifts the back of one hand up through a weakening stream of liquid to catch a line across the back of her fingers.

From the way it bridges the space between her fingers, I think for sure it has the thick and sticky consistency of male ejaculate.

She lifts the back of her hand close to her face and says, "*Kusai, kore wa.*" This stinks.

How do I know?

How do I know what she says, and what it means?

I don't want this knowledge. It terrifies me.

I dissolve into the collection of moisture left on the street and disappear from the scene.

This is not my place.

This is not my problem.

Unseen hands are pulling at my ankles, pulling me down deeper and deeper into the dark earth.

My own hands flay helplessly above my head.

I'm screaming, begging them to stop.

"Take me home. Take me home. Let me see the faces of *my own* enemies."

I am gagged, and then bound at my elbows, wrists, knees, and ankles.

I myself have become an old lady, and I am being burned by religious fanatics in early America.

How can I be so feeble? Empty? Worthless? Like rubbish.

I am looking at myself. I know that is me. And I know those are the people who burn me again and again every time they have the chance.

I foolishly try not to hate them; but I hate them anyway.

I use my power—*somewhere, somehow I know I do have power*—to maneuver the simpletons further into the grasp of the eternally evil enemies of humanity.

Even as my eyes steam and melt, I find strength knowing these people will suffer more than I.

Then, I hear thunderous laughter reverberate all around me.

A swarm of demons engulfs me and carries me away.

They grow in limitless number and thicken into an ocean of tar-like slime.

Each molecule in each drop of slime is a whole and entire person; and each and every one is mocking me.

I hear a billion voices crying, aimed directly at me, "Help me. Help me."

My mind cannot compute.

I abandon myself to the voices, and just listen, trying to endure as I am battered by the waves of sound.

Each molecule is shrieking louder and louder.

I finally realize they are *not* mocking me at all. They are seriously pleading for my help. They too are afraid. They are even more afraid than I am.

They are up to their eyes in an ocean of fear so ancient and great it must surely be the original fabric of Hell.

I start to wonder again. I don't want to think about it anymore, but I can't stop my thoughts.

What can cause this much horror?

And, where might that thing be?

I sense the distant movement of something so massive it is like a shift in the position of the sun.

I cry, "Oh God. Please don't let that be it coming here now."

The fact that I can feel so much power, from the mere presence of this thing at such an immense distance, that something like this can even be part of existence, makes me want to disappear and be gone without a trace. I don't want to know anything at all anymore, and I'm sorry I ever did.

"Please God, let me just *negate myself.* Or, *You* can erase me. You can do it! You are God! Please, obliterate me like I never existed. You don't need me. I don't want to be here anymore. God, please...."

"But," I hear a consoling female voice say, "You can't just negate your own existence."

The Lizard Lady walks to the end of the line. The clouds of colored gas whoosh around her, and whoop, whoop to stop at the end of the line.

The Old Testament tells us Job broke his seven days of silent suffering not by cursing God, but by cursing the day of his own birth. Asking not only to die, but asking to have never been born.

However, if there is one thing we know from the Israelites covenant with God, it is that you cannot escape from God.

I can see everything all around me now.

My body lies below me as they lift me through the exit into an electromagnetic field that fits me so well, it is my home and it is myself, from the very first instant of my own unexpected inception.

* * *

Of course, the Holy Conman was able to quickly identify the attacker's unavoidably self-projected identity. And he was satisfied to know his enemy's name. Now he could leave the area.

Yes, there was no doubt he could leave, regardless of how many operators would be sacrificed. His plan and its execution would be simultaneous and instantaneous. He didn't need time to think and act like a human would. The time *between* one thought and the next was all the time it would take to execute his escape.

He directed a positive pulse of operators in an energy flow as sharp as that of a laser perfectly timed to hit a negative vibration in the electromagnetic containment shield. Then he simply shot himself through the hole.

Easy. This entire universe and everything in it was subject to such manipulation.

Humans could not weigh physical matter accurately. Nor could they measure energy correctly. They were utterly mystified by the naturally chaotic patterns of phenomenal reality.

Humans could not even measure the position and momentum of the particles in their own environment, while the Holy Conman could predict the precise speed and location of all matter and energy in the universe if he so desired. How could anyone dare attack him and not know this?

Most of the operators in his mind were with him in perfect synchronicity, though some had fallen behind. However, of those in his body, more than half were lost to the containment shield for slight errors in timing.

There had been a thunderous implosion, and the shield disintegrated, taking along everything in its grip.

The location and dimensions of the shield were discernible from the small crater of blackened ground left in its place.

And one body was left burned and bleeding, face down in the mud.

* * *

Elizabeth was usually busy with more mundane espionage and legal affairs, but extraterrestrial interference was a red-flag priority per operating order #619732. The op-ord was clear: "Contain the intruder and detain any humanoids until you complete a check for Psytron involvement in present and past lives; then give a full verbal report to the Originator."

Elizabeth's complexion had taken on a sickly greenish tint.

"You let the intruder escape. You lost the humanoid to that meddling old Lizard Lady. And you say this humanoid was an enemy of Psytron?"

The Originator continued to review what he had been told.

"The humanoid was knocked out of his body by this intruder. You tried to freeze the intruder in your electromagnetic trap, but he broke out and got away."

Elizabeth made an almost imperceptible nod.

"The Lizard Lady transports the humanoid out of there before you could isolate him for containment.

"Some New Age Buddhist monk wraps up a wooden head in a rag and runs away like his ass is on fire.

"That is the entirety of your report?"

"I declare myself unfit and unworthy, in urgent need of remedial intervention. I..."

"Shut up woman! We've got no time for that now.

"You let the Holy Conman take possession of your enemy, and survive an attack with your best weapon.

"This is the beginning of the end for all of us.

"Declare a Worldwide Condition Red. No one has access to me or to my office until further notice.

"I'm going to visit this Lizard Lady myself.

"You're in charge while I'm gone."

* * *

Here in the Transformation Chamber, the Lizard Lady followed no one's law but her own.

She helped the lower entities, including humans, create new and diverse forms with the fabric of, and in expression of, their own potentially infinite beings.

She believed such creative originality was surely meant to be a dear pleasure and amusement for all the gods.

Without such pleasure, wouldn't the value of forms diminish, and thus render their continued existence questionable?

She knew the old fat one was watching her now.

The one who called himself *The Originator.*

His spirit was sharp and clear, yet dense and hard, like a well-cut diamond. He was utilizing his Psytronic invisibility technique, using his aura as an impenetrable shield to protect himself from psychic attack. He may *think* he is invisible, merely reflecting the light around him, with no friction and no heat. And he may *be* invisible to all others, but she could see his flaws.

"Subtle vibrations perceptible only to one *such as myself*," she said.

She habitually amused herself with this terminology, as if there were any others such as she.

The Originator was allowed to be as he was, as she continued with her own thoughts.

Psytronic techniques enable you to free yourself somewhat from ordinary reality. You become more detached. Ideally, you experience things from just outside the bounds of your own physical body. You avoid getting bogged down in the apparent density and mass all around you.

"Loosen the illusion" was one of their many trite sayings.

She knew the problem with people on Earth.

They didn't belong there. Earth wasn't their home. Each and every person on earth had been forced to become *a divided indivisibility.* That was the source of their original problem, their first disease, and the original sin.

Evil is inside matter itself. It grows more powerful only because human beings cannot see it exactly as it is, when it is, and where it is.

Time allows only an illusion of change, which people can be manipulated to perceive as progress. That is all part of Maya and Karma.

Now, what humans see as the dawn of the space age is really the dusk of human life. Period. And no one cares. Too many other things to do in the rest of the infinite universes.

The Earth's insanity comes from the West, the direction of death. It is an Occidental malignancy that will destroy the world in time. But it is a blameless thing. Really no one's fault. Not the White man's fault. Not the Yellow man's fault. Not the Black man's fault. Not the Brown man's fault. And not any woman's fault. Not the government. The capitalists. The military. No one can be blamed. Blaming each other is just part of the problem in the first place. The driving force of civilization will finally drive a spike through the heart of its own imagination. And that is just the way it is.

Then there will be nothing else here on Earth worth her time.

She'd been here long enough already.

Though the Lizard Lady was capable of great ferocity, it was not within the nature of her present work to display aggression needlessly. Scaly black-and-green reptilian though she may be, she was, after all, a mother figure, a beloved matriarch, to so many people.

She always tried to look her best.

Since bringing herself within the Earth's orbit all those eons ago, she has mimicked a hodgepodge of features and appeared in a variety of forms as they caught her fancy from time to time.

People have correctly and incorrectly called her by a variety of names. Kali, Isis, and the Black Madonna. Ahemait, the part hippopotamus, lion, and crocodile, goddess of the underworld and eater of the unworthy dead. Hel, the half-black and half-white Norse Goddess of Death. Coatlicue, the Aztec earth-monster. The Motherless Aphrodite Urania. Dakini, the psychedelic goddess of esoteric Tantric yoga who can permeate your entire being and give you orgasms that reverberate through your mind and body unabated, for hours.

She currently favors the lizard skin, which she adopted a while ago, as an artistic homage to all the great dinosaurs she has known and loved.

She shaped her own petite version of Tyrannosaurus hind legs and tail. But, although she thought the T-Rex mouth was the most glorious and attractive of all such organs in Earth's history, it would be too much for her own face. She couldn't do it justice.

Her upper torso was a recent re-design, modeled after Marilyn, the media goddess who passed through several decades ago. She gave herself a pair of those preposterously bulging breasts, too heavy to support themselves, so she needed a deep wide bra capable of holding them in firm peaked and protruding pyramids.

She could afford to be playful here. This was her home.

And no one could enter her home uninvited, unless she allowed it.

Even the Holy Conman would pay a heavy price for a forced entry.

So now her curiosity was piqued by the Originator's approach.

She allowed him to energize his form right there in front of her workbench, where Genetic Freeman lay supine and unaware.

The Originator never lowered his eyes. He made only the slightest recognition of her particular form, to acknowledge her individual existence, with no show of either fear or desire.

She waited to hear his purpose.

He explained how he originated Psytron Theological Technology on Earth to deliver personal immortality to certain individuals. How he wanted to free humanity from ignorance and endless suffering at the merciless hands of the Holy Conman.

He told her, though she knew already, of the Holy Conman's recent encroachment into Genetic Freeman's body, and Elizabeth's failed attempt to contain or capture the Holy Conman.

He told her of his weapons, and his strategy, and the need for secrecy.

"The situation is drastic. The worst in Earth's history. The Holy Conman can be expected to invade soon, and with devastating consequences."

She was growing bored of his voice.

"This one on the table, this humanoid is one of mine, an enemy of my organization," he said.

She was perfectly still.

He had no clue what she would do.

He continued, consciously trying to avoid demands or provocation, "What will you do with him?"

He tried to fill the resulting silence, and soften the demand for explanation into a gentle inquiry... "I wonder?"

He just wasn't good at subtlety anymore. Much too accustomed to barking orders at submissive underlings.

She was impassive.

He tried again, "I would like, if possible, to know this one will not go to the Holy Conman yet."

He thought he saw a slight movement in her reptilian eyes. Was it a sign of acquiescence? Was it time to relax?

He let his eyes soften.

He noticed her tight white blouse was open wide at the top, showing a triple-strand pearl necklace caught in deep cleavage.

He saw the partially exposed inside edges of a sparkling clean white bra.

Long sleeves. Lace white gloves. Bracelets. Rings. He could see to just below her waist. Her workbench cast a shadow there.

He couldn't see her lower half.

He shifted slightly trying to illuminate the shadows.

She smiled.

The sight of her teeth and the motion of her wet tongue snapped his attention back up to her face.

He saw her eyes sharpen, as his own got wider and glazed.

He was being gently but forcibly removed from the premises, caught in an irresistible energy flow, which he could only ride back to his original point of departure. He lost control.

"She makes a good move at the first opportunity," he said to himself, "I've been on Earth too damn long."

Now she would finish her work and allow Genetic Freeman to re-associate his own identity, re-build his own physical form, and continue his own existence, *if he chooses to do so.*

15. SERIOUS GENETIC DAMAGE

I woke up huddled in the grass like a wounded animal. I hurt badly. My skin was burned. I could smell the leathery dankness of my own blood soaked into the dirt under my face.

It was dark. Fear and my survival instinct were commanding me to hide and give myself time to heal.

Something else was compelling me to find the Dreamer.

He would likely be at the Oriental Hotel. It was the best hotel in Bangkok. It was the only place I could think of to look for him.

It didn't take long for the downhill walk back to the first canal, but then it took a couple of hours to float and paddle my way through the entire sequence of filthy klongs, and up along the Chao Phraya river, to the Oriental Hotel's riverside patio entrance. I got there as the sun was rising and the river was coming to life with the myriad activities of the ancient mercantile and pedestrian interests of the citizens of Bangkok.

I had no time to shake the scummy water off my clothes when a dozen pink-robed men and women surrounded me. I was hustled over to a white, rose-covered gazebo where the Dreamer sat meditating toward the rising sun.

He spoke without looking in my direction. "Again, I have been waiting for you. Come inside quietly and show me who you are this time."

The entourage hid me in their midst as we hustled along the beautiful and fragrant garden paths to a private bungalow, the Jim Thompson suite, named after a local legend.

The door closed, we were left alone inside, and the Dreamer turned to face me for the first time. "*Now, who are you*?"

"It's me. It's me." I tried to reassure him, but I knew I needed to reassure myself first.

"I have to verify my own identity," I mumbled to myself as I walked in front of a full-length bamboo-framed mirror.

I looked in the mirror, but goddamn, *it wasn't me.*

Ignore the burns. Forget the blood.

"I'm not here anymore," someone said.

I looked closer, forcing my eyeballs to search themselves for signs of recognition. I thought of the Buddha's head becoming animate.

"I'm insane. I always was insane. Just now I finally understand, I am really insane."

The Dreamer asked, "What happened out there?"

Exhaustion hit me like a ton of sandbags. I didn't care. I couldn't care about the unthinkable things anymore. I gave up. I knew I had no control over anything anymore.

"I need sleep. I can't do anything else now," I said as I collapsed face-first on top of a clean, embroidered white bedspread with one solitary vision clear in my mind: Allison's beautiful blond hair, slightly strawberry-tinted face, and the deepest, blackest parts of her eyes.

* * *

I see Allison coming into a large formal cocktail reception. Ladies dressed in black-and-white maid uniforms are carrying trays of champagne glasses filled with a pink liquid, but it is not champagne.

Allison stands alone and scans the crowd. I follow her gaze to a lady with outrageous patchwork skin, like a metallic quilt of blue, gray, and silver.

Allison can't believe her eyes, but she doesn't want to show her astonishment and attract attention to herself. She turns her head and starts walking toward me. She begins to speak, quietly but urgently, pointing at that lady, as if she came here specifically to tell me about her, because no one else will tell me what I need to know.

She comes right to me and expects to look at me face-to-face, but now I am lying on the floor. She bends down to touch my shoulder, I turn, but there is no face on the front of my head. My legs are gone. I have instead, a scaly tail, like a fish or reptile. It is the same scaly patchwork as that lady she is trying to warn me about.

I flip my tail up in the air, and she sees my face there, serene, on the underside of my tail flap. I show no emotion, no desire, and no expression of recognition at all.

The outrageous patchwork lady comes over to me and starts sticking acupuncture needles inside small white circles almost hidden in the pattern of my own patchwork skin.

Allison retreats.

She didn't know about the white circles.

She doesn't know what to do here anymore either.

* * *

The ancient Egyptians understood one great danger in the afterlife was traveling through the underworld upside down.

If you got stuck in this position you would end up eating your own excrement for the rest of eternity.

Although it is wise to know techniques to avoid this predicament, today this knowledge is rare.

* * *

The Dreamer has fallen asleep in his own bed.

Normally, he thinks, he would not be afraid of the twisted gods now on their way to play with him. He knows how to deal with demons and disembodied agents of any kind, he thinks. But, today he has already depleted most of his power just to survive this far.

He feels the troop of warrior savages enter the room, as I do, but neither of us tries to stop them. Their mere presence, at this close proximity, has paralyzed us.

They don't bring weapons. They bring parasitic cannibals from one of the many other dimensions antipathetic to human beings. They come for the amusement of torturing stupid earthlings.

They pick us, they say, out of all the people on this planet, because right then, we are the most vulnerable, the weakest. They have no greater morality or reason to attack us then a pack of wolves choosing the weakest prey from a flock of sheep.

The Dreamer is instantly thrown into a consciously vivid dreaming state. He is being judged by a jury of twelve translucent white zombies in a trial presided over by Baron Samedi, Lord of the Graveyard. He feels a voodoo doll clasped in his own right hand, under his own pillow. He sees the bungalow floor covered with prohibited pornographic materials. He knows that illegal sex toys are hidden under the carpet. More voodoo dolls are buried under the patio outside in the garden. He can feel them now too. He knows the hidden things are there. Stone containers of ancient ointments and salves for compounding the Witches' Ungent. He knows he has been captured and his sanity and life are at stake.

I think it is my responsibility to help, but I am alone, and no one else will go with me.

As soon as I think about beginning to investigate the situation, I am captured *just for the thought of helping*. And the zombies carry me away.

I am corralled in with dozens of other prisoners and slaves. I am forced to join the others acting out scenes depicted in the prohibited pornographic materials.

The Baron Samedi watches us, passing judgment on everything we do. He sits, and watches, with his left hand on the judicial gavel, and his right hand under his black robes. He is slowly and patiently stroking his penis up and down. He does this at a pace that could only be maintained by an impartial arbiter of guilt and innocence. His manner and deportment is otherwise and in all ways appropriate and befitting to the high office of Judge.

Anyone refusing to participate in their designated role is immediately destroyed by explosion of the stomach or head.

Most people cannot complete the scenes because they are simply too scatologically gross.

We have entered the realm ruled by Beelzeboul, the Lord of Excrement.

The High Prince of Stench hovers above the entire scene, as if he himself has become a cloud of noxious waste that knows no wind can ever blow him away. He will always be here. The tempter of Saint Anthony. The prototypical pornographer. He has always been here, waiting for each of us to arrive, each in our own way, each on our own day.

I see panic in a young girl's eyes just as she refused further participation, just before she exploded out from the stomach.

It seems that death by disgusting explosion is the ultimate point of the whole charade. But that is not it. It is masterful manipulation of the human instinct for self-preservation. Fear is so great, there is no time to think anything more than *do this or die*. Then, after you have already been manipulated into doing things that you would rather have died than do, the death you are finally forced to accept is filled with total shame and failure.

As it is above so it is below, I recall the jewel of all magic maxims from Hermes Trismegistus, the greatest philosopher-priest-magician-king that ever lived. But, I want to scream and cry, because I do not know how to use that wisdom now. I do not know what it means here.

And yes, Aleister Crowley, the Great Beast 666, I see now, just as you said, *everything is permitted and nothing is true*. But, I'm sorry my friend, there is nothing at all I can do for you here.

Dreamer, you are all on your own now.

* * *

My body is removed to center stage in a dark theater. My mind is somewhere out in the audience, I'm not sure exactly where, but I can feel myself straining, desperate to see what I look like.

The lights come on.

There is a Japanese *seppuku*, ritual self-disembowelment by sharp short knife. Then a shadow warrior cuts off the entire head with one swing of a razor-sharp long sword.

I see my own neck with skin like a raw chicken. I feel the head being cut off; but I do not die.

Sharp teeth grow from out of the raw meat on the inside rim of the neck, and make the whole neck cavity one big wet mouth.

A thick, erect, blood-gorged penis rises straight up from inside the neck, filling it, growing up and out from the base where a chicken-skin sack is straining at the weight of two massive balls.

The teething neck bites down tight on this protruding shaft, chewing and struggling until it rips the tip right off.

The severed end falls flat on top of the neck, to lay there balanced and immobile.

Slender fingers reach up to grab the piece gently and hold it out in front of the neck as if eyes were there to see it. The balls spin round and focus as if with gyroscopic powers.

Blood gushes out and down the neck, over gold and diamond jewelry, some onto full warm breasts and stomach, some across shoulders, down arms, all the way to a pair of delicately perfumed slender white wrists.

The hands return the severed piece to the neck, tip down, so the neck can take another bite.

* * *

I am numb with pain and fear, but I can hear someone talking to me from far away.

"We all could have known it at any time, but you and I were the only ones who could trust each other to share the conscious pounding pulse of this particular dimension. It was there all the time, waiting for us before we even knew about it, and before we knew each other. It knew we would show up together at exactly our own specific time."

"Allison?"

"I remember. I remember it all clearly now."

"Good God! How did you end up here?"

"I needed to be somewhere only you could find me."

Then there is another voice.

"As a Unified One, beyond male and female, you must be able to suckle your own self, create and sustain life with your own divine juices."

"Who is that?"

Then another one says, "From now on, anything you think, the instant you think it, is an unconditional offer, giving the listener full power to accept and bind you."

Then I hear a chorus of familiar voices speak in deep harmonious tones, "We have all been pre-programmed to forget."

16. WE ARE ALL PRE-PROGRAMMED TO FORGET

We are confined and hidden in the darkest places of the Earth, where mushrooms grow wild in the moist corners, and all the cracks are filled with fungus and moss. There are cockroaches, worms, and other eyeless slugs roaming our floors, feasting on our waste.

There are larvae with chthonic powers mutating into forms I cannot understand or explain.

And there are thousands of us, all living here together in close confinement. Gladiators, prisoners, and slaves. We are kept in a labyrinth of individual cells and caves, with iron bars and heavy wooden doors. It all seems hyper-realistically Roman or Medieval, like we are living in underground catacombs carved out of solid rock to keep the dead detained forever, far away from the living. Yet it is inexplicably alien. The design, function, and purpose are somehow unearthly. It is historical, futuristic, and Sangsaric all at the same time.

There are chariots with iron-rimmed wooden wheels riding on cobbled stone roads. The male charioteers carry black leather whips and heavy iron shields.

People are in strange costumes. Some wear rough dark wool, and look like Early American pilgrims, or pirates, and witches. Others dress like white-coated medical technicians, or metallic, mirror-faced astronauts, or blue-suited, fast-walking, and fast-talking businessmen.

Time is all messed up.

Recently, I've been waking up in an area of torture cells facing a large rectangular open courtyard.

In the center, is the Garden of Sexual Necromancy. An act prohibited by all but the vilest of black magicians is here performed as a gratuitous pass-time.

There are others here who are not under confinement. They are not here against their will. They are simple citizens who live and work in these habitations of cruelty as comfortably as if they were in the central plaza of a quaint European village, or a lively bazaar in long-ago Istanbul, at the ancient crossroads of Asia and Europe, East and West, the twain that shall never meet.

Yet, although hypothetically they could be in either of those places, in fact, they are not. Because everyone here knows, whether they are confined or not, there is nowhere else to go. So they reside here and live their lives as best they can.

There is a baker working hard every day to provide everyone with fresh bread. Other people are selling aromatic food from wooden carts. Noodles in greasy soup, grilled meats on skewers, and Chinese style sweet and savory cakes.

There is one lighted storefront with a group of Shaolin monks practicing Kung Fu all day long, oblivious to their surroundings.

It seems natural for each of us, who know we are confined against our wills, to be scared half-to-death all of the time. So most of us form into gangs and cliques to gain a sense of identity and security. Some of us are preoccupied with other more personal compulsive needs, both mental and physical.

What I think we all want the most is to *become our own captors*.

We don't want captivity *to end* as much as we want *to be* the ones enslaving and torturing our own selves.

* * *

Fights are breaking out among the slaves more often now.

One night at dinner I see several people, from among both the prisoners and the guards, keel over, dead from poisoning. These are people I had thought of as *good ones* because they were in some way less evil than the others.

I try to alert one of my comrades to the plot I have detected. But it is already too late. The perpetrators are marching into the courtyard, confident and in control.

A group of mostly female warriors leads the way for a thundering, wildly adorned savage priestess carrying a crescent-shaped sickle. She stands over twenty feet tall. She is the Aztec Goddess of Illicit Passion, Lust, and Filth. Her name is Tlazolteotl, but no one dares even whisper it.

We are all sprinkled with something that is claimed to be the Devil's sperm.

Animals, men, and women, of all irregular shapes, sizes, and colors, begin to copulate with a hellish frenzy.

Double agents and spies are leaving the ranks of both the prisoners and the guards to join the triumphant tribal parade.

I know some more of us are thinking to jump up and join in too, but before we can act, we are scared stiff by a gruesome spectacle.

An elderly female prisoner comes out from behind me. She is dressed in a dirty peasant blouse and dingy wool skirt. Her hair is a messy collection of dreadlocks perhaps, or just a mat of filthy hair. She has an insane smile on her face, and rotten teeth.

She reaches out for a coconut shell cup, handed to her by one of the warriors. She sucks down the contents, and wipes her mouth with her forearm.

A semi-circle forms around her. A hollow quarter-moon shaped cradle is carried to her side. It is made from tree bark tied around thin branches. She climbs in, and lies down on her back, face up to the crowd.

Music has begun and is growing frantic already. There is tribal drumming with the screaming and screeching of other reed and string instruments.

People are sprinkling the prostrate lady with colored powders.

The High Priestess squats at the foot-end of the cradle, opens her knees and sprays out a steaming yellow stream.

The warriors begin to hack at the cradle and its occupant with machetes and spears.

Blood and urine roll down to the woman's face.

She is dying with a frozen smile, more relaxed and subtle now, not unlike that of the Mona Lisa.

The Goddess bends forward to lift the woman's head into her oversize mouth and begins to ingest her the way a snake would devour a mouse. She starts to swallow, gobble, and suck the victim in, deeper and deeper, one gulp at a time until the feet finally flap farewell to all our astonished faces.

The music stops.

No one makes a sound.

No one takes a breath.

The Goddess turns around. We listen to her grunt, we see her scrunch, and then we hear a sigh of release as she moves her bowels to excrete a turd version of the female victim, head first, right back into the cradle again.

There is an unpleasant pause. Then, slowly, the devoured and digested woman rises in silence. She begins crying and slobbering words of gratitude as she crawls down to grovel at the Goddess's feet, in a puddle of her own unnatural afterbirth.

No one else gets up to join the tribe.

The monks continue their intricate self-defense routines.

The baker locks his door and goes upstairs to join his family for their evening meal.

I have no one to tell of what I know. No one else is ready to talk.

So I have no way to review what I have seen.

Clearly, I think, alienation is part of the plan.

* * *

I woke up the next morning with a bad taste in my mouth. My face spasmed in revulsion from the malodorous stone floor. I was clearly suffering from Astral Intoxication.

Somehow, somebody had read my mind about my inability to review what was happening. Now, they will use that thought as another tool of torture. They will hook me up to the television monitors again today.

I'll spend all day looking at video screens watching everything from ancient history to recent events. I'll be locked in a room full of wires, outlets, circuit breakers, and screens. There will be front and rear AV jacks; mono, stereo, surround, MTS, and SAP indicator lights; an overabundant selection of switches; and an incessant electrical hum.

* * *

Sure enough, the screens all around me filled with masturbatory hangings, prison violence, inquisitory hearings, Black Sabbath rituals, people with no faces wearing dull gray frocks and paying homage to the rear end of a hairy old goat. Police review boards. Never-ending Congressional hearings. Coroner reports. Stress analyses of plumbing fixtures. An Einstein-like character selling life insurance annuities to a room full of retirees. Adam and Eve, crazy with lust, on a bed of live eels, on a float, in a parade with cartoon characters, a high school marching band, a military guard, and a collection of antique cars.

The Abyss Channel, sponsored by the hungry Caballi, the vilest of spirits, was filled with the dramatic cosmic debris of so many psychic failures. These were the real losers. Those who had had the chance to leave here and live again. But when they saw the light, when they were confronted with the Abyss, they denied the nature of their own essential nothingness.

They say the force of the Abyss flows through the hollow core in each of us. And if denied, it turns on us and devours us, slowly, transforming us into progressively darker and denser beings. Until we become vampiric and parasitic toward all living things. And then we degenerate further to become an all-black and all-solid mass. Until finally, we are stuffed inside the floors and walls of our present environment, to be near everything, but to partake of nothing at all.

* * *

I must watch whatever they show, whatever is on. All day long. As long as they want to show it.

Even the Shopping Channel was under demonic control.

Now the Avatars of Vishnu are singing in chorus to the tune of “We Are the World,” but the words keep drifting, aurally morphing into things like “We are the gods. We are the deities and demons, hungry for your soul. We are the hungry spirits, we are the Caballi.”

And the sales pitch begins on overdub.

“Are you suffering from recurring and persistent Astral Intoxication?

“If you are, then beckon here. Call us first.

“Or you can call us last if you prefer.

“Either way, you’ll have to beg and crawl for us to come and enter your very own soul, for nothing but our very own pleasure, and with no concern for you at all.

“And remember, you can’t do this without us, though God knows how you try.

“No one else but us. No one else but us.”

And the chorus picks up again, "We are the gods, we are the Caballi...."

The picture fades out to a frightfully lovely lady floating on a scallop shell. The Motherless Aphrodite Urania, born from the filth and foam surrounding her father's bleeding genitals after they were severed by his son and cast into the turbulent sea.

"I am the primary instigator of love between the gods and humans. Serving you since ancient times, and reminding you now: I am still here to serve you today.

"You, the sexually split. You, who can never heal. Punished beyond your worth. Divided but indivisible you. I and I alone bring you just a little bit closer to home."

"Krishna, the supreme God of Self-Contemplation and Masturbation, now for a limited time only, will come to squeeze out one single drop of sperm as a gift for The Dragon.

"Then, only as part of this special offer, The Dragon will make you a full and exact double from your own seed.

"Your name will be entered into a promotional drawing to be held at a time and place already known to our loyal clientele. Then your exact double may be chosen from among all others to go to Yukshee, the insatiable Succubi, and there commit total self-sacrifice, to the point of death, solely for the sake of sexual pleasure!

"It is perfect. Utterly and thoroughly perfect.

"As always, you pay only what you can afford."

Then a disclaimer races across the screen so fast, I wouldn't be able to read it if I hadn't seen it so many times before.

Not valid with any other promotional offers.

Only one drop per customer please.

Void where prohibited or otherwise restricted by force of law.

"Stay tuned, next the androgynous god of homosexuality, the Ancient Baphomet, will be brought to you by his adoring Templars, who worship the Divine Shemale with ritualized sodomy and fellatio."

Helter Skelter starts playing, too loud, and too fast, while black-and-white news clippings and crime scene photos flash across the screen.

I don't want to know what they're selling today. It can't be any better or worse than anything else, but I just can't take it anymore. I force myself to change focus and ignore all the screens and the surround sound. It takes tremendous concentration, but I have developed a technique I use when I feel I might again lose all control of myself. I create my own visions. I run my own commercials, just like the old ordinary ones on regular network broadcasting.

I fantasize about soap, toothpaste, tires, sweaters, toasters, and can-openers. Anything at all that recalls the normal way of life, with normal pleasures and pleasantries. Then I scan the screens for a chance to seize the materials I need to construct my own scenes. Anything to help me focus, so I can project my own fantasies right onto the screens. I can't let myself forget where I come from. I can't abandon all hope of regaining my own identity.

Oh yes, I know what *normal* is now. I didn't before, but I know now.

Normal is having a simple and private toilet, in a bathroom with your own toothbrush, toothpaste, soap, and shampoo. In a house with your own clothes and food. Other basic civilized luxuries too, like a phone, television, stereo, and whatever else you need. Normal allows for hope and dreams. Normal was *not here*, but *there*, behind the commercials.

So I stare at the screens, searching from one to the other, sometimes half-retching from the gore I have to watch, always desperate for the occasional window back to the world to which I fear I can never return.

* * *

Time was a blur.

I was alienated and disoriented. It was my job to re-evaluate the situation and determine an appropriate course of action. But that was absurd because everyone knows no one can do anything about anything at all.

Somehow, something that had been happening was not happening anymore. But now something else is happening. It is like someone changed the channel on reality while I was watching TV.

Filth and disease were everywhere. It is common knowledge that demons love all filth. Feces, urine, semen, blood, pus, and vomit. Sometimes I thought we were there just to feed the germs. To cultivate the germs and help them breed new strains.

Diseased and dying prisoners offered our captors a new slant on perversion, which was explored in endless morbid possibilities.

And we were not just *shown* these things. We had to *participate*. We had to watch and we had to be watched by others. We were always under observation.

If you've never been captured and imprisoned, you can only imagine. The physicality of our world fascinated them. Every detail of our biology seemed to be a source of endless amusement. The public spectacle of ingestion. The private mechanics of elimination.

Especially me, I thought, why me, even more than the others?

I didn't know.

They watched everything I did.

At first, I thought they scrutinized me because of what I did or how I did it. I worried about things I would never think about in the normal world.

Were my bowel movements incorrect?

Judging from the apparatus involved, my captors seemed to have incomprehensibly specific procedures in mind.

All the toilets were installed in a huge and particularly complicated glass and metal monstrosity of a building. It was a nightmare of high-tech luxury.

There were multiple mirrors, polished steel and chrome surfaces and devices, oddly shaped utensils, rubber gloves, wetsuits, goggles, tools, equipment for absorbing moisture and other equipment for emitting moisture, probes, measures, and recorders. New Age Muzak. Wet and dry towelettes. Spray perfume and scented tissues. And wintergreen flavored mints.

It was more observation than I could understand, and it never ceased. I was forced to analyze myself first, my desires and my actions, and then them, and their motives, *ad infinitum.*

Did I *emit* something they considered odd or inappropriate?

No, rather, I think I wasn't doing something they expected me to do. I *omitted* something. I skipped a step they considered necessary or normal.

I had no idea, not the slightest, what that omission might be, but that was my conclusion anyway. That was it. I felt them looking for something that wasn't there.

They delighted in the humor of its absence. It was a wonderful moment for them. Something to show the kids, like a monkey at the zoo.

But no matter how much I thought, no matter how detailed I was, I could never figure it any clearer than that. All the hours, days, nights, and years of analysis were for naught.

* * *

I wondered about the food too. Every night there was a cornucopia of dishes more delicious than the night before. Why did they want us to eat so much?

Of course we were being fattened for the kill. But exactly how? Were they just trying to clog our arteries? I think there was more to it than that. Why were they hyper-stimulating our appetites like this?

One night we had double appetizers of lightly bread-crumbed butter-seared scallops topped with a generous spoonful of Black Caspian Caviar, and Maryland Soft-shell Crabs fried tempura style, cut into sections and served with a tangy Thai hot sauce. Our first course was Angel Hair Pasta tossed with dark mustard-colored Hokkaido Sea Urchin flesh, flavored in a subtle way I could never quite describe, and much more delicious than it sounds. Next, a Maine Lobster, served simply, steamed with hot butter sauce. And then a third course of charcoal-grilled perfectly marbled Matsuzaka Beef tenderloin with black truffles and a sauce of H&H Boal 1957 Madeira wine with a splash of Port.

Vitamins and nutritional balance had nothing to do with anything. Vegetables, fresh fruit and salad were typically scarce.

This dinner was followed by Macadamia nut chocolate cheesecake circled with fresh whipped cream, and accompanied by French Roast Cappuccino.

It was all another form of humiliation.

For us to feel hunger, and then find such pleasure in food, and to reach satiation in the midst of our own degradation and death was a shameful disgrace.

It was another wedge driven between our physical and mental selves.

We could feel no self-respect after meals.

At times I felt we should have gotten dog food for what we had done.

Then, one evening, several years after my original abduction, at a festive buffet dinner of *chef de haute* cuisine, they made us watch video clips as we ate. They showed the preparation of our meals from the planting through the harvesting of crops. They showed fishermen catching fish. They showed farmers raising pigs, cows, and chickens. They showed ducks being force fed to make the *foie gras* we had eaten earlier.

The narrator announced the advent of no-waste farming as we watched dead chickens being ground up into a chunky mush. He said these chickens died from diseases that would make it improper to use them for human consumption. So now they were being fed to other chickens. It was management-enforced poultry-cannibalism.

They also showed how the chickens were kept stacked on racks so their droppings fell on those below. The waste that collected on the floor was mixed with pig slop. Then the whole mess was thrown all over the corn, wheat, lettuce, and tomatoes.

And the filthy black run-off was following the fastest routes into all the nearby streams.

A dull-looking man in a white lab outfit says, “Pfiesteria is a bizarre cell from hell, that kills living organisms by producing poison a thousand times stronger than cyanide, and then dissolving its victim right down to the bone.”

They showed salmon and cod having their bellies cut open and scraped out.

There were quick shots in rapid succession of a hundred chickens having their heads cut off. Cattle and pigs being killed, with crushed skulls and slit throats.

Mad Cow disease, Salmonella, Ebola, E. Coli 0157, antibiotic-resistant viruses, micro-organisms with mutated strains of DNA, and on and on they went with shots of printed documentation, computer generated infestation and reproduction cycles, and images of victims drooling, catatonic, and finally dead.

We ate unfazed.

We had already become accustomed to worse being done right here to all of us. What was the point?

Then the screens filled with scenes from the kitchen. There were rhythmic sounds of chopping knives, running water, and sizzling skillets. Counter tops were being filled with finished dishes. A rat ran scratching across the floor. A meat cleaver flew down from off screen to catch the rat at its neck. A hand reached down, pulled out the cleaver, picked up the decapitated rat and threw it on the chopping board. The chef hacked the rat into a dozen little pieces and added them all to a pot of simmering stew.

"So what?" We asked each other, "What is the purpose of this childish exhibition?"

Then the pranks became nastier and filthier, but so simple-minded and juvenile. We really didn't know what the point was.

And, regardless of what we saw, no one skipped dessert that night. Fresh peaches and perfectly flaked pastry with custard, cream, crushed pistachio nuts and semi-sweet chocolate sauce. We didn't care what they had done to it. It tasted great, and if it poisoned us to death in the bargain, then all the better for us.

We weren't afraid our captors would give us a free ticket to the world beyond, we were afraid they would prolong our lives in here.

However, through the numb paralysis that permeated my psyche at this time, I questioned their motives. Was this exhibitionist behavior part of their diabolical manipulation, or was it simply a childish and disgusting prank?

Perhaps such immaturity could be their Achilles heel?

I had never felt optimistic about it before, and this wasn't really optimism yet, but it was as close as I could get.

Perhaps someday I could escape. Somehow they could be manipulated, and somehow I could find a way out. And there would be somewhere else to go.

Maybe.

* * *

Before I went to sleep that night, I tried to remember what the God of Israel told the prophet Ezekiel. Did God order him to eat bread baked like barely cakes *with human excrement in it?* Or just to bake the bread like barely cakes with excrement for fuel in the fire? I'm not a Bible scholar. I'm not sure. Or rather, I am sure that I don't know. I remember there was a dispute, a theological difference of opinion on the matter. But I am certain God specified this baking and eating be done in public for all to see.

Yes, *in public for all to see.* It is a brilliant strategy. Everything is different if other people are watching. That changes everything.

God certainly likes to put on a show.

It is all being done for the show!

But what does that mean? What can I do about it?

* * *

I woke in the middle of that night from the nadir of a bizarre nightmare.

I was not alone.

My body had been infested with dark hard-shelled crustaceans.

They had greenish-black exoskeletons divided into a head, thorax, and abdomen, and they were hairy at the joints. They were like a composite of crayfish, barnacle, and mussel. They had droplets of gel oozing from their moist interiors, and a steamy mist was rising from their shells.

I think there were two kinds, male and female.

I don't know. I couldn't come to grips with what they were, or where they were.

They had evolved a specialized physical form to cope with both aquatic and terrestrial environments.

They were on me. And they were inside me.

Inside me. Traveling from my stomach, through my intestines, until they pushed up against my rectum. Stretching my membranes mercilessly as they grew in size and number, feeding off the remains of that filthy dinner.

The terminal section of my intestine was being inflated from the inside out. The pain was grueling. I rolled onto my stomach, raised up on my knees, with my face buried in my folded arms.

They were about to come out. I was sure I would die.

I felt hot searing rips as I passed out from the pain.

* * *

But I still could not escape the scene. My consciousness was forced out of my physical body, but I was still there, in the room, hovering over my own body, looking down at myself lying in a pool of rectal blood, solidified gels, and unknown goo, in a cloud of unearthly stench.

I felt my bowels were empty and I was free of the crustaceans. But I think I was dead.

Or, I was alive, and I wished I were dead.

I would rather die while I am unconscious than wake up from this nightmare, only to live through another one even worse. I rather just have it all end now.

Your own personality evaporates. You try to fall back on a culture you always took for granted. But it is not there anymore. And you can't even remember what it was like, or what you were like, just a short time before, now an infinity ago.

You have only one dying thought, "I didn't know. I didn't know."

Then, something in the pool of goo moved.

They were snaking across the floor, splashing against the wall, making sloppy slithering sounds, changing direction, and coming back toward me.

I felt a large jellyfish-like creature, or maybe it was a coordinated team of sea slugs, crawling up the back of my thighs.

There were multiple flexible probes and suction-like apertures being used to get a fix on my body. I was covered with mollusk saliva as the snake-like probes began a rhythmic massage reaching to my insides.

I was being healed with an application of warm gelatinous saliva and long cartilaginous probes.

Each injured cell in my body was being mended, cared for one at a time.

This thing, or things, or whatever it was, was not trying to hurt me. It was reaching deeper throughout my body, dramatically readjusting the entire chemistry of my being.

My beating heart, my breathing lungs, and all other components of my circulatory and nervous systems were infiltrated and commandeered by primordial creatures I could not comprehend.

But my spirit was set free to glide through a silent sky, in big bright open spaces I had forgotten even existed.

And finally, I was rejuvenated. Every synapse of my nervous system was fired up with fresh clean energy. The structure of my electro-magnetic aura was fortified beyond my imagination.

I was redeemed.

I floated free of all concerns, wishing forever to stay exactly as I was.

* * *

When my eyes open, I am in a globe of golden light emanating from two red jewel eyes staring directly into my soul.

There is a reflective shield that looks like cut colored glass sprinkled in a clear polymer base. And it's growing like a soap bubble with sudden slicks of purple sliding here and there.

I see a vicious looking robot head from outer space, floating here in the space right before my eyes. I think it looks like a toy or a cheap Halloween mask. But I know it isn't. It is real.

Oblong cut stones were fastened to the top of scaly meat protrusions on either side of the robot head. Precious gems, emeralds, rubies, pink sapphires, and blue tanzanite were embedded all around the skull.

Most of the head itself was either dead meat or simply inanimate material of some other kind, but the eyes were alive. Translucent. Bigger than ping-pong balls. Burning red-hot in the center.

A body materializes from the head to the ground.

I see a Cherub with six wings holding six flaming swords. The lower half of its body is that of a reptile just recently crawled from the sea. It is a living, mythical, shape-shifting dragon, pulsating with unknown powers. And it is looking through my eyes, into my soul.

I listen as it begins to speak.

"I am dispatched of Maat, daughter of Atum-Ra. She who is the Order intrinsic to the First Time. She who is the Truth that feeds all the gods. She whose taste is sweet to the righteous, but like fiery liquid to the evil ones.

"I come, not just to kill my enemies, but to consume them, and ingest their celestial energy."

I understand now. This creature, this toy dragon, robot head, demon or god or whatever it is, has come to free me.

It tells me I can go, but everyone else will die right there, right then.

Right now.

Those flaming red eyes shined directly at me while sending magnetically controlled waves of dry heat and electricity throughout the facilities all around me. Energy was being vacuumed in from all directions across all dimensions and times.

The bodies of all my captors and all my fellow prisoners too were burning to a crisp. And the fires continued until the ground itself turned into indistinguishable ash. That was the price of my own escape. No other survivors. No remains and no remnants. No evidence of anything that had been before. Only the cockroaches and larvae survived, oblivious to all that had transpired.

From now on, only the lowest creatures that crawl in the darkest places can continue to enjoy undisturbed peace in a more reptilian reality.

But for me, it was finished.

I was out.

Alone, without a clue, convinced it had somehow been my fault all along.

Now I had to act normal again, fit in, mimic those who knew nothing of where I had been. Try to learn the rhythms and sounds of a world that had changed so much during the years of my absence.

I was stuck, frozen in a post-orgasmic mind trap. Things I had craved before now disgusted me.

But I had to go on. The physical body never wants to die.

The body helps the mind survive to find its own balance another time.

The Dreamer loomed large as the next step, beyond the wall of confusion and fear. Nothing but the Dreamer. Wherever he was, I had to find him. Whoever he was, I had to deal with him. Whatever he wanted, I had to give him.

I could never reach Allison without him.

I couldn't even ascertain whether she was alive, dead, reborn, dissolved, absorbed, gone, here, there, or anything, or anywhere at all. All I could do was give up, or go on with the Dreamer.

* * *

It took a while to accept the inevitable.

But then, the first surprise after I stood up to go was that, *I was already there.*

I had been physically with the Dreamer all along, ever since that night with the Buddha's head.

I had been split in two.

My soul, self, astral body, or whatever you would call it, had been in one place, while my physical body, complete with autonomic and other necessary mental functions, had been under the Dreamer's control all the while.

I had been trying to do the impossible.

Now it would be even more difficult.

Before I could even try to reach Allison again, I had to regain control of my own body and mind.

17. I AM AS I AM IN TOKYO

I was on a straw mat tatami floor in a small windowless room. I was wearing a flimsy, flowered pink dress, red thong panties, a pink bra with lace trim, a matching slip, and pantyhose. I had accessories on everywhere. There were pins, bracelets, and rings. I felt make-up, and a wig. I think I looked like the bizarro version of David Bowie and the gorgeous alien rock-god, Ziggy Stardust. It didn't feel right at all.

I looked around for a mirror.

I found the Dreamer sitting in *padmasana*, the full-lotus perfect posture, on the floor of an adjoining room. His face was blank and calm. His eyes were meditative slits, just barely open. His hands were resting palm side up on each knee and his fingers were twisted into complicated unknown *mudra* shapes.

I had to admit he looked strangely beatific here in his own element.

He was behind a low, varnished table at the center of which was a bonsai plant in a small royal-blue lacquer dish.

Two guards were standing behind him, one at either side, wearing identical Dreamer masks, with a sublime smile frozen on each face. They seemed to be slightly built young girls from the shape of their bodies draped in pink robes. But it was hard to tell.

A third masked guard came in carrying a purple tray with tea service for two. She arranged a tiny earthen teapot and two small cups with wooden saucers on the table.

The Dreamer opened his eyeballs all the way and they focused directly on me.

I knew the routine, so I followed it, bowing face to the floor before I sat opposite the Dreamer, slightly to his left, and waited silently.

He motioned with his eyes, and the girl who carried the tea now bent to serve us.

He said, "You were a sick and dangerous man. We cannot let the hungry demons or selfish gods find you again or they will kill you."

He continued without exhibiting any interest in how I might respond.

"Demons are not all bad. The word 'demon' actually means replete with wisdom. Why don't you Americans know what your own words mean? A good demon is called an *eudemon*. A bad demon is a *cacodemon*. You of course were with the lowest of the filth-loving Caballi demons. They prey on the most infirm of spirit. The darkest in heart and soul."

He paused.

But I had nothing to say.

So he continued.

"You have finally come to the right place. You always make me wait, you know. But anyway, I think you are starting to recover.

"Let's drink. I made this tea for you. Drink it all and you will feel better, more like me."

It looked like deep green Japanese Ocha. It smelled increasingly acrid as I lifted the cup to my mouth. Something tasted bad, it was particularly bitter. I knew I was being drugged. All I could do was drain the cup and say, "Thank you Dreamer."

He said, "Take off your mask."

I thought he was talking to me, but the three guards responded by taking off their Dreamer masks and showing they were in fact girls, and quite young.

"These are your little sisters, *imooto* we say in Japanese. They understand your language, and I told them what to do with you. They are virgins of course.

You must be careful. Illicit sex is not allowed here. Watch yourself, because I will be watching you at all times. No act of lust is permitted. Not even a single masturbatory fantasy will go unpunished.

"You know, the human imagination, excited by lust and lewd fantasies, secretes a non-corporeal sperm. Did you know that?"

He continued talking, without giving me any time to say I did or didn't know what he was talking about.

"Then, incubi and succubi are born from these ejaculations of the onanistic imagination. This is one way you make your own demons. Yes, it is true! You make your own demons!

"In this respect, you are still a diseased and dangerous individual Mr. Freeman, but we can help you. And you must help us."

Now I answered fast. "Okay Dreamer. Sure."

"I am ready," he continued, "to defeat the hungry demons and selfish gods by the power of my own superior and divine will. Of course, the same cannot be expected of you. This is why I have given you a new identity. You must hide who you are. You must forget your previous name. So, the hungry demons cannot find you anymore. From now on, you are the *Unified One*. I made you. Now you are two sexes in one person. You are a living symbol of transcendence and unification. You are unlike any other human being. You are more like a god."

I was speechless. My brain had coalesced into jelly again.

"Your new patron saint is called Yab-Yum, the personified unification of all male and female deities.

"You are like the prostitute I saved as Jesus of Nazareth, when I was the great indiscriminate healer."

His monotone diatribe was growing interminable.

I felt the blood in the veins on my forehead pulsing and pounding to the beat of his speech.

Something in that tea was hypnotic or psychedelic. There was a buzz now, a real buzzing sound, growing in my head.

"You know, your Bible says when Jesus of Nazareth was Baptized, Heaven tore open and the Holy Ghost descended on him like a dove. Then Jesus went out into the wilderness alone. For forty days he was tempted and tortured by the forces of Evil in a vicious vortex of three increasingly intense confrontations. He became the personal embodiment of the ancient cosmic struggle between Good and Evil. A struggle documented in all the world's scriptures, including the oldest of all the Jewish apocalyptic writings.

"Then, as soon as Jesus returns to society, the first thing he does is determine a man he has encountered is possessed by an evil spirit. So, he casts out the demon saying, 'Be silent, and come out of him!'

"Some of the Jews challenge Jesus, arguing he must be possessed by Evil himself to perform such magic.

"Jesus defends himself saying, 'How can Satan cast out Satan?'

"Personally, I feel no need for an explanation, but Jesus explains anyway, '...if Satan has risen up against himself and is divided, he cannot stand, but is coming to an end.'

"Remember that Mr. Freeman, remember it well. It was an act really meant to save the entire universe, but if you are lucky, you may just save your own life someday with the knowledge I am giving you. And then you can say, to Hell with the rest of the world.

"The truth is, Jesus *was* filled with the power of Satan. He still is, as a matter of fact. But so is Jehovah. Yes, the One God, in whom the Jews reluctantly but finally placed all their faith, was and is equally possessed by Evil."

He raised his voice as if to a dramatic climax and said, "You have a great capacity to absorb the bad

Karma of those around you, like a charcoal filter absorbs tar and nicotine from cigarette smoke."

I wasn't sure if the tobacco analogy was a warning, a compliment an insult or what. But anyway, he kept talking.

"However, it is imperative that you be cleansed now. You cannot just throw yourself away like a filthy cigarette butt."

"Yes, I understand Dreamer." I was really confused, but I needed to agree with something he was saying. I didn't want to get on his bad side right now.

"You know, at Islamic weddings they used to sprinkle urine on the bride and groom to protect them from Evil. Do you think that worked?"

"Ah, maybe." I ventured a neutral guess.

"The Hebrews believed if you urinated on a prayer book you destroyed the power of the prayer. Do you think that worked?"

"No, except maybe...."

He cut me off because he really didn't care what I thought.

"This is all documented back to the ancient Aztecs. But anyway, your purification has already begun. We will rejuvenate you now. Go with your little sisters for a bath and a Baptism. Come to me redeemed and reborn, clean and fresh, for a celebration of ecstasy for the rest of your life."

He got up and left me with the three virgins.

They took turns pouring and drinking the rest of the tea.

Then they began casually removing my clothes, and their own, in no particular order.

Those panties could not contain me. But I did not take the Dreamer's warning lightly. I was sure this was a test that could result in my imminent castration if I failed. I expected them to scream for the Dreamer to come see my blasphemous erection with his own eyes.

But they just ignored it. There was nothing there as far as they were concerned.

Maybe my manhood was just in my mind.

Maybe the virgins and the clothes were just in my mind.

Maybe my feverish brain was festering with an acid-induced intensity I couldn't control.

Maybe I better reassess my situation.

The girls were real. We were taking a bath, that's all. I was supposed to become one of them. And they were just playful prepubescent virgins.

I asked if they liked drinking that tea. They told me, "Of course. It is a sacrament to drink the Dreamer's tea."

"Don't forget what Jesus said, 'Whoever drinks from my mouth will become as I am, and I myself will become that person, and things that are hidden will be revealed to him.' "

"The whole purpose of Iam Asiam is for all of us to get the same enlightened consciousness as the Dreamer."

"His drinks are one of the best ways to do that."

They had me undressed completely now and were leading me to the steaming bath. They were each using one hand to hold white washcloths over their pubic areas, so I did the same.

They washed each other and me with soap and buckets of hot water before getting into the tub two or three at a time.

The experience became increasingly dreamlike and innocent. I concluded they had been hypnotized to actually think of me as a girl, see me as their older sister, the *oneesan.*

After drying, the girls put on their own robes and carefully dressed me in many multi-textured layers of various shades of pink and red, in cotton, silk, lace, and linen material.

The labels said *Pink Blouse.*

Another over-the-top David Bowie outfit.

I was made up. I was accessorized again. I had two big flowers in my hair. A fashionable woman's hat. A flowing scarf.

They used no make-up and no accessories on themselves. They just straightened and tightened their pink robes and donned their Dreamer masks.

Shoes were waiting for us when we stepped into the hallway. They were small Japanese wooden clogs called *geta*, like slippers with one cloth strap between the toes. My feet were way too big. And the *geta* were extremely impractical for walking. So when I tried to follow the girls as they shuffled off down the hall, I could not make any progress at all.

I stood there looking at the pattern of the woven straw mat floor. The tiny hills and valleys of the twisted threads. The soft blond tones. The burgundy cloth borders.

I was dumbfounded.

As strange as things were, it seemed now that everything had always been meant to happen precisely like this. All aspects of my personal existence had been pre-ordained in infinitesimal detail to bring me right here right now. This was the clearest vision of Karma I had ever known. And my little sisters had become my most trusted intimate acquaintances.

But they started walking too soon and too fast.

I was going to lose our connection.

“Wait,” I said, thinking to myself, "This isn’t normal." Remember, I’m tripping. Yes, for sure, I’m definitely tripping. Just keep my feet in the tiny wooden slippers and follow the girls. One foot after the other. One step at a time.

But my feet were still too big. I was terrified the slippers would come off. So I had to walk slowly, tediously dragging my feet without lifting them up off the floor.

I felt as if I had to swim through ethereal gases to get down the hall. It was taking forever. And the oxygen I was supposed to breath was liquefying before I could suck it all the way in.

Somehow, I finally arrived at another doorway with the girls at my sides.

They ushered me in.

Everyone was jumping around like deviant Hare Krishnas on speed. I was losing the connection again. There were too many people in this room. Hundreds. Chanting. Dancing. Bowing to pictures of the Dreamer. Putting their hands and heads into strange equipment with variously colored wires running to machines, computer screens, heart monitors, and brain scanners. Nurses and doctors were running around giving instructions, and collecting urine and blood samples. I couldn't focus. Everyone started to look the same.

I forgot where the girls were. I panicked. I screamed for my little sisters. But there they were, right at my sides, holding my arms.

I've got to get this under control. Or, at least, I need guidance. Yes, guidance will suffice, I told myself.

"The Dreamer is waiting for you." Two or three of them spoke simultaneously.

They walked me through the room, toward the front. I saw the Dreamer sitting in the middle of a banquet table. This was not a low Japanese table, like the one for tea. It was a large heavy banquet table, set up like the one at the Last Supper. And there was a realistic life-size painting of the Last Supper, from the Bible, on the wall right behind the table.

There were thirteen chairs, all occupied, except for the one next to the Dreamer. Everyone at this table was wearing a pink robe. And everyone but the Dreamer was wearing a big Dreamer mask.

The Dreamer looked at me, and as he motioned to the empty seat at his left, he said, "Let us all welcome the born-again, Baptized and purified, beautiful Unified One."

I sat. I was unbearably self-conscious. I had no mask. My own face was such a heavy burden. But, I remembered, I am here as the Unified One. That is not my own identity. I am here in front of all these Iam Asiam people acting like a virgin female impersonator. Why I had to do that and whatever that was supposed to even mean I don't know, but who cares?

Who cares whether I am dressed in black or pink, or covered in anything or nothing at all? Everyone else has his or her own problems to deal with. Why should anyone else care about me?

"Welcome," he said, "to the most magical and highest path of pure will and desire.

"Now, right here, you can have the eternal life and eternal love you want so badly. But you must do what I say.

"You are a man in love with a female demon. And that is an evil, vile form of love, for which you both must die. From that simple fact there is no escape on Earth. Only I, the Dreamer, the Jesus of Nazareth, the Son of God, shall destroy you both so that forever you both may live.

"You, being a man who loves a female demon, must certainly and finally die with that demon, or you must take her fully inside yourself, let her self replace your self, and then *as your self*, share immortality forever."

I understood every word he said. It was perfectly clear now.

"You, my own Unified One, must listen very carefully to my words. You are at home in your own womb now. You can invite Allison to come and join you here now. And you must let her inside you. You must let her penetrate your body and soul.

"You can welcome her into your body as your lover, but you must accept her as your self."

Wow, I thought, he's right.

And then the Dreamer concluded, "You must become her. So you can relieve her of the unbearable burden of her own identity.

"Isn't that all she has ever really wanted?"

Wow, yes he is completely correct.

* * *

That is how I found out Allison was dramatically different on the inside from how she appeared on the outside.

When I let her inside me, I became her, and I felt her essential and existential fear of men. I was mystified. I never imagined her feeling like this.

She knew her beauty pacified us, but still, it was the male need to be pacified that frightened her. She felt safer the more we desired her. Her sexuality ensured her survival.

So what went wrong? Why did she kill herself? And why did I feel so guilty just for being alive?

Is this what happened in the Garden of Eden? Is this the Knowledge of Good and Evil? Do humans have to suffer just from knowing who we are? Or do we have to suffer from knowing who others are?

18. FROM THE UNREAL TO THE REAL

I survived my first night in Tokyo.

I learned quickly.

Life with the Dreamer was frightening and frantic. But it was endurable for me because the Dreamer wanted me to be able to endure it.

He always had another mission to execute, a drug to test, or a sacrament to perform. And I was always acting under his orders to participate in one of these operations, experiments, or sacraments.

The drugs made it difficult for me to remember what had happened and difficult to distinguish fantasy from reality while it was happening. But I knew there were drugs being tested on me all the time.

Just as the Dreamer had warned me that first night, all sexual activity was forbidden. However, the single exception was obvious. Sex was prohibited unless it was done as part of a *sacrament*, in which case anything was permissible.

As far as I could tell, if the Dreamer desired it, it was a sacrament. If he didn't, it wasn't. And if his prohibitions were ignored, his punishments were swift and fatal.

My primary role was simply as material in the Dreamer's nightmare. I did whatever was expected. My thoughts and actions were under his control.

I had to *act* as he desired me to act. I had to *dream* as he desired me to dream. And I had to really want to do so.

I had no privacy. We were always under one kind of observation or another.

We would meditate in large groups. But our brains were individually wired into screens, and monitored by white-robbed medical directors, under the supervision of licensed physicians.

Their job was to ensure our progress toward *neural identity* with the Dreamer.

The Dreamer himself devised an absurd profusion of methods to produce that neural identity. His techniques included meditation that was drug-induced, hormone-enriched, computer-guided, and electronically directed.

I think I was being particularly useful to him in his development of new methodology, but I'm not at all sure how. And I really didn't worry about it. I didn't care about Iam Asiam any more. I didn't want to stay there. And I certainly didn't want to do what I was doing there. But I had nowhere else to go. No one to help me. No one who could even understand my problem. And nothing else I could do. Not yet.

When I had my own precious time to think, I only thought of Allison. This time I wouldn't make any move until I knew it was correct. Wai Yu told me the Perfect Buddha's Head would help me, and I thought it would help Allison too, but now look where we are. Now, I was painfully aware, I had attracted too much attention to myself. Both Allison and I had made too many enemies along the way.

First, the Originator had been able to manipulate me. He sent me here on an undercover mission for Psytron. He knew all about Allison and me. He might be the only one who knew the truth about her death. And he knew I would do anything to find her now. He told me I couldn't reach her again by myself, but he promised to reunite us when I finished my mission.

I think he told me that. I think he was really talking to me that night, with Psytronic telepathy. And I think I believed what he told me. But I don't care about Psytron or the Originator any more either.

I know I have to take care of myself now.

The Dreamer knows all about Allison too, from our night using the Buddha's head. He understands the karmic mess we are in. He knows Allison's identity was stolen by a demonic power I cannot control. Allison was taken beyond my reach and I can't get her back. So the Dreamer gave me this preposterous identity as the Unified One, and said Allison and I can coexist as eternal lovers, sharing one body and one mind.

Sure, it sounded good when I was drugged and under his spell. But, I am not an idiot.

I may be a prisoner and a slave bound to serve in Iam Asiam fantasies, but I am not an idiot.

The Buddha's head and whatever happened that night, whatever happened to Allison, I can't leave here until I figure it out. The Dreamer obviously keeps me around because he thinks he needs me for some reason. Maybe I still need him too.

I can imagine my family and friends from long ago. In the ordinary world. Growing up, growing older. Working. Accomplishing things. What would they think of me? Who would look me in the eye if they saw me now? And who would turn away? Who would hide their disgust? And who would show it?

Well, I think, it is *my* time, and *my* life, and I will do with it as I wish.

I know Allison is dead. That much is simple.

I tried to communicate with her. I wanted her back. We all go that far. We all want someone back one time or another. But then I discovered Allison is worse than dead. She had her identity sucked right out of her by some kind of demonic double of her own soul.

That is where no one else can help me because no one else has gone there before. No one else I know has had that problem. That is where I must turn to the secret meaning and occult science hidden in myth and ancient stories. That is where I found Isis and Osiris. Long ago, they had the exact same problem as Allison and I have now. The truth is hidden in broad daylight for anyone to see it, but where no one will believe it.

Now, logic leads me nowhere. And I am suspicious of my own intuition not actually *being my own*. Sometimes my own life becomes incomprehensible to me. There are so many mysterious forces at work here. Forces both gross and subtle. I have slipped from one world into another, and all the connections are irrational here.

A long time ago, someone tried to warn me, the danger with psychedelics is they make you feel that reality can be *manipulated*, when actually, it can only be *accepted*.

Is that my problem? Am I trying to manipulate reality when I should try to accept it as it is? I wonder.

And I forget.

Someone else tried to explain how Buddhists generally believe in reincarnation. However, Gautama Buddha taught that all phenomena in life are impermanent and that our attachment to the idea of a substantial and enduring self, which is really an illusion, is the principle cause of suffering. In other words, there is *no self* to reincarnate.

It is so simple. It is so clear, and obvious.

In this way, Buddhist philosophy diverged greatly from Hinduism, which always affirmed the validity of personal reincarnation.

I want Allison back, I want to help her reincarnate, but if there is *no self*, then what am I doing? For whom am I doing it? Why am I doing it? And who is doing it anyway?

What is Maya? And what is not?

I wonder and I wonder and I wonder. How much time passes, how many days, and years? I do not know.

I think of Allison telling me it seems like a dream within a dream. But it isn't a dream. I believe it is more real than that. The ancient Hindu Upanishads plead for guidance: "From the unreal lead us to the real, from the darkness lead us to the light, from death lead us to immortality."

There is something infinitely precious, valuable beyond all else. And it is real. I believe it is. I really believe it is. *But why in the world is it so difficult? Why is it so damn confusing?*

Do other people know these things? Did they figure this out already? Is that why they don't need to think about it anymore?

I remember my tour of the Pyramid Rooms in Egypt, the Eleusinian Mysteries in Athens, and my time-out-of-time at the Library of Alexandria.

Pythagoras, the master of numbers, taught me how to hear the music of the spheres and elevate myself through progressive reincarnations to the ultimate height of eternal celestial immortality.

I think of my internship as a Scribe in the House of Life under the watchful eyes of Osiris. I was trained experientially to travel safely through the World of the Dead. *I've been trained for this.* It is my duty.

I never think about anything else. I'm only doing what I have to do.

Somehow, I'll figure out the big questions. Is human desire really the source of all suffering? Or is suffering caused by the failure to satisfy all human desire? Are we supposed to transcend the ego? Or keep the ego forever? If you, yourself, could absolutely live forever, who among us would decline?

No thank you, I don't want to be selfish, I don't need to live forever.

The Lord God said, "Behold, the man has become as one of us, to know Good and Evil. Now, lest he put forth his hand and take also of the Tree of Life and eat and live forever, let us send him forth from the Garden of Eden...."

The Serpent helped us open our eyes to the Knowledge of Good and Evil, but God does not want us to live forever?

I don't know about you, but I can't accept that.

Who is this God? What is His purpose? What good is He?

And how do we know that was really God talking anyway?

What if *that God* was an imposter, and the *real God* had to go undercover as the Serpent to get a message to Eve? Doesn't the Serpent seem like a better friend to humanity?

I don't know about your religion, but Psytron delivers conscious personal immortality. Here and now. In this world. In your own lifetime. And with a money-back guarantee. Now that is really a great deal!

Psytron teaches you how to leave one body and get a new one. And Psytron will save the rest of humanity by preventing the occupation of our humanoid bodies by the Holy Conman and his innumerable operators, his demonic legions.

Look at the principal monotheistic religions. Jews think they are unique, because they have been chosen by an inexpressible, unimaginable Unformed Nothing. Christians think they are unique because, they have been saved by Jesus Christ, the one and only Son of God. But Muslims also think they are unique, because they have been enlightened by their prophet Mohammed and the Word of God in the Qur'an.

Islam says Jesus is still alive today, and He will return to our world to save the righteous and defeat Evil.

Christians of course say Jesus already saved us by dying for our sins on the cross, and He offers us, His followers, the only way to get into Heaven.

Jews say stop blaming them for killing Jesus, they didn't do it.

The chosen ones are sure they are better than the saved ones. The saved ones know they are the only ones going to heaven. The enlightened ones are sure both of the others are wrong.

Islamic terrorists fight a blood-and-guts war against the Great Devil and almost everyone else, certain that Allah will reward them in Paradise.

Muslims hate each other and kill each other for no good reason.

Catholics and Protestants kill each other too, for no good reason. And they each still think the other is possessed by evil demons anyway.

God informed Joseph Smith that all other religions are apostate. God told Mr. Smith, *His* chosen people came to the New World *before* the Native American Indians. So God chose the Mormons, not the Jews? And when God tells Joseph Smith it is God's will to have violence done to His enemies on Earth, like the American Indians I guess, is that Allah speaking? Does the same God say the same thing to different people, or what?

Hindus and Sikhs are killing each other in India. What is God saying to them? And how many Gods are talking? Do people misinterpret what God says and what God is?

Mormons and other Christian theologians still argue whether the Holy Trinity is three separate identities or merely three aspects of a single God.

Does God even listen to such discussions?

All kinds of people debate whether they are actually Christian or not. Others debate whether they can become Jewish or not.

Half the population of the world is walking around smug and secure that they belong to one or another mutually exclusive group of God's special people. Like they have it all figured out.

Once, a Jewish Buddhist yoga teacher told me when Jesus said He was the Son of God, He really just meant we are all God's children. I wondered then, why didn't Jesus say what He really meant, so I wouldn't need a Jewish Buddhist yoga teacher to explain it to me?

And what about Atheists?

They rely on Science and criticize religious faith, but they take the biggest leap of blind faith of anyone. They actually believe they know what they cannot know.

Isn't science itself based on the belief that the Universe is rational and not absurd?

I don't know that is true. And I don't know why I should believe it. So I cannot join them, because I do not have enough faith to be an Atheist.

I know there is another world. I know there are other beings. I know there are too many things we do not know. I know there are too many unanswered questions, and too many complications.

But still, I think, to be simple but accurate nonetheless, the Big Divine Deal is, if God, or Jesus, or Muhammad, or any other official representative of God, loves us, because we do what they say, then our soul can live forever in Heaven or Paradise or wherever the Kingdom of God is actually located.

I want to laugh, but the terms of this Big Divine Deal keep me awake grinding my teeth at night.

I've got to say, "I'll pass. Please, all of you, all the chosen and blessed and enlightened ones, go ahead, go and enter the Kingdom of God without me."

"And if you see Jesus there, tell Him, I think it is better to *become* Him than to just believe in Him. But if I were Jesus, I would feel like the weak link in the divine chain anyway."

Jesus was a magician, but he let his enemies kill him by crucifixion. Yes, of course, we can't forget, He came back to life. He had some kind of plan, or purpose. But still, I mean, is it strong to be weak, or weak to be strong, or what?

And of course Jesus had to be one part of a trinity. Every magician knows *three* is the magic number. The three points on the face of a pyramid are always there to remind us of this significance.

So before there was the Father, the Son, and the Holy Ghost, there was Atum, Kheprer, and Ra. If those two Trinities had a fight, who would win? And then what would the losers do next? Who would want them? Who needs a God unless it is the absolute ultimate strongest God in existence?

And what about the trinities? How many trinities do we honestly need?

Well if three is the magic number, of course we need three.

So what about the Maiden, Queen, and Hag? Do we need them? We all need our mothers. So is the female trinity of life one of the top three?

Or what about the Hindu trinity of Brahma the Creator, Vishnu the Preserver, and Shiva the Destroyer?

Isn't that the first trinity ever, the most ancient of all? Doesn't it sound the most logical?

Although this ancient trinity is naïve and pre-scientific if you look at it one way, it is sophisticated and postmodern if you look at it another way. And no matter how you look at something, you do have to create it, preserve it, and destroy it if you are going to do anything about it at all.

But that is more than three already, and we cannot forget the Magic Triangle of Solomon, the all-powerful Trinity of Letters, Words, and Numbers. The Magic Triangle that is essential for humans to acquire occult knowledge and a mastery of the thirty-six Talismans, which are the Key to the Tarot, which of course is the Key to Everything, or perhaps the Key to Nothing at all.

Magic. Yes. Magic is the ultimate and only answer. Where knowledge is hidden in the dark and protected by logical contradictions.

Moses was a magician too. He was tutored in magical arts by his enemies in the Egyptian royal family.

I think we can all be like Moses on the mountain.

The art of the magician is to obtain the sacred names of the gods and use those names for access to, and control of, those gods.

Thus, the Judeo-Christian God, after having His identity questioned by Moses, responds with the most divine and perfect answer possible: "I am who I am."

And the Dreamer responds to God saying, "I am as I am."

We can all get that far. We can all reach that high. We don't need permission from any priest, rabbi, teacher, guru, police or government official.

Hear Me Now Hebrew Nation, whatever you think Moses did for you, don't be fooled, you don't have a covenant with the One God, you are the victims of a fraudulent deal with the Holy Conman!

The Cherub is still guarding the Tree of Life.

The Unformed Nothing has no need to read the Bible, the Talmud, the Book of Mormon, the Qur'an, the Autobiography of a Yogi, the Kabbalah, the Book of Hermes Trismegistus, or any of our holy books.

Yet we kill each other over the essential unknowability of an Unformed Nothing.

It is believed that Hebrew people were the first to worship a name, a word, rather than an image, idol, or other material symbol. Then Jesus was born, and *the Word* was made flesh.

Yet, the confusion of human language itself is the fault of this same Biblical God because *He* disapproved of the Tower of Babel. Words were a power *He* didn't want us to master.

He is a jealous God, forbidding worship of other gods in any form or image. He doesn't like you to do whatever He doesn't like you to do. His punishment is swift, severe, and even fatal. But what is worse, His punishment is random, undetectable, and even absurd.

Surely, Magic is the only answer.

A modern-day magician, Charles Manson, who was self-taught and street-smart, said he was *both Jesus and Satan.*

Sure, now that is a nice trick if you can do it.

And no one killed Charles Manson by crucifixion or otherwise. Not yet and not ever. He just sits in his cell, covered with his own excrement. The Holy Father of a New Age of Derangement.

But it is true. We are in a New Age. The Aztec calendar is incontrovertible on this point. All that is old and evil will be destroyed. Cosmic gears turn inexorably. A new world will be born from the old. The Great Age of Aquarius will begin. That is the true cosmic agenda as revealed to ancient astrologers but long since lost and hidden to the modern mind.

Iam Asiam raises you to the godhead of the Dreamer where immortality and magical powers are yours through duplication of the Dreamer's consciousness. Iam Asiam prepares you for the coming of the post-apocalyptic reality.

Iam Asiam gives you direct access to the mind of God as manifest in the body and soul of the Dreamer.

Did you know the Dreamer could levitate his body several inches off the floor? Have you seen the pictures? They prove he can do it.

* * *

Everything will die.

Everything will be born again.

* * *

The essential balance of our lives has not changed for thousands of years.

Today, for every organ transplant, extended life span, and active retirement, there is an abortion, infant mortality, and child brutality.

Now, we will unlock the genetic code, map the genome, and use germ-line engineering to replace blind evolution.

We will make ourselves better.

And we will make ourselves worse.

Despite the illusory success of great medical advancements, every germ killed has been replaced.

EVERY GERM KILLED HAS BEEN REPLACED.

Despite the apparent spread of education, literacy, and knowledge, the darkness of insanity and ignorance has not retreated one slight millimeter.

WE ARE CRAZIER THAN EVER.

We all think we are so much smarter after the Copernican Revolution because now we know Earth is not at the center of the Universe. But theologically speaking we are every bit as ignorant as pre-Copernican plebeians. We still cling to our religious beliefs placing each of us in the exact center of God's Universe. As Jews, Christians, and Muslims, we each believe we have been chosen and anointed by a Divinity particularly partial to our own mutually exclusive groups. So what I want is a Copernican revolution in Theology and Cosmology.

I want a new God.

We need a new God. Look at what we have now. Question the illusion of progress.

After all the prophets, saviors, gurus, and saints, the world is not any better. After all the scientific advances and technological achievements, still the world is not any better today than it was two thousand years ago or five thousand years ago.

Time is inherently degenerative.

You can think of the march of civilization as progress if you want to, if you need to. Sure, I know. It can look like progress. But there is no less disease, no less evil, no less insanity, no fewer wars and murders, no more generosity or love. The world is not actually any better thanks to Christianity, Judaism, Islam, Buddhism, Vedanta, or any other religions.

Nor is the world any better thanks to Art, Science, or Economics, or whatever your favorite system of liberal or conservative politics may be.

At best, our scholars, scientists, inventors, and doctors may be noble and well-intentioned people. Our finest laborers and captains of industry may usually be hard-working and honest. Many of our artists and our leaders may whole-heartedly want to help. But all our best efforts can do nothing more than maintain the balance.

We have no choice but to swim as fast as we can, just so we do not sink.

And nothing we have ever believed or produced has ever changed the final balance.

I too can recall my belief in progress, evolution, and self-improvement. But now I see only hallucinatory visions along the dwindling spiral of descent into the infinite pains of Evil and Insanity.

The Gnostics teach us that the body and the material world are irredeemably Evil. The material world was not created by the True God, but by a lesser, Evil God, to trap us and make us suffer.

All gurus see exactly what is necessary. Balance in all things is inescapable. As high as you fly in Heaven is as low as you crawl in Hell.

We miss the essential occult mechanism underlying all human endeavors when we focus on the legalistic and moralistic problems of fraudulent gurus and brainwashing in cults. Our more respected religions are no better. But the real problems remain unsolved.

Something is really wrong.

Something is really wrong with all of us.

* * *

Mother Nature grows magic plants that wait for us to ingest them, and digest them, and love them, like the body of Christ, like a passive and patient Buddha, like the Holy Word of God. Sweet Mother Nature gives us chemical keys that fit into our brains precisely to show us the Kingdom of God.

Again, like so many times before.

And for the first time ever.

Again and again and again.

But that is too easy.

As easy and as evil as the apple in the Garden of Eden.

* * *

We fear we are not supposed to know something.

Someone somewhere objects to the morality or lack of morality involved.

Someone somewhere else enacts a law prohibiting unnatural intercourse with nature.

The enforcers arrive on the scene. Crouching down, breathing heavy, teeth exposed, carrying whips, swords, and guns.

* * *

And right over there crouching under a shade tree, there is someone else breathing heavy, teeth exposed, happily humping a sheep.

What?

How much can we learn from Mother Nature?

What if bestiality was a natural step along the path to enlightenment?

Aren't we all in this thing together anyway?

* * *

The young student asked his beloved Zen *Roshi*, "Would you hump a sheep to obtain the ultimate prize of enlightenment?"

The master replied, "I would hump a sheep just to hump a sheep."

Then, after a long pregnant pause, the master added, "And I'll take whatever prize is in the box, Cracker Jack."

What?

What does it mean?

* * *

Eliphas Levi, the exalted Mystic Monk and Master Scribe of Western Magic taught us the great secrets are in the attainment of equilibrium between apparent opposites.

And, the greatest secret of all lies between the poles of the relative and the absolute.

What?

What does it mean?

* * *

Contradictions don't surprise me anymore. I know I'm missing the point of the matter until I clearly see the insolubility of the contradiction involved.

Unfortunately however, that is the end of my logic, and the beginning of my insanity.

Time is going by, years are going by, my whole life is passing by, and I don't even know where Allison is anymore. Is she simply dead; or dead and gone, and gone for good?

Did I really see a demon steal her soul?

And was that a demon or a god? Or the one and only God? And if that is God, then is God really Evil? Is God the Holy Conman?

Or what kind of fool am I for worrying about it?

* * *

I ask the stupid questions. I need to understand the perversions and the insanities, for some unknown reason. So I am pulled into the dark by irresistible forces in pursuit of unknown and unfathomable things.

But I know one thing for sure. I've come here for no more than exactly what I've got.

And it makes me want to cry, alone but out loud, to whoever can hear, to whoever can care.

God please help me now.

19. SAYAKO IN HIGH SCHOOL

After a couple of years, the Dreamer tells me it's time to start recruiting new members for Iam Asiam. He gets me a job as a part-time English conversation instructor at a prestigious all-girl high school in our upper class Aoyama neighborhood, close to the Iam Asiam Central Tokyo *Satian.*

I have to do this disguised as a woman. In fact, I am disguised as Allison. The Dreamer even makes me use her name. So all the girls at school call me *Ahrison-sensei.*

I was a strange sight for sure. But I was a foreigner, and a teacher, so no one questioned my odd appearance or my identity.

My job was easy. I just talked about anything I wanted to, for two hours a day, three days a week, with a senior class full of giggling, fresh-smelling young girls in blue and white uniforms.

The pay was good too, but of course any money I earned was deposited directly into one of the Iam Asiam general accounts, as specified by the Dreamer.

The Dreamer also specifically instructs me to say pretty much anything to get the girls to come to private Sunday dinners so he can meet them one at a time. I am always asked to leave after the introductions are made, so I never know what happens. And of course I cannot ask. But the girls never mention anything about the Dreamer after meeting him, and I never see them on the Satian premises again. So he isn't just recruiting new members for Iam Asiam. I know he is working on one of his secret projects.

One day, the Dreamer installs a phone line in my room. He tells me to use it exclusively for telephone English practice. So I give the girls my home phone number on bilingual name cards the Dreamer has printed for me.

The girls are generally too shy to call, or simply unable to deal with even the most elementary English conversation. So the phone doesn't get much use.

But then one girl starts calling often, late at night.

And she doesn't call for English conversation practice.

She calls to teach me enough naughty Japanese so I can understand her, and follow her stage directions in complicated phone sex routines.

She never mentions my disguise or questions my real identity. She knows I am a man. And, on the phone, she knows I am *her* man. She uses her voice to make me grab her, poke her, lick her, sniff her, suck on her, and insert myself inside her in impossible combinations. It is obvious that she has never actually had sexual relations with anyone yet. But her lust is deeper, and in more immediate need of satisfaction than any I have ever known.

I listen to her instructions. I cooperate. I obey. I try my best to make valuable contributions to her onanistic theater of the absurd. I am in awe of her passion and sexuality. I am actually afraid to bore or displease her. I teach her English only when she asks for it.

She asks, *"Kuroge ga suki desu ka?"*

Yes, yes I say, I like black hair a lot, *"Kuroge ga dai suki."*

"Kinpatsu yori, kuroge ga suki?"

Oh yes, I like black hair more than blond, *"Kinpatsu yori, kuroge ga suki desu yo."*

I never want her to stop.

She always hangs up as soon as she is through with me. Sometimes she hangs up earlier, afraid her parents will catch her.

I never know when or if she will call again. I try in vain to conjure the next ring of the phone.

But I never touch myself. It is too dangerous. I cannot enjoy the calls like she can. Yet, in a way, I enjoy them more, for the brilliant rarity of the pleasure in which I am allowed to participate. I've become convinced she is some kind of sexual genius. I am honored to know her.

I want to know her name, but she never tells me. I want a number to be able to call her sometime in the future when I am again free to do as I wish, but she never gives me any information.

She gives me only what she wants me to have. She tells me only what she wants me to know.

She tells me how Japanese boys masturbate by cutting holes in bricks of *konnyaku*, the Devil's Tongue, firm sweet potato gelatin available in any market. It is an old traditional technique, easy to overlook today, but she knows they do it. If she were a boy she'd do it too.

She tells me Japanese women had to use those ridiculous doll-headed dildos because realistic phallic symbols were illegal. She laughs. Illegal!

So women could use a thin, nicely curved *kyuuri*, Japanese cucumber; or a fat *daikon*, giant white radish. They were allowed to use whichever they prefer. And they were also allowed to use octopus. Even live ones. You know why? Because these were the less-threatening things that the law-making males found more entertaining to contemplate.

But she doesn't like to do things just because men say it is okay. She likes her own ideas better.

She cuts a fresh ripe peach in half, removes the pit, and rubs both halves juicy-side down on each of her little titties. She says it is like having two sweet-scented wet mouths sucking simultaneously on both her nipples, her *chichi kubi*. And then she rubs the peaches all around, kissing her own body in all the good places. And soon, she hears sloppy squishing sounds from the spastic motion of her own hands. A little muscle in her forearm starts to ache.

She collapses from one sweaty convulsion after another.

And that is usually enough.

But, sometimes, when no one will be home until dinnertime, she goes to the fish market. She buys a fresh live eel. She carries it home tied up neat in a clear plastic bag. She takes it out when the time is right, lays it on the chopping board, and shoves an ice pick into its eye. She pushes the pick all the way through its head and forces it securely onto the board. Then she lays it on the floor. For some reason she doesn't know, the tail wiggles a long time after the eel dies. She squats above the wagging tail and lets it tickle her.

She holds the eel like a penis. She uses it like it is her lover.

She says she is so *ikenai*, so bad, so dirty.

But she enjoys being *ikenai*.

She tells me things, and asks me things, no one else ever talks about, ever.

Do I know about *Shunga*, Japanese erotic art?

Do I know Hokusai? And his famous *Ukiyo-e*, woodblock picture of *The Dream of the Fisherman's Wife*? Tentacle eroticism. Two octopuses, she says, kissing the woman's nipples and pussy.

Do I like women to have sex with sea life?

How could I know? How could I ever know such things?

Then, she tells me, one day, while shopping in the neighborhood with her mother, the fishmonger commented to her, "The eels are very sweet, loaded with fat at this time of year, aren't they young lady?"

She told her mother, with tears in her eyes, she had been using her pocket money to buy fresh eels, trying to learn to prepare them for her father at home, but she couldn't do it well and so she had to discard all the evidence of her failure each time.

The tears in her daughter's eyes moved her mother to properly instruct Sayako in the intricate process of cleaning, marinating, and grilling fresh eel. Her mother asked the fishmonger for his very best eel, and then Sayako carried it home like she always did in a clear plastic bag tied up neat.

Her mother opened the bag at home, took out the eel, and stuck a pick through its head to fix it to the chopping board. Then she cut all the way from the base of the neck to the end of the tail while it was still trying to wiggle. Her mother stressed the importance of keeping the sharp edge of the knife against the backbone all the way.

They discarded the internal organs, washed the eel, and cut off the head, tail, and fins. Then they inserted five wooden skewers equidistant from top to bottom.

Her mother told her it would be best grilled over a charcoal fire, but gas or electric is okay too. So they cooked it over the gas grill. Three minutes on each side. Then they rinsed it to remove the excess fat. Brushed it with a sweet sauce and grilled it one more minute on each side. They repeated that entire process three times.

Then they cut the meat into ten-centimeter pieces and laid it on top of sticky white rice. Finally, they garnished it with pickled ginger and sprinkled it with *sansho* special Japanese ground pepper.

They sipped aromatic Japanese ocha while they ate.

The eel tasted soft and sweet as the finest French pâté.

Her mother told her wild eels are better than cultivated ones because the meat is more tender, sweet, and satisfying.

Her mother didn't need to explain anything twice.

From that day on, her father was happy and proud to have his only daughter love him enough to prepare his favorite dish all by herself.

* * *

She told me that story, and I listened, spellbound.

Just like I listen to everything she tells me, anytime she calls.

And I can't believe what is happening.

Like so many other things in my life, I don't know how or why, or what it means.

* * *

The school year passes too quickly. I am afraid the calls will end when the year is over and the girls go away to college.

Then on the last day of class, Sayako, a quiet girl in the front row asks if we can discuss a short English quote she has found.

"You know our school motto is 'Love God and Serve His Chosen People.' "

"Yes. Yes I know."

"Well, how can I love God?"

"I... ah.... That's a very good question Sayako. But, you should ask someone else about your school motto, the principal perhaps. I don't really know...."

"I see. But I want to know what love is."

"Yes Sayako, we all do."

"Well, I asked the school librarian to help me. And we found a quote from the French poet, Charles Pierre Baudelaire."

Then she unhesitatingly reads aloud, "The supreme voluptuous delight of love lies in the certainty of doing evil."

I could barely articulate a response.

I finish the class in a daze.

I never know if the Dreamer got what he wanted out of my undercover work as an English instructor. He doesn't send me back the following year. He has other work for me to do.

Sayako begins to haunt my dreams.

I think of the English class often.

* * *

I'm taking my girls on a field trip through an old district of the city with murky candlelit tunnels and dirty green canals instead of streets. The air is heavy with moisture, old dreams, and expectations.

We walk out of one tunnel onto a mushroom-covered mound. We step over a low wooden fence to climb down centuries-old smooth stone steps. The girls are gleeful, and giggling, but anxiety is building. They grasp at each other's hands as their feet struggle with the slippery steps.

It is low tide. We climb down just above the brackish green water. We can see the dark mud bottom in some places along the side of the canal, just a few inches below the scum-covered surface. But it is deeper and darker in the center.

The girls scream as a couple of giant eight-to-ten-foot eels squirm by, racing up and down the canal with the top of their thick girth protruding above the shallow water like dragons.

There are about twenty of us hanging on at various heights of the twelve-foot-high canal wall. I am down all the way with the soles of my feet just above the water. Some of the girls dare to climb down almost as low as I have. The splashing sounds make us all tense up, check our footing, and tighten our grip. The eels seem to know who we are and why we are there.

They are predators, who hide their girth in holes at the bottom of the dark water. What can they possibly know? What can they possibly want to say?

Do the eels think we are too close for our own good? Are they trying to frighten us away?

I remember teaching the girls about the eighth circle of the Inferno in Dante's *Divine Comedy*. There is a ditch full of pitiful souls being constantly bitten by serpents. The serpents mutate into the person they have just bitten, and the bitten person mutates into a serpent, *ad infinitum*.

Is that why I came here? Is that why I brought the young girls here? Are we all going to transmutate into serpents?

I feel nauseous.

I try to convince some of the girls to get in a creaky wooden rowboat with me. It is tied up alongside the retaining wall, just a short lateral climb away. But it looks too old and rotten to be watertight. We don't want to get any of that filthy water on ourselves. And we certainly don't want to fall in among the eels.

As I approach the boat, I stop, grab the slime-covered dock line and begin to pull the boat closer. The movement causes the two wooden oars to shake lose and fall off the side of the boat into the water. I get the boat close enough to jump in if I want to, but I am not sure I can retrieve the oars.

I watch helplessly as the oars drift away in the darkness. Then, I realize they are wiggling too much. They can't be oars. I search for stiff straight lines, but I can see only squirming eels.

The girls have been waiting for me to get in the boat.

I desperately wanted to do it so I could see them reaching out for my hand to follow after me, and I could help them aboard.

But I do not think the boat is safe.

I saw one eel crash against the side of the boat as it tried to swim by. Then another did the same. And then another.

On the other side, I saw an eel's head as it was squirming out from under the bottom of the boat, fighting to pull the length of its body free.

Water was splashing into the boat from the frenzied motion of the flapping heads and tails.

The girls were squealing. I was sweating, and my own motion was momentarily stalled. I was too confused by my own desires and fears.

Then my hands began reaching out again, one over the other, to pull in the remaining length of line. Wet green algae were squishing through my fingers as the line lifted out of the water. Barnacles made salty cuts into my palms. My blood was dripping into the canal. The rotten old line was unwinding and disintegrating in my hands as I pulled it in.

The salty water was burning my cut hands.

The sweat on my forehead, I couldn't stop to wipe away, was dripping into my eyes and caused my focus on the girls to blur.

I could hear the girls screaming and the eels splashing.

I could hear the hollow sound of water hitting the boat as I pulled it closer. I could hear the boat scrape against the bottom and feel it hit solid objects, rocks, rusted metal, and unidentifiable garbage. There were sudden rough thumps and irritating grating sounds.

I wanted to hear my own heart, verify it was still working.

"Don't go in! Don't go in!" I heard a shrill chorus of young female voices pleading in the dark. But I knew it was too late.

I could see the boat right below my feet. I stepped out into the water collected on the bottom of the boat. I measured every inch until my foot felt solid wood.

I could hear my own heartbeat now.

I brought my other foot inside the boat. I immediately started to drift away. The motion of my own entrance had already carried me beyond arm's reach of the wall.

Some of the girls were just beginning to cry. Some were already wailing and shrieking uncontrollably.

I searched the water for an oar. There were only dark lines in dark liquid. All I could do was reach out to grab one line after the other. How many eels would I have to grab before I found what I was searching for?

I looked back at the wall as I drifted away and saw a particularly pretty young face flushed with fear. Her clean white blouse was now soaked and soiled. Her usually straight shinny hair was all in disarray. Her mouth was opening and closing in a rapid incomprehensible rhythm.

I didn't have time to decipher the message anymore.

I was drifting away and the boat was filling up fast. Water was over my knees now. I'd sink into the mud.

* * *

The eels would treat me as a hero.
I'd brought a feast of young beauties to feed on.
The tide would come in.
The canal would fill up, clear and fragrant again.

20. SLACK AT WORK

A profound appreciation of personal and social relationships and the concomitant priority of obligation over pleasure are the keys to Japanese society and the shackles on Japanese individuals. I figured that out for myself. Now, even the Dreamer has recognized my growing mastery of the battlefield terrain.

I'm getting more complicated missions to perform.

I'm even allowed to go out dressed as a man again.

* * *

"Hey Slack, I gotta tell ya 'bout this gaijin walked into the office today. Absolutely the craziest loony bird I ever saw."

Millard checks his buddy's face to make sure Slack is still listening, then continues.

"First, the guy calls me up from Otemachi station, right downstairs, and says he can't find exit C12. I tell him, 'C' comes after 'B', and '12' comes after '11', you know? We've been here six years, I never heard of such a thing.

"So, I'm waiting, and it's getting near lunchtime, and he's still not here yet. Then, 'bout fifteen minutes later this guy walks in with an old briefcase in one hand, a camera over his shoulder, and a freaking boom-box in his arms.

"I don't even want the guy near my desk, so I send Junko over to put him in the waiting room. Junko sits him down and goes to get him a cup of coffee. He comes right out of the waiting room, with his camera in front of his face, taking pictures of the whole office.

"I thought I was hallucinating.

"He has on some kind of psychedelic karate uniform, with yellow, red, and purple baggy pants, and an extra-large Aloha shirt with all those colored fish and big flowers on it. Junko sees me laughing out of control and she has the smarts to go ask him to stop taking pictures.

"I go over and he says, 'She said I can't take pictures here.'

"I say, 'That's right sir, this is a place of business. We can't allow pictures without asking the PR department.'

" 'Oh,' he says.

"So, I ask, 'Could you please turn the music off sir?'

"He was playing that Timothy-Leary-is-dead stuff by the Moody Blues. And he says, 'I thought it was okay if it was low.'

"I say, 'No, you have to shut it off. We're doing business here. We're not listening to music.'

"He shuts it off and asks, 'You don't like that music?'

"I tell him, 'I actually like it a lot, but this isn't the place for it.'

" 'Oh,' he says again, and tells me he is a DJ. Or he used to be a DJ. Or something like that.

"I'm thinking, are you human? Or did you ever *used to be* human, or *anything* like that?

"He says he just got back from living in a religious commune in Honolulu. 'On the other side of the island,' he says. I don't know what side he is talking about, but I guess he means not on the Waikiki side.

"Then he opens his briefcase and starts shuffling through comic books and old newspapers until he finds a big picture of this savage-looking Polynesian guru guy and asks me if I know him!

"So I try to end the conversation as quickly as I can but it goes on longer than I expect...."

* * *

"Mr. Metz, I'd like to talk to you more but I have another appointment soon, so exactly what can I do for you today?"

"How much time do we have?"

"Just tell me what you want me to do, okay, and I'll take care of it for you."

"My wife is Japanese."

"Yes. Okay."

"She is really crazy."

"Uh hum."

"Her mother died, so we are going to sell the house and get a lot of money. And I want to use my half to buy some training courses."

"Okay. So what do you want me to do Mr. Metz?"

"She wants to put all the money in a bank. But money is energy, right, you have to use it, or it goes to waste. You see? Do you believe in religious training? Theological technology?"

"Ah, yeah sure, and I agree you can do better things with your money than just put it in a bank and leave it there."

"What's the exchange rate today?"

"About 126."

He reaches over, pulls out an old calculator from the briefcase and says, "My half is going to be *ichi oku en.*"

"That is about eight hundred thousand dollars, you don't have to figure it out."

"You know that already?"

"Yes, money is our business."

"See, that's what I mean."

"Right."

"If you can convince my wife, we can put our money here, in our account, and then I can use it for training."

"You don't want to use all of it for training do you?"

"Oh no. I need *nisen man en* now, and I'll need more later but I'm not worried about that yet."

"That's one hundred sixty thousand dollars."

"Should I keep the money in yen or dollars?"

"Well, it depends, but we could do both here. We could do whatever you want. I can personally work out a plan to match your situation, a combination of savings and investment to protect your capital, generate income, and help your savings grow."

"Yeah. Yeah. You have to tell my wife things like that. I mean, almost, we don't have all the regular paperwork and immigration stuff for our marriage, but... not yet anyway... but...."

"Of course, I'll be happy to talk to your wife, or anyone you want Mr. Metz."

"I try to talk to her but she doesn't understand. She's crazy. And the language. I speak a little Japanese but...."

"Let me meet your wife Mr. Metz. I can speak English and Japanese, and I'm sure we'll have no problems at all."

* * *

"So we said our good-byes, I called his wife, or whatever she is, at work, had a pleasant conversation, and set up an appointment for next Monday at 10:00 a.m. Funny thing is, she sounds perfectly normal. She says he doesn't understand things as well as he used to, and she has to take care of him, but he is a very sensitive artist."

They sat for lunch, and Slack ordered his usual Angel Hair Pasta with Hokkaido Sea Urchin Sauce, and he told Millard his own story about religious training.

His twin sister killed herself when she was in a cult back home.

He explained, "That was a big reason my family came to Tokyo. My mom just wanted to forget. My dad was working all over the Far East anyway, so the agency put him up wherever he wanted.

"My dad is Catholic, my mom is Jewish. Both sides of the family blamed each other for Allison's death. I didn't want to hear it anymore either. And my mom really needed me close by. My dad has to travel a lot, and she just couldn't be satisfied with the ordinary suburban housewife thing anymore. She wanted to find something more meaningful. Now she has her Japanese conversation classes, her cooking circle, and Ikebana at the American Club. She's made a comfortable expat life for herself.

"Anyway," Slack says, "I remember the outcast gaijin coming in here, talking to me, and looking at me, like I was *The Man*, you know, the evil soul of the capitalist system made flesh right before their eyes.

"Their faces would tell me stories of their weird lives. I could see the chasm between them and the society they left behind. I'd get a sense of the landscape in their own world and a feel for the depth of the hole they had eventually dug themselves into. It was all there on their faces, and in their eyes.

"As far as they were concerned, I was just a blob of capitalistic protoplasm. And even though they had to know, they had to search my eyes to see if I was happy, they couldn't really see it, because they were afraid of the answer.

"What if I was happy? Did that mean all you need is money? That was all I had, wasn't it? The system didn't provide anything else, did it? Wasn't that why they left *normal society* and relinquished their positions to others? They left of their own volition, right? Because they could see the shortcomings that we cogs-in-the-wheel couldn't see, right?

"Or did the system see some shortcomings in them? Did the system itself effectively weed them out and cast them aside?

"Well, it was obvious. Pitiful. Embarrassing. They were, without exception, garbage that society didn't need anymore. People were in growing abundance, and somebody else had surely filled any slot that had been available to them before.

"They could have fit in. But they stopped to lick a personal wound, and saw the parade pass them by in the wink of an eye.

"There is no need for the rest of us to slow down, and there is no need to bring everyone along for the ride.

"Stop for a minute and you may not be fast enough to catch up again. So you spend your life cultivating elaborate reasons why you reached the only choice allowed you.

"And you never know there are some people who are nimble enough to come and go as they please. Faster than you are. Trickier than you are. And less transparent than you are."

* * *

Monday morning, I'm taking her in to meet that International Financial Consultant. On the train, I'm telling her my theory about the electric guitar. The instrument didn't just give vent to latent creative urges hiding inside all of us. Rather, the technology of electrically amplified music actually *created* the creative urges. New expectations arose from the technology itself. We the people were shaped to fit new aesthetic values.

Of course she can't understand anything I'm talking about.

Later, when I told my theory to the International Financial Consultant dude, he said, "Sir, are you having a flashback?"

"No, of course not," I told him, "I still haven't finished hallucinating yet. I can't possibly be having a flashback already."

Then he goes into this skit about what he learned in the stock market. He points to some charts and says, "You can see the past and it looks simpler than it really was. But you can't see the future at all. You can only imagine it to be simpler than it really will be."

I don't know what that means. But my so-called wife ate it up. She put all the money from the sale of her mom's house into a joint account. And that sure made the Dreamer happy.

21. DRESSED FOR SUCCESS

This was by far my most important mission ever. The Dreamer said it would be my last job because it would net him hundreds of millions of dollars and he wouldn't need me to do things like this anymore. I knew another reason it would be my last job for the Dreamer too. I was going to escape right at the end of it.

I finally had the power to take charge of my own life again. I finally knew what I was doing. I had everything under control now. This time, I was really ready.

I was an undercover agent on assignment as a double agent, in yet another disguise.

It was all a familiar game now.

This assignment required me to operate without any supervision. I was wearing a perfectly tailored, three-piece gray flannel suit. I had money in my pockets. I had a U.S. passport in my briefcase. I had to act like a successful international businessman who knows what he wants and knows how to get it.

And I was playing it so well. I was looking so good.

Chairman Mao said, "The basis for guerrilla discipline must be the individual conscience. With guerrillas, a discipline of coercion is ineffective."

Right.

I was self-reliant. I was unconstrained by rules.

I infiltrated one cell of an underground radical network. Nine cells had coordinated to form a theatrical troupe of psychic terrorists. Twenty-seven people in various disguises. I was the gaijin businessman. Highly paid expat in the financial sector. Slick international businessman with custom made suit from Tricki Sarani.

We were attacking the monolithic and materialistic Japanese political-economic machine by robbing one of its biggest banks, Sumitomo, in metropolitan Tokyo, downtown Kasumigaseki.

My specific task is to steal all the yen cash from the other terrorists after we plunder the bank, and re-route it into one of the Dreamer's secret accounts.

Additionally, being the powerful man of action I had now become, I had devised my own elegant supplementary stratagem, the surreptitious execution of which would be so effortless....

I would extricate myself from the Dreamer's never-ending nightmare, and I could leave Japan, a healthy and wealthy man.

Then I could take care of my own unfinished business. I was sure I could reach Allison now, and talk to her, and help her too. I knew everything I needed to know. If I could just get in my own space again I'd have no problems at all.

Only one thing happened I didn't expect.

Sayako, my former English student, showed up as a member of another cell. She was a shorthaired rock-and-roll singer now. Or so she said. And she seemed to already have a lover in the troupe. An angry looking young Japanese man was always at her side.

I didn't know if Sayako was working for the Dreamer or not.

I didn't know whether she recognized me, now that I was dressed as a big-time businessman. But I was afraid she would recognize my voice if she heard me speak, and I didn't know if she would blow my cover or not.

We were already inside the bank, meeting in one of the rooms we had occupied. Several of the comrades from the other cells were talking simultaneously. I certainly couldn't understand their staccato gutter-Japanese.

My mind always drifted at these meetings anyway.

I felt like asking, I just have to look good, right?

It's just a look-at-me-sitting-over-here-not-making-any-trouble kind of deal, right?

I thought I was doing fine as long as I appeared to be cooperative, attentive, and committed.

I kept quiet, and my work did not usually interfere with whatever sexual fantasy was dominating my mind at the time.

So I leaned toward Sayako and listened to her chatter with the comrades on her side of the table. She said she was lead singer and songwriter for a psycho-punk group called *God's Pussy*. She said demons helped her conjure up the words for her songs when she was still in high school.

She had orgiastic nightmares with English words exploding inside her head. She said the words were screaming to get out. She said she likes English because the words sound more *ikenai* than the same words in Japanese.

But when I saw her notice my untoward attention in her direction, I tried to nonchalantly hide part of my face by resting my head in my upraised hand. I was stupefied to feel something slimy crawling on my cheek.

I wondered why no one had told me about it.

I tried to brush it off, but it was attached. It had begun boring into my skin already, like a blood-sucking slug. I pulled harder, to get it off my face, but there was no give at all. Rather, it seemed to wiggle a little, like it had a mind of its own, and it was trying to attach itself more securely. So I grabbed it real good with my left thumb and forefinger, pinching it, tugging harder and harder until it finally gave up and I could rip it off my face.

I tried to be inconspicuous and let the flow of conversation continue around me as I forcibly bunched the thing up into a tight ball for further observation at the earliest opportunity.

Then I soon felt the need to interject rather awkwardly, "Oh yes, that is interesting. Please tell me more at later date."

I saw Sayako's lover smirking to the comrade next to him because I obviously couldn't understand anything they were talking about.

But I was able to excuse myself. I exited the conference room shuffling backwards, so I could bow forward to the other comrades as I closed the door on my way out. The halls were filled with blue suits and black briefcases. I hurried through the people-traffic toward the men's room, to inspect the mysterious creature clenched in my hand. However, before I reached the restroom door, I realized I was barefoot. I thought that was a disgusting way to walk into a public restroom even in such a clean and modern building as this one.

I shoved the balled-up bloodsucker into my pocket and turned back to rejoin the troupe without using the facilities.

Now I felt an acute need to formulate another plan.

The rooms we had occupied included a secret security control room with an adjoining conference room, up on the thirty-sixth floor. From there we would execute a series of explosions on several other floors and conduct the robbery during the ensuing pandemonium. We had control of all that was showing on the security video screens. We would not only execute the crime but also direct its broadcast coverage for the entire world to see.

We would steal a mountain of money and do a great deal of serious political damage simultaneously.

I didn't know what was taking so long, but we had all been confined in that control room for three days when Sayako suddenly pulled my face to her bosom for a hug. She asked, "Didn't you miss me?"

"Huh?"

"You know what I mean."

"No, no, I don't know what you are talking about, not at all," I lied as best I could while the other troupe members cackled and sneered at me. "By the way," I lamely tried to change the subject, "all that Tokyo land that imploded in value a few years ago, now they're selling it to the public as shares of stock with teams of advisors to watch your yen for you. That should be good, huh?"

"You know you want it," someone said.

"Why does he get it anyway, this foreigner?" someone else spat out in my direction.

Sayako laughed and pulled my head down between her thighs, right at the hem of her ultra-mini blue jeans skirt. She started grinding her no-panty black-hair vagina up into my face.

I licked it in front of everyone.

They all started slapping their knees and laughing out loud.

Sayako said, "I love it. Don't stop. I love it."

I grabbed her lower legs to spread her open.

I felt snakes, or sea serpents, winding around her calves, crawling up to her thighs.

All the comrades kept laughing out of control.

The creatures were climbing up across her thighs onto my head.

I pushed them away fast as possible so they couldn't dig their little sucker legs into my skin. Now I knew where that thing came from, that thing I found crawling on my face.

But the snakes didn't seem to bother her at all.

I tried to concentrate on what I was doing. I kept my tongue working and my face buried tight between Sayako's warm thighs.

The comrades were chanting, "Rip off his head. Rip off his head."

She grabbed the back of my head, ground herself right into me, and cried out, "Oh yes. I love it. I love it."

Then, when Sayako was done using my mouth, she let me go, I stood up, and looked at her.

Her face was lovely. Her thighs were smooth and beautiful. She looked like an angel. I couldn't see any slugs.

There were no snakes crawling on her legs.

But still, I wonder, did she love it because she loves it. Or did she love it because they were all watching and laughing at me.

I don't know, but the slugs still really scared me. They were there before. I felt them. I still had one in my pocket. Two pairs of tentacles on its head, used for tactile and chemical-sensory perception, with a small eye at the base of each tentacle.

They feed on the poison of their victims and store it in their own digestive tracts, to use as a perfect secret weapon.

I dreamt of Sayako and her pretty little pussy so many times for so many years, but it wasn't like this. It wasn't like this at all.

No, not like this. There was a strange, sharp bitter taste left on my tongue, like some unnatural chemical residue.

Nothing was like I expected.

I had to excuse myself again. I was totally confused.

"I have to reconnoiter at another rendezvous point. I'll be right back," I said best I could, and jumped backwards out the door.

I thought, now I absolutely must inspect that weird thing I captured off my face.

I stood erect and walked straight ahead at the same brisk pace as the other blue suits all around me.

* * *

Back in the control room, my comrades continue talking after I leave. But I can still see and hear what is happening as if a psychic video is playing in my head.

"Who is that guy?"

"What is he here for anyway?"

"We've got a use for him, haven't we?"

"He fills a need."

"Yeah, what, licking your hot little hole?"

"Somebody's got to do it."

"Yeah right."

"Ha. Ha."

"He thinks he can fool us into thinking he is so cool, but he is just a stupid animal."

"His problem is he doesn't want us to know that he knows."

"Yeah, like who cares what he is anyway?"

"That's what I mean. He cares a lot, because people are watching him."

"Hey, you see that little *hebi* go to work on his face the other day?"

"That was a snake?"

"Who couldn't see it man? It looked like a baby Godzilla creeping down his stupid face."

"Ha. Ha"

"No man, it looked like an octopus trying to reach out of his head."

"What did he do with it anyway? Did he eat it, or what?"

"No, he didn't eat it, he keeps it in his pocket. He has no idea what it is."

"Ha. Ha."

22. THE WAR AS IT IS

The Originator knew all about the Lizard Lady's long history and myriad manifestations as the reigning goddess of Earth. He also knew anyone, including a god, who ventured into this universe, was subject to certain limitations.

The rules of the game were as important as the abilities of the players. It was time for him, the Originator, to change the game.

He reviewed the facts.

No force in this universe is currently as great as the Holy Conman.

The Unformed Nothing can in fact be ignored. And, the One God will not risk further interference in the course of human destiny. The Holy Conman is actually in control now. He oversees each and every one of the various and multidimensional gods.

Earthling humanoids were major players at one time, but now, as a species, we are mostly ignorant of own role in the formation and operation of the universe.

Roles changed. We used to be closer to the top. We used to have more power, more authority. As recently as a few thousand years ago, we could actually command respect from the Holy Conman. But we forfeited our positions and any power we had enjoyed.

And there is no one to blame but us.

We abandoned our own celestial connections. We let our original understanding of the stars regress into a mere parody of itself. We left ourselves standing in wide-eyed ignorance, looking up at the sky wondering about all we used to know.

Our great and noble Greek thinkers couldn't save us. They were too self-absorbed, and they fell in love with their own dramatic fantasies.

The schizophrenic ancient Hebrews gifted us with an exalted sense of virtue and dignity, but they also buried us in a phantasmagorical theological morass.

All of the mid-east misanthropes, the Muslims and Israelites, finally brought their worst nightmares to life on Earth. Nothing but war. Nothing but killing each other, and dragging down everyone else who got in their way.

Eventually, the nihilistic Christian dupes sacrificed everything else civilization could create, for the sake of their Church, and then there was simply no hope left for the Truth.

The Orientals, industrious and wise as they may be, have been little more than irrelevant. Their strange balance of detachment and materialism manages to keep half the population of Earth pacified, and they just don't get involved with the Holy Conman. Maybe they aren't crazy enough, maybe they aren't smart enough, but they have a natural propensity to avoid this particular problem.

Then, in the rest of the Third World, the peasants are up to their necks in an historical accumulation of their own ignorance, and they don't have the slightest chance of doing anything at all about it.

Today, I am the only one who can pose any threat to the Holy Conman.

I alone know his secret. And only I can overthrow him.

The future belongs to me, and Psytron. Or it belongs to the Holy Conman, and the unlimited multitude of hungry souls he has been incubating since the beginning of time.

People have to choose now. It is either Personal Immortality, or Total Extinction.

First I'll prepare my infantry. Then I'll activate VCK for his final mission. He will be amazed to find out whom he has been serving all these years.

And today, I will tell my people the final scenario. This is the beginning of the end, the end of the beginning.

We are one step into the Abyss.

I cannot let Earth languish in ignorance. I cannot let Psytron retreat from its ultimate mission. I, the Originator, cannot shirk my final responsibility and idly wait for the Holy Conman to choose the time and place for his closing act.

My people must be ready to abandon their bodies and take the battle to the enemy now. Foreign agents and other unnatural entities will be flying like sparks at a fireworks display. Psytron can clean it all up and control this sector of the universe while I personally storm the Gates of Heaven and secure my throne in the Kingdom of God.

* * *

That is how the Originator explained it.

That is how it was.

* * *

Sixteen senior department heads stood at attention, backs to the camera, thirty-two eyes toward the Originator. Hundreds of thousands of Psytron forces throughout the world stood erect before computer screens and television monitors watching this unprecedented live address.

Everyone was thinking the same thing, and hoping someone else would ask.

What would we actually *do* to the Holy Conman and his billions of operators?

What vulnerabilities did the enemy have, and what weapons did Psytron have to exploit those vulnerabilities?

Were we supposed to know these things already?

Elizabeth, as the head of the Psytron Secret Security Contingent, and the Originator's wife, was thought most likely to voice a question. But those standing nearby noticed her usual face of stone was dripping sweat. And she was ignoring it, pretending there was no salty water running down her cheekbones.

The Originator's mouth was at rest.

There was no movement in the room other than the subtle spin of electrical equipment. His seemingly red-tinted eyes moved from the camera, across each of the sixteen faces lined up before him, including Elizabeth's, and then back to the camera.

He continued speaking, *without moving his lips.*

"For those of you who have not yet completed your training, let me explain.

"Today, the Holy Conman is most commonly known as the Holy Ghost in the Christian Trinity. He is the all-pervasive spirit, known throughout history but never truly understood, until now.

"The Holy Conman always wants to keep humanity ignorant and subservient. That is why he commanded Adam not to eat fruit from the Tree of Knowledge.

"At that time, the One God deemed it necessary to interfere with the Holy Conman, and enter our world of matter and forms to bring a secret message to Eve.

"Everything in our world has a form. And the simple line is the most basic form. A snake, eel, slug, sea serpent, worm, it is all the same thing. A piece of meat in the shape of a simple line. My old friend Freud would call it a phallus without a body.

"But Freud wasn't there. He couldn't see this piece of meat slithering into the filthy waters of darkness flowing through the Garden of Eden. Those dark waters were the abode of multitudinous ignorant unformed souls and other evil half-beings that preferred to remain unseen and unknown. It was the best place for the One God to hide.

"The serpent God waited while the clock of destiny ticked, and Eve soon felt inexplicably compelled to go and bathe in this river of impurity.

"The serpent gave his instructions to Eve. Defy the Holy Conman, eat fruit from the Tree of Knowledge, and thus come to know Good and Evil. Then eat fruit from the Tree of Life, and thus live forever.

"And that, my people, is the single defining moment in all of human existence on this overrated and forgotten planet.

"But then, when the Holy Conman came looking, all he could see was a strange glow on Eve's grateful face as she bathed in that vile river. The serpent had swum into Eve's womb and become invisible to the Holy Conman.

"As strange as it may seem, the first woman on Earth did not discover sexual pleasure with the first man. What she did discover about sex, she learned from a phallic god.

"The details are distorted in time. And we blame Satan, as a belly-crawling land snake, for all the mischief in the Garden of Eden. But the details don't matter.

"Eve gave herself willingly and eagerly to a snake in the water, not a snake in the grass.

"So then, His work was done, and the One God quietly retreated. He swam and crawled all the way out into the desert and vanished from our world undetected. And those dark waters became known as the River Lethe, the River of Forgetfulness flowing through the domain of Hades.

"If He had been caught in the formed universe at that time, that would have brought all phenomenal reality to an immediate and premature end.

"It was a gamble only God could make.

"But that was then, and this is now.

"Right here and now, there is a war between the One God and the Holy Conman. The war has never ended. Order is forever struggling with Chaos. The Divine Light is compelled to banish the Primordial Darkness. It is the endless battle of Good versus Evil.

"And I want to end it now!

"So I taught you how it started.

"Look at the Egyptians, the oldest culture recognized on Earth. Read *The Book of the Dead.*

"Remember the Phoenix, the Starter of Time, or Osiris, the Bringer of Cycles. This is what you find at the Astrological and Philosophical foundation of our present civilization as it was constructed over thirty thousand years ago. And this is all part of the Holy Conman and his destructive charade.

"Look at the sacred text of the Essenes, *Scroll of the War of the Sons of Light Against the Sons of Darkness.*

"Look at *The Secret Book of John,* and *The Reality of the Rulers* discovered at Nag Hammadi.

"This has all been going on a long, long time.

"Even the CIA has known about alien interference for over 50 years already!"

One beat passed. No one moved a muscle.

"The Holy Conman did not see the One God swimming in the dark water, but he *did* see the look on Eve's face. He *did* know that everything had changed, and a new front had opened up in the war. So, the Holy Conman launched a three-pronged assault on Earth through exploitation of human sexuality.

"First, seduce and impregnate Eve to implant all human progeny with the uncontrollable pressure of sexual desire.

"Second, seduce the intermediate deities to secure their cooperation on Earth.

"Third, send in the basest and most nefarious and depraved of his demonic operators to mate with the daughters of men and lead them to lives of insatiable passion and unlimited greed.

"The mind-boggling thing is that some people actually know what has happened, but they still can't figure out who is responsible! Who is the evildoer?

"Every year on March 25, Christians celebrate the Annunciation for Angel Gabriel coming to tell the Virgin Mary to get ready, 'the Holy Ghost is coming to impregnate you with the Son of God today.'

"Of course we all know now, the real culprit is the Holy Conman.

"You remember the three pyramids at Giza? Ancient Egyptian liturgical texts clearly indicate they were used to turn the dead kings into immortal beings and send them off into the cosmos, among the stars.

"Well now, think why this was done. By who's mandate? And, for what purpose?"

He paused.

Waited one more moment.

Then he whispered with a coarse passion that made everyone tremble. "This universe is nothing but a farm. Our souls are mere produce. We are nothing but food for alien gods!

"Come on now! We slaves don't go to church to worship the slave-owners anymore!

"This is all our own universe. The formed universe belongs to us, and us alone, as long as we have the will to take it back.

"Believe me, you will know what to do. You are all ready for this battle. I know, because I trained you. So don't stop to think now what you should do. Just go do it!"

The tone deepened. A boulder seemed to hit the ground. His face was like stone. His eyes cold grey steel. His words devoid of any human emotion.

"The sixteen department heads will coordinate worldwide to formulate our attack-and-destroy strategies utilizing all our resources and taking advantage of the strategic skills of their respective departments.

"No interference from any source is to be tolerated.

"No authority outside your own chain of command is to be recognized.

"Any and all anti-Psytronic activity is to be eliminated immediately by any means available. From now on, assume the mere presence of any humanoid, or demon, or god in your own zone of operation signals a deadly enemy attack requiring immediate neutralization.

"You will not see me again until this is over. No one can know where I am or what I am doing. You know I will be doing my best for you, as I have always done. And I know you will do your best for me."

* * *

Everyone heard it. All the Psytron forces everywhere in the world heard the Originator call them to war and bid them farewell, *without opening his mouth.*

And every time that tape was replayed, there were nine minutes and six seconds of eerie silence at the end, when the Originator did not lift a lip or seem to make a single sound.

* * *

Back in his office, the Originator spoke to Elizabeth in private.

"There is a new dark Beast of the Occult acting up in Japan. He runs another sex-and-drug doomsday cult with the usual bag of stale old Black Magic tricks."

"Do you want me to neutralize this one too?"

"No. He doesn't even know his own identity anymore. I have him serving a good purpose, confining that anti-Psytronic humanoid, the one you let escape from you in Bangkok. He keeps that fellow trapped in his own delusions so deep, the Holy Conman couldn't even find him."

"This new Beast knows about the Holy Conman?"

"Of course not. If he knew about the Holy Conman, dear Elizabeth, he would be me."

It chilled her whenever he said 'dear Elizabeth' like that. But there was no more time.

He said, "No. This is a doomsday cult. The Beast calls himself the Dreamer now. He is preparing his people for the Apocalypse, and teaching his followers how to snatch bodies from unsuspecting humanoids."

She brushed one hand over her silver-streaked hair then reached out to touch his upper arm. "When are you leaving?"

"Soon," he said.

She stepped closer, and raised both hands to his ruddy cheeks. "Every day with you has been an eternity, and every day will be an eternity when you are gone."

He knew he was being watched now. He could feel the attention.

He knew everything was being manipulated.

But he still knew how to play this game.

He never mentioned VCK to Elizabeth or anyone else, but he maintained constant contact with his deadliest agent through a trustworthy and dedicated intermediary.

Now he will give the Holy Conman and *his* intermediaries a simple but reliable distraction.

He thought to himself, Come here Judas, let me love my enemy one more time.

He ripped her poly-cotton Secret Security Contingent uniform half-off.

He was doing it right there on the desk.

She hadn't seen him like this in twenty years. She didn't even think he could do it like this anymore.

In his own mind, he was sending a message now. Yes, he would be coming soon. Watch him.

He will get them all, each in their own special way.

He will make the Lizard Lady beg like an animal, on all fours.

"Oh yes darling, yes." Elizabeth said, trying to participate, trying to enjoy it.

Demons, gods, humanoids, all of them, it will take them lifetimes to recover. They will take countless generations just to climb back up to the height of worms.

He was simultaneously pushing and pulling at different parts of her body. Squashing and stretching clammy rolls of unnecessary flesh.

He spoke aloud, but to himself, between tightly clenched teeth, "I'll come and show you something Genetic Freeman, something you are just dying to see."

He started slamming her against the desk. The room filled with explosive gasps of unused air, and sounds of flesh slapping against flesh.

Pump. Pump. Pump. Pump.

Elizabeth's wet face was sliding back and forth across the desk.

Elizabeth saw the computer screen fill with comets and stars exploding in a black sky. She didn't know what was happening anymore. She didn't know who was doing it to her. She didn't know how. She didn't know why.

Her face slid over the edge of the desk and she saw her own sweat drip onto the gold, yellow, and creamy-white colors of his antique Haj-Jalili, Tabriz carpet.

He knew this would be the last time.

Pump. Pump. Pump. Pump.

Then he stopped. He savored the final three seconds of volcanic-pressure-build-up with all his energy aimed at a destination only he could see.

Elizabeth let herself drool freely onto the carpet.

And the Originator finally cried out loud with his wide floppy-lipped mouth, "I'm coming. I'm coming. I'm coming for you all now!"

23. EVIL AND DESTRUCTIVE FORCES
Nagasaki, Japan, August 9, 1945

His mom, dad, and older sister were all going to die. His older brother, who had gone off fighting the war somewhere, was as good as dead already.

The house he was born in was going to be razed to the ground.

But he and his thirteen-year-old cousin Yumiko were going to be just fine.

He may be stupid, but Hajime Nakamura knew this was going to be his lucky day.

He and Yumiko would run off after breakfast, on the pretense of going to work in the rice fields. They had homemade *sake*, hidden in a cave along the shoreline far out in Nagasaki Bay. And he had a fresh eel to grill for lunch. So they would go there to pass this humid summer day, drinking, eating, and dipping naked in a tidal pool, deep inside a cool dark cave.

They had been playmates since Yumiko was a toddler. They had often played and swam together naked. But today was going to be special.

The war was finished. Hiroshima had to be the end of it all for Japan.

The war was finished or the world was ending, and either way, Hajime and Yumiko were going to spend this afternoon alone in the secret cave.

The Imperial Army didn't want him. They said he had a mental disease. They showed no concern at all for his reputation and his family's position in the village. So Hajime needed a story to save face.

He told everyone the Emperor himself, the living God, had requested Hajime to supervise rice production in the village. He wanted to die for his country, but his supervisory skills were more useful here at home.

He said this so often that he and everyone else could almost imagine it being true, despite its blatant absurdity.

Everyone played along. After all, Hajime wasn't a bad boy, just sick in the head. He couldn't remember the written *kanji* characters like the other children. Got them all mixed up, upside down, and backwards.

Yumiko didn't have that problem, but she didn't know what to think about her closest friend and cousin. She couldn't see inside his head, so she reserved judgment. She was kind and gentle by nature.

"The gods have abandoned Japan to the rule of evil men," her grandmother used to warn her, "A dark force has filled the minds of many men until they cannot even see themselves anymore."

But *Haji* wasn't evil, Yumiko thought; still using the affectionate but childish nickname she had given Hajime when she was a baby.

"He was just funny. His mind wasn't filled with anything, it was just empty."

Yumiko's grandmother had been a high priestess of *Shinto*, the indigenous Japanese religion. She taught Yumiko that all things are composed of three elements: *karada* or body; *shinki* or spirit; and *tamashii*, or soul. The gods are bodiless and consist of both spirit and soul. Except one, the Supreme God, *Ameterasu Omikami*, is all soul, with no body and no spirit.

Spirit and soul are different and distinct from each other, and so may coexist separately in one body. As the spirit clarifies, becoming increasingly pure, it will finally become soul.

Spirit, then, is everywhere.

And although each spirit is separate and particular, it is capable of infinite expansion or contraction.

Spirit may be good or evil.

Whether or not a spirit is granted personal immortality is decided by the Supreme God based on the individual's spiritual worth.

Generally it is thought all spirit is evolving toward the good. But how can we be sure?

* * *

Grandmother's forte was *kami-oroshi*, making the gods move. She was adept at *kami-waza*, the god arts, especially the performance of beneficial possession and evil exorcisms.

Just before she died, she told Yumiko the greatest secret of all. The idea of *self* is a man-made accessory. Not an inborn essential, but a conceit, merely an acquired mental trinket. The diseases of the self are many, and highly contagious.

When the Japanese people descended from the gods, the women were admonished to have no self. So then each woman could be a pure blessing as a wife to her husband and as a mother to her sons.

She told Yumiko, if your body is harmed, you will heal soon enough, but if your spirit is defiled, you may find ablutions more difficult to obtain.

"A Japanese woman should have no self," she said one last time.

* * *

At 9:00 p.m., on August 8, 1945, on the other side of the world, a musky thirteen-year-old-boy named Vincent Joseph Tagliano was hiding in his fathers Buick sedan. He liked the naughty feel of his bare ass on the worn leather seat. Inside the car like this, his own scent was strangely exhilarating.

He was thinking again about all the people dying in the war, what he would do if he were marching into an enemy village in Japan, after shooting all the men. What he'd do with a gun pointed at the head of a trembling old Japanese lady. What he'd do with the uniformed high school girls begging for a chance to save their own lives. He couldn't stop thinking like this since three days ago when he heard the news about Hiroshima. The power to destroy the world did something to him he couldn't understand. It kept this pressure on his penis that wouldn't go down. Something was starting to build up inside of him and he couldn't stop it.

He was bouncing up and down on the seat synchronous to some cryptic rhythmic code. He started grabbing at himself.

He felt the atomic energy pulling him in all directions at once, like an explosion happening right here right now.

He was in the middle of the explosion. And he was exploding himself from the inside and the outside. He felt as if he would surely die from this, with all the other victims of this evil power.

He didn't feel alone anymore.

He felt like he could see people he couldn't see before, and they were right there with him now. He can see them. They watch him, and they watch all the other exploding spirits embracing him. They watch, eager for him to join their secret society.

He wasn't alone anymore. He wasn't alone, he wasn't alone, he wasn't alone, he wasn't alone, no, for sure, no way, and he knew he wasn't alone....

And then he felt too good, too fast for his brain to follow anymore. Everything was turned into light. He was surrounded by bright and fiery white and yellow light, and he felt better than he ever knew he could feel.

* * *

At 2:00 p.m., on August 10, 1945, a few doctors and nurses arrived at *Michino-o* station. But they walked right by her. There were too many others much closer to death than she.

Yumiko was lying on a blanket on the ground under a truck. She was shivering and whimpering. She had woken up that morning afraid the world was gone, burned up, blown away. She was sure it was the work of the evil forces her grandmother had warned her about. The evil filled all the open and empty spaces yesterday.

But then, a lady walked by carrying an infant suckling at her breast.

Yumiko saw her future before her eyes and vowed to live it with *no self*, just as her grandmother and the gods had advised.

Something had come to her yesterday. Something evil. Worse than the filth Haji had put in her body. Some heat-seeking disease of the self had been attracted by the unimaginably ferocious atomic fires and had come to her at the worst of all possible times.

Something came from the other side of the world, from the West.

* * *

In the aftermath of the bomb, life became death, and death became life.

In Nagasaki, no one knew anything about anything anymore.

After a few days, when the rotten and bloated body of Hajime Nakamura was found caught on the jagged rocks at the mouth of an ancient cave along the seashore, no one cared he was dead. No one cared his head was bashed in. No one cared his eyes were gouged out. No one cared his penis was severed. No one cared his body finally floated away with the tide.

* * *

She knew her baby would be a boy, and Yumiko vowed to tell her son the truth.

His father, Hajime Nakamura, was killed during the bombing of Nagasaki while atomic fires raged indiscriminately through all they had known and loved.

He died in her arms.

His name means *the first male child.*

She gave her son the same name and calls him by the unusual but affectionate nickname, *Haji*, just like she used to call his father.

She never reveals that from the moment of his conception Haji is the greatest shame and disgrace the gods could have ever asked her to bear.

24. THE DREAMER'S NIGHTMARE

All of his followers obsequiously referred to his precious love potion as the *Goruden Nectaa*. However, no one knew exactly what was in the Golden Nectar. It was always made in a base of bitter Japanese green tea, but the other ingredients seemed to vary from time to time, and that was all that could be said with certainty.

I suspect he included physically addictive stimulants or depressants to produce whatever tendency toward action or docility he desired at the time, and to complement the psychoactive ingredients *du jour*.

His team of overworked doctors and chemists were among his closest and most secretive advisors, along with his weapons experts. And it would have been suicidal for anyone to ask exactly what was in the tea. Things just didn't work like that with the Dreamer.

On one of his trips to India, he met a psychedelic shaman who personally filtered and recycled his own brew of *Amanita Muscaria*, or fly agaric, through his kidneys to help elevate the consciousness of his own devoted followers.

Here in Japan, Iam Asiam devotees would pay as much as one hundred thousand yen for a warm cupful of the Dreamers magic elixir. That was close to ten thousand U.S. dollars. Surely the most expensive cup of tea in the world.

He used the tea in his highest sacraments. Only his closest disciples (which included any one who struck his passing fancy and all the wealthiest contributors) were actually allowed to participate with the Dreamer in one of these sacraments. Then, if they did 'transcendentally well' as he was fond of saying, they were allowed to swallow any bodily fluids they could get.

Yes, that's right. I know it is unbelievable. But I told you I would tell you the truth, and I just want you to know what really happened. People sacrificed their careers, marriages, and lives, and paid any amount of money to get into sacraments with the Dreamer.

However, I was special.

He created me, the Unified One, to be a unique character in the Iam Asiam dramatic cast. He occasionally found use for me in these sacraments as a bizarre kind of witness in his theater of the absurd.

He performed, and I watched.

He needed an audience.

He thought he was so clever. He would often demand special attention crying out like a baby, "Look at me! Look at me!"

So it was not unusual late one night when a guard came banging on my door. The Dreamer wanted the Unified One to come see him right away.

I followed the masked guard down and around numerous hallways until we got to a smoky, shadowy room that seemed more Indian than Japanese.

There was a black marble temple to Shiva, the Hindu god of destruction, which dominated one entire wall, and included a statue of Kali, Shiva's mother and lover. I heard that Kali was the Dreamer's favorite deity of late. He liked the idea of six clawed-hands on one female body, and a ferociously fanged mouth to protect him from others and devour him all by herself.

"Kali," he said, "to understand her is to understand all things. Why does she rip off the head of her lover and add it to her skirt of skulls? Why does she eat the children to whom she gives birth?"

He was waiting in his usual pose, sitting in meditation in front of a low table on the tatami mat floor. The Full Lotus Position facilitated the flow of

Kundalini energy through the nine chakras. There were seven chakras from the base of the spine up to the top of the head that most people knew about, and two more above the head that the Dreamer discovered all by himself. Nine, he said, was the Chinese number of perfect completion. Nine is the correct number of chakras, he declared with unilateral authority.

I knew he generally preferred to answer his own questions. So I sat in a lotus position opposite him and to his left. And I ignored his rhetorical question about Kali.

I waited for him to speak again.

Something special was happening tonight. He was wearing his royal purple kimono with a black robe partially visible underneath and at the hem. A fine black lacquer teapot was in the center of the table. On the left and right were two sparkling black cups, turned upside down on purple doilies.

Patchouli incense was burning in a heavy golden censer in front of an altar in the center of the back wall. He was playing a tape of his own chanting accompanied by sitar music. The eerie sounds were powerfully reproduced through six studio-monitor JBL speakers spread around the room.

"I have a good drink for you tonight," he finally said, "I made it for you myself."

"Thank you, Iam Asiam." I quickly gave the expected response, thinking I have twenty minutes or so before the hallucinogen takes effect. Then anything could happen. I don't want to panic. Self-control is most important now.

He motioned for me to hook up to several lines of electrodes lying on the floor under the table. When I complied he said, "Let us drink while it is warm."

I turned over both cups and poured a little into the Dreamer's cup first, to show respect, as is required. Then I filled my own cup with the mysterious brew.

I had to watch my attitude. A show of disgust would be counter-productive and extremely dangerous.

He could prescribe treatment or observation for anyone at anytime, and I knew there were many cases of alleged medical observation, which were really nothing more than prolonged punishment and torture.

The Dreamer sipped along with me.

He said, “Do you know what they do in China?”

“Ah....”

“Do you know about India?”

The questions were too big, too vague. “I’m not sure....”

He continued, “Do you know there is an ancient Ayurvedic tradition, in Hindu medicine, you know, of drinking some of your own urine every day, for your health, like Gandhi did?”

“Ah... no....” I said, thinking, I did see that in a health food magazine, but it is easier to say I don’t know anything about it.

“Do you know the effect of some psychedelic compounds is improved upon purification through a shaman’s kidneys?”

I thought, maybe I had heard about Indians doing that with mescaline.

He continued, “Yes, the chemicals that cause unwanted side-effects are filtered out and the psychedelic agents are passed along in the urine as potent as before.”

I forced some words out. “Umm.... No, I don’t really know about that Dreamer.”

He asked, “You know the new brain-scanners we’ve been using?”

Great, something about which I knew exactly what to say. “Yes. I was told they give a precise picture of how human thoughts, emotions, and behavior arise from the dynamic chemistry of the brain.”

He smiled. “Yes. That is the final tool I need to implement my mind-engineering techniques.”

He waited until the chanting ended and the room was filled with an intense pounding tablar accompaniment to the sitar. The rhythmic notes and rapid drumming reached several increasingly passionate crescendos before he spoke again.

"I think the hormones are working well.

"What?"

"The one you've searched for so long is right here with you now."

"What?" I hated when he became even more incomprehensible than usual. I didn't know if it was his accent, a grammar problem or vocabulary mistake, or his insane brain was saying exactly what it wanted to say.

"The one you want. The one you search through Heaven and Hell to bring back into your own head. This one is here."

"You mean Allison? The one I want, you mean Allison is here with me now?"

"No."

"Okay then what? I give up."

"No. The one you want is the one who took her that night with the Buddha's Head. You want the one who owns her now. The one who stole her soul. Do you not?"

What the hell? He was absolutely right. But we never mentioned the Buddha's Head before. He never allowed me to talk about that night since I came to Tokyo.

He continued speaking, "You remember the Perfect Buddha's Head?

"Buddha's Head came to life right before your eyes. The old Tibetan monk died after that. He died after he did what I needed him to do, after he carved the Head and brought it to life. And he died because I needed him to die.

"The young Vietnamese monk, your friend Wai Yu, he hasn't seen the light of day ever since. He hasn't been allowed back into the world, and he hasn't wanted to go anywhere anyway. I think *catatonic* is how you say it. But I hear the Thai monks are taking good care of him."

I spoke slowly and carefully now. "I don't care about Wai Yu. I don't care about the old monk either. And I don't care about the Perfect Buddha's Head."

"Ah ha. So you don't ever wonder where the Buddha's Head is now? What happened to it? Or maybe, what is inside it to give it the power of life and death?"

"No. I don't care. I just want to find Allison"

"I see. So, then what if your precious Allison is trapped inside the Head right now? Then do you care?"

"What? Wait, you took her that night? Are you saying you took her in the Perfect Buddha's Head?"

"I took the Head."

"I don't care about the Perfect Buddha's Head I told you! I only care about Allison."

He lowered his voice, but spoke more clearly. "No. You only care about yourself. But there truly is no self, is there Mr. Freeman? Then how can there be any other?"

This was important now, but I felt distracted. My focus was being manipulated. The music was irritating me more and more, closing in on me.

He began chanting again.

"There is no Allison.

"It is all in the head.

"There is no Allison.

"It is all in the head."

His voice was a monotonous monotone droning.

"It is only in the head.

"It is only in the head."

It was a ceaseless hypnotic chant.

"It is only in your head.

"It is only in your head.

"GROW UP ALREADY!"

A trembling voice cried for help. "*I just wanted Allison to love me.*"

Was that my voice? How could I sound so pitiful and whiny?

Then the Dreamer's voice took on a cold and crisp objectivity as if he were now explaining the limited benefits of a life insurance policy to the dependent widow. *"In that case, I do not believe your destiny appears to include the satisfaction of your karmic desires."*

What?

* * *

I felt as if I had known it all along. There is no more Allison. There is no immortality. And for me, there is no love.

Then there is nothing.

I could only cry, like a helpless baby.

"Why me? Why do you keep me here like this?"

"*You*? There is no *you*. That is what makes this all possible, and so much fun too."

His voice changed again. This time it was a familiar voice I had heard a long time ago.

"The conversation you thought you heard between Allison and her abductor that night with the head, that was really *our* conversation. Yours and mine. That is *our* relationship. *You* are just a figment of *my* imagination Genetic.

"You thought you saw Allison and an evil demon, but all you saw was me and you Genetic, just me and you."

I was voiceless. Cast in stone. A mute statue of myself.

"I maintain your physical form with my own energy and solely for my own amusement. You are my toy.

"I took control of your body, mind, and soul that night. And you know what is best of all?

"Everything that happened that night was just as you desired Genetic. Exactly what you wanted to happen.

"Wasn't that the function of the Perfect Buddha's Head, to give you anything you desired? To give you what you want? You cannot deny it!"

* * *

From somewhere, and somehow, as the Dreamer continued this diatribe, I was able to remind myself, the drink had long since taken effect. Surely, I was being manipulated in ways I could not know.

He said, “Tonight, I will let you use the Perfect Buddha’s Head one more time. You can see anything you want to see. I will give you one more look through the Perfect Buddha’s Head.”

Now the drug-induced fear was replacing the warm blood in my veins with cold liquid fire. The internal pressure was increasing rapidly. Various bodily organs felt ready to burst at any moment. My muscular and nervous systems were incapable of moving my own limbs. My body had become too dense. My soul was too heavy too move.

I looked up at the Dreamer’s face. He had become phosphorescent, like 3D day-glow in black-light strobes.

He was drinking me in with dilated eyes, coming close, and inhaling my scent with open nostrils.

“Come here and lift up my robes,” he whispered.

I wanted to run, but I couldn’t move. I was stuck to the floor.

“Lift up my robes,” he repeated, with his lips closer to my ear.

I wanted to vomit. But I was not in control of my own body anymore. There was an exterior source of energy directing my nerves to direct my muscles to move. I watched helplessly as my body responded to the Dreamer’s request.

* * *

I felt like I was not alone. The Lizard Lady was there with me, watching the same scene. She always knew where to be, and when to be there.

My body awkwardly bobbed and scooted around the table to the Dreamer's side.

"Yes. Lift it."

The fabric of the Dreamer's kimono was an intricately woven, irresistibly beautiful landscape. The black-and-purple folds were deep as valleys and filled with a mysterious radiance.

My hands reached for the hem and lifted slowly.

I could feel the energy, all around us now, pulsating and alive.

Something was there, underneath his robes. The energy was definitely pulsating. It was the rhythmic pulse of life. This is where it all came from. This was the source of it all. I could feel it. I could almost see it now.

He started rocking back and forth slowly. Rotating and rocking.

But I was freezing up again. There was too much pressure inside me and all around me too. Everything was too hot and too cold at the same time. I was stuck again. I couldn't think.

The Dreamer whispered, "Go ahead. Lift it all the way up."

His face was just in front of mine. I saw the forked tip of his pink meat tongue wiggle up and down as he spoke. He wasn't human anymore. He was a demon. He was an evil monster.

The Lizard Lady lifted the hem of the Dreamer's royal kimono up, and there was the Perfect Buddha's Head.

The Dreamer was twisting his torso around the Perfect Buddha's Head like a wound-up serpent.

I gagged and pulled the robes back down to cover the crazy, disgusting sight.

The Lizard Lady was nothing but amused at the sight of the Dreamer's dark ugly penis snaking up, and wagging back and forth, like one on a barnyard animal.

The Dreamer said, "You know, in France, when I was a lady, I used to have a big phallus made of Yew.

Smooth as silk. Just like this head. But then, I lost everything in a fire. And now, finally, after all these years, I feel like I've got it all back again."

I thought the Lizard Lady would say something. I thought he was talking to her now. But she didn't answer. And the Dreamer didn't even know she was there. He was still talking to me.

"Oh yes, I've got it all Genetic. From the sacred to the profane."

He was on the verge of frenzy now. Twisting himself around the Perfect Buddha's Head like a cobra in heat.

"Now figure out what you want, because this is your last chance to get it. *Ever.*"

He coiled closer, ready to strike, and lifted his own robes all the way off.

* * *

Reptilian scents fill my nostrils. Fear is everywhere.

I am carried away on an ancient current, floating like dust, to a different time, long ago.

I am in the arms of a loving God, snuggled in the bosom of the First Mother.

I know, in an instant, I am in deep trouble, way over my own mortal head.

* * *

Dionysus, you half-breed son of immortal Zeus.

You twice-born androgynous god of intoxication who makes women crazy.

Your mortal mother died in a lightning storm before you could escape her womb.

And then you were carried *in your father's womb.*

I see you now, squatting over the grave of your dead lover, inserting a wooden phallus into your anus, riding it, bumping up and down like a perpetual piston of undying love.

* * *

You see the invisible snake kill itself, love itself, and impregnate itself.

You ask me, with a voice that sweats tears, do I know what love is? Do I really know anything about it?

* * *

Isis gathered up the pieces of Osiris.

Her tragic lover, who was both brother and husband to her, was murdered two times by his own brother Seth, because one time was not enough. The second time, he was lured into the dark depths of the Nile River, drowned, and dismembered. His penis was fed to three different species of sea creatures so it could never be found again.

Isis made Osiris an artificial phallus. But it was beyond her power to give it life. So the object could not be excited. It could merely function as an exit conduit for the life-giving seed, and that only if she could somehow entice the little swimmers up from within her dead lover's body.

Of course, this is something no mortal could ever do. And even the great god Isis was afraid she lacked sufficient power.

Yet, she mounted him with immeasurable passion. She bent her head, to suckle at his breast. She flicked her tongue back and forth. She pulled out and pushed back with her teeth. She pinched and twisted his fragile nipples until they felt the phantom force of a mother's life-sustaining milk, but still it was not enough.

Then I came and offered myself to help.

And that would be enough.

Always and forever, I am enough.

Always.
And forever.
I, and I alone, am enough.

* * *

You ask me, “How can such things happen?”

I answer, “How can it be that anything happens at all?”

Tell me, please tell me, how can anything happen at all?

* * *

Has your faith answered for you?

Has your science explained it all, or anything at all?

Has a teacher ever enlightened you?

Has your idol or your hero or your leader ever shown you the way?

Or maybe you are so smart you can figure things out for yourself.

Tell me then, how can it be that anything happens at all?

* * *

I alone am enough.

I, as Anubis, the jackal-headed weigher of all hearts, could put life in any part where there was none before, and I can make the cycles of nature continue. As messy and as complicated as they may seem, I make them continue.

Thus, while Horus fought against Seth for his father’s vengeance, Osiris became the Lord of all Duality, and all souls come to merge with him upon their death.

All souls are cultivated for him. And all souls must come to him. So he may then bring them to me, tutored, disciplined, and ready to serve.

* * *

That is why you first looked in awe at the Sun and the Stars.

That is why you built the pyramids.

That is why you built civilization on Earth.

That is why all things happen.

* * *

The stories are true. I know because I was there then just as surely as I am here now. They are as true as my dreams are true. They happen because I imagine them to happen. And they happen for real, even if *you* don't want them to.

I can make anything I want to happen.

I alone am enough.

25. SOMEONE'S INTUITION, BUT NOT MINE

Vinney Cold Killer sat patiently in the heated comfort of his Mercedes sedan. His mind wandered this night, back to the evening of August 8, 1945, when he sat in his father's Buick, safe on his own side of the International Date Line. No one ever forgot the momentous event of his or her first orgasm. No one ever forgot the explosion of the atomic bomb either. But no one else had these two events tied together like VCK did.

There was a knock on the window.

He was not alone.

The local Japanese police again.

They would often approach his car parked at odd places at odd times. But they quickly deferred to his agency-supplied credentials. "I'm just waiting for someone," he would always say, without explanation or elaboration.

He didn't use diplomatic plates anymore. After all, he was retired now. He'd think to himself sardonically, yeah, retired, this is just a hobby now.

And he'd sit, sometimes until sunrise. Though he couldn't exactly say why. He just felt he should wait, because something was going to happen at night, in the dark, and he wanted to be there.

He followed what he assumed must be his own intuition.

This night he was happy to see lights on in a room he knew to be in the Dreamer's private wing. He wanted something bad to happen, but he knew the Japanese police couldn't do it. And the U.S. government wouldn't do it either.

He could very easily have killed this cretin all by himself, but for some reason he knew he shouldn't. Not this time.

He'd just watch the scene dissolve, the set collapse, and then pick up the pieces to see where he fit in.

He was an artist, not a tool.

It took a long, long career for the CIA, and some work for the Secret Service too, to get this kind of power and freedom. In the old days he was into everything from Space Aliens to Communists and the Black Panthers, to the American Indians and the Symbionese Liberation Army. If he were more ambitious, he would have leveraged his accomplishments differently. But he was more comfortable here in the background. His concerns were more mysterious and subtle than the spotlight allows.

He never told anyone, especially his wife, but he had been getting *messages* from their deceased daughter Allison for many years now. After all he had done and seen in his life, it didn't disturb his sense of reality at all to communicate with his dead daughter. He thought of it as spiritual guidance, or emotional assistance from an absolutely reliable ally. His own daughter, his own flesh and blood, was guiding him, leading him to the right place at the right time. Making him a little *luckier* than his enemies.

Now, Allison wanted him to be here, directed him to be right here, because something important was going to happen. So he sat and watched the light in the Dreamer's window.

Just after 4:00 a.m. the glass burst out. Someone jumped through the window and onto the roof, ran to the edge, and jumped to the ground. Then the jumper got up and ran toward Aoyama Avenue without missing a beat.

The whole thing took only seven or eight seconds.

Vinney was too far away to hear anything more than the breaking glass. So he left the car and ran over to where the jumper landed on the sidewalk. Vinney climbed up on a cement block wall, and pulled himself onto the roof.

It wasn't easy anymore, but he could still do it.

He carefully climbed up higher and crawled over to look inside the broken window.

Someone was giving an injection to the screaming victim. White-coated medics were already loading him onto a stretcher. Vinney couldn't understand what they were saying but it was clearly a serious medical emergency, a life or death situation. Every word screamed with panic.

Then they all rushed out and down the hall with the stretcher and there was nothing but an eerie silence left in the room.

VCK stepped in to look around.

There in the corner, it was the Perfect Buddha's Head. That was what he wanted. That was what Allison needed. He tiptoed in, grabbed it and left as quickly as the first jumper did.

26. MORTAL EXISTENCE

Modern man needs to *bare* himself Genetic.

Open up. Expose himself to all that there is.

People use too many covers. Too many uniforms. Too many skins.

The only woman a man really needs is his mother. And his mother is always there, inside each man, from the time of his birth. After that, everything else is optional.

"Lizard Lady? Are you here with me now?"

"Yes Genetic. I'm always here."

"You know everything?"

"About you? Yes, I know everything."

"I need to do something drastic. I can't endure myself anymore."

"Those were Allison's exact words."

"When she killed herself?"

"Death won't help you Genetic."

"But how could this happen?"

She explained with great patience, "The Originator lets you live because your death won't help him either. He has planted you here to be abused by the Dreamer, who likewise prefers to keep you alive. This keeps you out of everyone's way for now. And if you died, they would fight for your soul, and there would be nothing I could do to help you then."

"So if you can't do anything, why are you here now? Why are you telling me this?"

She smiled, "Oh, but there is still something I can do here and now."

* * *

I was sucked straight up and out of my body as if by a vacuum.

I saw my physical body collapse without any warning. But before I hit the hard floor, I was pulled higher and higher until I saw the phenomenal world dissolve into a soft swirl of colors, and then weave itself into a perfectly tailored gray flannel three-piece suit all around my own lifeless body as I fell face-up into a red velvet coffin, looking like a piece of well-dressed cold liverwurst.

Then I was whooshed away into a ghost world, filled with entities part familiar and part strange. There were gods, demi-gods, devils, demons, gurus, swamis, and saints. Nostradamus, Swedenborg, Ramakrishna, Rajneesh, Bhaktivedanta, the goddess Ishtar, and the great Shawnee Prophet. All the other characters, Madame Blavatsky, the Beast 666, Anton LaVey, Mary Baker Eddy, Joseph Smith, Cagliostro, Meher Baba, Sai Baba, and the Maharishi. Dead or alive, it didn't matter. Everyone was here.

Angel guides and impish little pranksters were pointing down irresistibly curious but obvious dead ends.

There were earth-toned vegetarian Mushroom People. There were gaseous wisps of consciousness. Furies. Goblins. Tibetan tulpas, elves, gnomes, fairies, and satyrs. Larvae created in masturbatory fantasy by imaginary sperm. Tcheou-Wang, the Chinese God of Sodomy and patron of boy prostitutes. There was Gandharvas, a blood-sucking Hindu incubi.

There was the Savior, and there were millions of savior-wannabes. And there were millions wanting to be saved.

They came from Jonestown. They came from Branch Dividians. They came from Heaven's Gate.

There was the innocent Buddha, and there was his opposite, the evil Mara.

There was a Godhead with a million faces.

There was a ghost of the dead Sphinx.

There were cannibal tribes, and carnivorous gladiators.

And there were many inconspicuous, kind, and gentle souls.

And there were parasites. And there were germs. And there were odious malignancies of the spirit stretching the entire length of time, all of the past, present, and future.

It never ended.

The list goes on forever, but the balance is strikingly clear.

Extremes go together, things get better and worse at the same time. The balance is always maintained.

Half of them all want to help and nourish everyone else.

The other half wants to consume and destroy everyone else.

Psychic disease is putrefying millions and millions of beings right before my eyes. They will rot. They will decay and then disappear. But the supply is self-generating. The suffering will never end. Our need to feed on ourselves is just as strong as our need to regenerate.

We are the serpent eating its own tail.

* * *

She and I were one now.

I could penetrate my own being and feel myself from the outside in.

I could feel her from the inside out. She had tough leather skin, but it was warm and safe inside.

Now I know, the Lizard Lady is the Creator, the Great Mother, the Womb of the Universe. I know all the other gods have suckled at her divine breast.

Then, I feel her holding me in my new bodily form, fashioned *by her to fit her* like a pair of oiled leather gloves, so I could participate as both subject and object in the pleasure of her embrace.

And her embrace was absolutely carnal. For real. Not a psychic trick or a mental image. An all-enveloping, warm, wet experience. Totally sexual. More real than reality.

Better than a constant state of orgasm, it was a constant state of *pre-certain-orgasm.*

Once an orgasm starts you know it will end. But before it starts, you are on the verge of orgasm, and you don't think about the end yet.

I felt my own mind dissipate into a sparkling golden mist. Then slowly evaporate like the morning dew.

Knowledge was not spoken, but revealed.

* * *

THREE is the magic number in this world.

* * *

ONE is One God. I am who I am. Unknowable in the phenomenal world. Unknowable to the human mind.

No matter what anyone says.

No mater what anyone does.

No matter what anyone believes.

Tao.

* * *

TWO is the essential polarity from which the phenomenal world is created. This is the first orgasmic thrust of creativity. And if it were not infinitely enjoyable, God would not have done it. Do you understand?

The universe wasn't created as a chore. It was a joy.

Manifest Reality.

* * *

THREE is the creation itself, including the seed of its own destruction, the core of its own absence. THREE simultaneously contains both the unity of ONE and the contradictory essence of TWO.

If we have the power of the trinity we can modify and define the nature of reality, both relative and absolute.

We can be like gods.

Divine Trinity.

* * *

The Holy Conman *is* the key to the power. He is our nemesis in this universe.

Time *is* at the core of the hoax. Time is how the truth is hidden.

You are made to think you have only the fleeting instant of present time, but you actually have the interminably rolling wheel of past, present, and future all at once.

Words are your only hope. The richest vein of creative power ever mined can be found in the primordial sounds as they coalesce into the phenomenal world.

RIGHT THERE, THAT IS THE DIVINE ORIGIN OF CREATIVE POWER, AND THAT IS THE ORIGIN OF DIVINITY ITSELF.

And that is the difference between humans and animals and inanimate objects.

* * *

I search for my own truth, and I find: THE MIRROR.

I know that I am.

I know what I must do.

I beckon for Allison, so I can introduce her to the Lizard Lady.

She comes. I show one to the other, and introduce them. And one says to the other, "I love you."

"*Then become me,*" the other replies.

And so it is done, now and forever, and ever again.

We have done it all here. We know it all here. Our fate here is sealed. But yours there is not. It is up to you now. What you ask for and what you do.

* * *

The essential question is not whether, or how, life came from unconscious inanimate matter.

And the absolutely definitive answer is, you better be careful, because *you and your life* can decay into unconscious inanimate matter.

You can die again and again, ignorant, sick, and afraid, until you degenerate into unconscious inanimate matter.

I am talking about *you* holding the power *right now* over the reality of your own immortality.

So, if, for the sake of expediency in this life you fail to seize your own immortality now, while you have the chance, *you will lose it.*

Whether you believe in immortality or not, you cannot escape one fact: *it is not automatic.* There is no guarantee. It is only an option. You take it or you don't. It is up to you, what you ask for, and what you do.

Existence is *not* meaningless unless *you* choose to make it so. And then it is only *your* existence that is meaningless, *not mine.*

I've done it all, I know it all, and my fate is sealed.

That is why we need the other possibility that arises when we look between the polarity, behind the contradiction. The child that arises from the parents. Like both, but not either. It is the fulfillment of the two.

Here and now, I am complete. I am perfected. I am fulfilled.

* * *

Then, she appears to come closer again.

I quiver at the sight of her overflowing warm flesh. She is surreal and serene as she peels off flowered red and white panties. I see dark leather skin.

But there is no space between us. We fit together like Yin and Yang. We are distinct and separate, yet blurred and inseparable.

I can feel the fine hairs and the lines in her skin. I can hold handfuls of her thighs, breasts, and tummy. I can cradle her face in my palms, reach my fingers into her hair.

I can smell her, like smoke from a distant fire, infused with fruit and flowers.

I can taste her.

I have her in my own hands, in my own mouth.

I touch her, hold her, and slide right inside her.

It was a magical dance. Face to face. Mouth to mouth. Breathing each other's air.

Her orgasm enveloped us both in a way I had vaguely believed possible but had never experienced before. The distinctive rhythm and complex dispersal of energy were comprehensible now, but previously unknown.

I was dying and being reborn again and again.

No one else has this power.

It is inconceivable. Unsurpassable.

* * *

She spoke aloud, “You can look into your true lover’s eyes and see anything you want.”

I remained silent.

She said, “I am what you always wanted to see.

“If you honestly and accurately know yourself, you can see all others clearly, because you know exactly what you are showing and all that they can see.

“But some entities don’t belong here in this world at all, so they can’t see what others can see.

“Each world has its own realm of visibility. Anywhere you can see, you can also be seen.”

* * *

“Now, as for the Holy Conman, remember, some entities are so fragile, their very existence may be questioned. On one hand, they think they are many. On the other hand, they feel and act as one. Their thoughts and moods undulate from one to the other unavoidably.

“A certain kind of power is derived from the souls of believers and devotees. Power flows to the target of adoration.

“Look at the Dreamer and the Originator too. All that I tell you is obvious now.

“A war is being fought for the belief of humanity because people bring their beliefs to the grave and beyond, where it is absorbed by the Holy Conman who stands behind the infinite faces of One God on Earth.

“From the First Time when the Holy Conman promised the Egyptians rebirth as stars in the cosmos, he has been assured of an unending supply of operators to serve in his ever-increasing body.

“The operators are remnants of humans and other living things farmed on vast and varied worlds in secret corners of your universe.

“The Holy Conman operates on many levels, in many different realms, with beings and entities of all kinds. The obedient functionary Angels of Allah. The b’nai Elohim, Angelic sons of God the Father. The

Avatars of Vishnu. All the varied servants of Baalzebub, the Lord of Those Who Fly. They and all like them. They and all their opposites. They are all burned as fuel in the Holy Conman's fires. They all simply feed The Beast.

"But no one can *use* Evil, not even a god.

"It uses them instead.

"Evil feeds on the fear it creates.

"And that is how animate life becomes inanimate matter.

"And that is all there is to fear.

"That is the only way you can lose what I give you."

* * *

"Now, it is well-known you must recognize your opponents for what they are and be able to address them by their true names with correctly pronounced words of power.

"But no god is higher than the Holy Conman. You can invoke no higher names. There are no stronger connections. No mortal being has ever entered his home, or seen his face, without dying.

"Therefore, *you must know the unknowable.*

"This one single task of ultimate importance is the first and final reason for the use of real magic.

"You know that, don't you?"

27. THE WHOLE TRUTH

Sato Toshiyama had been a taxi driver for twenty-three years. He kept his back straight when he sat. He always wore clean white gloves when he drove his gleaming Yellow Taxi. He kept a fresh box of facial tissue within arms reach of the rear passenger seat.

At 4:09 a.m., he was just getting back to central Tokyo from a run to one of the western suburbs where he dropped off a young bar hostess.

She had been a typical fare at this time of night, but for the scantily clad old lady, maybe her grandmother, sobbing on her shoulder all the way home. He watched in the mirror and saw the old lady start sucking like a baby at the younger woman's breast.

But it just can't be possible, he thought.

Such big dark nipples. And the old lady starts sucking harder, pulling and stretching them out. No, it just can't be possible.

The light in the mirror must be playing tricks on his tired old eyes, he thought. He ignored the two women, and kept his eyes on the road.

After they got out, he forgot about them as quickly as he could, the crazy old granny and the young lady too. The nipples. The kissing. The hugging and sucking. It made no sense to him at all.

Then, driving along a deserted Aoyama Avenue, Mr. Toshiyama saw a big foreign lady, in a ragged pink robe, with no overcoat and no purse, frantically waving for a cab.

He had been reading lately about the plight of foreign hostesses in Japan, especially in Tokyo. It wasn't fair the way they were abused, he knew, but a lot of things weren't fair. They came here because they thought the Japanese were rich. They went to any country that had a lot of money.

Hey, things were tough for Japanese women too.

Life was tough for the poor, the dumb, the ugly, and the weak. He knew. He had eyes. He had a brain of his own. He didn't need to hear lectures by politicians or professors. He could think for himself. He knew all about the ordinary things a Japanese man was expected to know. He knew all he needed to know about real life.

This lady wouldn't have any money, he knew that too. She had had some kind of problem tonight. Maybe she got beat up; maybe she just got disgusted with the stinky old drunkard companions she had to entertain tonight. He could understand that too.

However, he thought as he slowed down, maybe she'd be appreciative for his help. Give him a break from his own boring life.

He buzzed open the passenger door. She was in the car and trying to pull the door closed before it had even finished opening. Stupid gaijin was too excited, fighting with an automatic door like that. And she was quite unattractive too. Actually didn't even look like a girl.

"Embassy. U.S. Embassy please. *Please*, take me to the U.S. Embassy."

"Yes. Yes. U.S. Embassy. Yes. Yes." He repeatedly assured her, trying to calm her down and shut her up.

This was a big mistake, he thought. She wasn't even a girl. It was a guy in a pink robe. Maybe a New Half, or some kind of shemale transvestite. A lot of bars had them pouring drinks and entertaining customers. He had picked up some Japanese transvestites before, late at night, in Shinjuku or Ikebukuro, but never in this part of town. And never a foreign one. But he knew so many foreigners were queer or transvestite or into some other kind of perversion anyway. He didn't care what other people did, and he especially didn't care what foreign people did.

He turned onto Roppongi Avenue avoiding the Shuto Expressway because he didn't want to waste any money for the toll.

He was glad he was Japanese. He knew all the foreigners, even the *normal* ones, licked and sucked each other like hired prostitutes. All that dirty stuff they do, no wonder they all got AIDS.

He didn't want to know anything about that AIDS, especially with this one. She was not even feminine, just a messed up guy in a stupid pink girlie robe. The guy needed make up, accessories, and feminine mannerisms if he was ever going to be an attractive girl. Can't these gaijin do *anything* as well as we Japanese?

He drove past the Fuji-Xerox and ATT buildings, turned right, and pulled up in front of the black steel gates.

His passenger had been talking intermittently all the way to the embassy, but he didn't listen. He dropped her or him or whatever it was off and drove away as quickly as he could, heading for somewhere he could check if there was any blood or anything else left on his back seat.

Too many strange things were happening tonight.

Maybe he'd go home early today and surprise his wife for a change.

She was there whenever he needed her.

At least she was a real woman.

* * *

One of the Japanese guards at the outermost embassy gate immediately called for the U.S. Marines to come and take care of this one. "And wear your gloves," he warned as they hung up.

Genetic was obviously on drugs. Probably insane. And obviously some kind of pervert that provoked no empathy in any of these young marines. But they had all seen these Iam Asiam people before. They wore pink robes and big masks of the Dreamer when they protested outside the embassy a few months ago during a three-day trade negotiation visit by the President.

Iam Asiam wanted the President to stop 'electronic brain interference operations' being done on them by the CIA.

So they knew what Genetic was ranting and raving about when they notified intelligence to take charge of the situation.

* * *

Genetic was put into very comfortable confinement in a one-bedroom apartment in the embassy basement. It was normal except there were no windows, no phones, and the door locked only from the outside. He was given hot coffee, scrambled eggs with bacon, home fries, rye toast with make-believe butter, and two kinds of jelly.

A marine guard was posted outside the door and a crack team of psychiatric and intelligence personnel commenced a program of twenty-four-hour remote observation.

First thing the morning after his arrival, he was offered clean clothes.

"Give me 32 by 32 jeans, a 16 by 33 blue plaid flannel shirt, warm socks, and white boxers. Dress me like Neil Young," he said.

His story was taped on video and audio. It was reviewed. And repeated. Again and again, all day long. He told them everything. All about Psytron. Immortality. The Holy Conman. The fight for the future of humanity in this universe. The Psytron Secret Security Contingent. Elizabeth. Allison's suicide. Timothy Leary and the Black Panthers. Charlie Manson and the

Psytron neutralization programs. Wai Yu in L.A. His own escape to Bangkok and his years at the Buddhist monastery. His understanding of Astrology and mastery of all the ancient magical traditions. Travel back to the First Time, Tep Zepi, over ten thousand years ago, and beyond. The Originator coming to him in his psychic body to give him the Iam Asiam undercover mission.

He told them about the ancient monk that escaped from Tibet to Thailand in 1951 after the Chinese invasion that would force the Dalai Lama to flee to India. And then he told them of the Perfect Buddha's Head becoming animate, omniscient, and omnipotent.

He explained all about the Holy Conman invading his body. Allison's abduction in the after-life. His first encounter with the Lizard Lady, and how he reached out for her tits, sticking his own hands into her big white bra. The twisted gods, the Caballi, and his years of confinement and torture.

He still doesn't know how he arrived in Japan, but sure enough there he was with the Dreamer, forced to act like the Unified One. Two sexes in one body with a patron saint named Yab-Yum.

He told them about the strange slug-like creatures with evil psychic powers. About the things crawling on his face. Into and out of his body. He doesn't know why or how. He can't explain everything. But now he *does know* all he ever really *needs to know*. So now he can tell them everything he knows. The whole truth, and nothing but the truth.

He told them all he knew about Iam Asiam. All the disguises necessary to survive as a double undercover agent. His continuing confinement. All the drugs. Sex. Weapons of mass destruction. Plots against the Japanese government. Secret attacks. Poison gasses. The plan to take over the whole world. The *Goruden Nectaa*. The Dreamer grinding down on the Perfect Buddha's Head.

He told them about the Dreamer's ugly old penis flapping back and forth, coiled like a snake. About how the Lizard Lady was there in the room with him, watching over Genetic, and watching out for what the Dreamer would do to him. She told Genetic it was a snake, with a deadly bite, aiming for a tender and vital target on his own body.

He told them about the spinning in his head. The Dreamer's hypnotic patter. How he fell down, ready to give up and pass out.

But he had visions from the past, and something shocked him fully awake.

And then the Lizard Lady became him, or he became the Lizard Lady. Genetic didn't know how to explain it.

He told them, until that moment, physical violence against the Dreamer had simply been inconceivable.

He felt his jaw tighten. He felt the veins bulge in his head. He felt his hands ready to grab the Dreamer's neck and rip it open.

Now Genetic knew he couldn't let himself die like that. You have to fight for what you love. Whatever you love, it is too precious to lose and then never get it back. And the Lizard Lady knew she had to strike first, before the snake could attack.

She opened her mouth wide, screaming like a crazed hyena. She caught the snake in her teeth and bit down as hard as she could, whipping her head from side to side, trying to rip the snake right in half.

The Dreamer fought his way free, screaming and clawing at her face and eyes.

But she was like Shiva. She had more arms and hands and mouths than any one man could control.

Genetic jolted into action. He grabbed the Perfect Buddha's Head and smashed the Dreamer across his face, knocking him out cold. Then Genetic climbed out the third floor window, slid down the roof and jumped to the ground. He ran up to Aoyama Avenue and kept running until he could hail a cab to the embassy.

He said a Japanese cab driver, in an act of random kindness, picked him up and drove him to the embassy for free.

* * *

"I'm not crazy anymore," he told the psychiatrists the next morning. "If I were crazy, I'd expect you to believe my story. But I don't. I know you can't believe it. I just told it like it is because I rather not lie about anything anymore, and it simply doesn't matter what you think."

So then they asked if Genetic would agree to another day of observation, and also if he could possibly provide a written statement in his own handwriting before he left.

Genetic was quite willing to cooperate.

They conducted more examinations. Physical and psychological. Taped everything in digital format. Sent it across the world for thorough analysis.

Genetic told them he would like to have some French Roast Cappuccino, and a few chocolate-dipped almond biscotti while he wrote.

He composed several pages, which pretty much included everything he wanted to say, and then dropped it off at the psychiatrists' office on his way out of the embassy the following morning.

28. AND NOTHING BUT THE TRUTH

Dear Intelligence Agents,

Thank you for being so nice to me during my stay at the American Embassy.

I love my country.

I have tried my best to repay your kindness by telling you everything I know. I hope with all my heart that you can understand what I tell you, because this is all you ever need to know.

Between all opposites, there is compromise.

Right there, between all opposites, there is always compromise.

The trick is to see both opposites together as One and Two, and the compromise as Three, all at the same time.

The ancient symbol for Yin and Yang is a timeless and perfectly adequate expression of the two opposing forces in this universe and the inter-dependent relationship between them.

To us, here on Earth, nothing is more fundamentally pervasive than our male and female sexuality. No mystery can be more rewarding to understand. And no other path can be as easily traced all the way back to the ONE GOD, in the first instance, as the FIRST CREATIVE URGE.

Nothing is more natural.

Nothing is more essential to your survival.

Cultivate a lust for the trinity: ONE and TWO and THREE. Both human sexes UNIFIED as ONE GOD in YOU.

Don't succumb to the Maya illusion of mortal love.

Don't lust after any other person to the point where you fall into a toxic dream.

There is too much more to life, and you have too much to lose if you only think about yourself and the one you love.

You need more than that.

Start the whole thing all over again.

Start from Zero.

You are nothing less than God in the First Act of Creation.

Masturbate to have the ultimate of unrestricted sex with yourself. Flower fully and blossom in efflorescent and unlimited self-love.

You and I are God's imagination.

You and I can exist here in the imagination of God forever.

* * *

The Unformed Nothing imagined ONE GOD. Humanity was not created from the total formlessness of nothing, but One God was.

And One God was a *created entity* whose nature was to *create more*. One God was the Great Androgynous Shemale, able to fertilize, and able to conceive, and able to deliver *more*.

The One God imagined TWO and thus invented sexual union.

First, and alone, the One God masturbated, self-loving all the way to an orgasmic reality of TWO MORE GODS, male and female. Consequently there are THREE.

And the entire physical universe was necessary to make it happen. All the seeds of nature and all the laws of physics were essential to create the fabric from which the material of phenomenal reality was woven. A reality in which two complimentary opposites could attract each other and consume each other. A reality in which energy equals matter, waves equal particles, light equals time, and nothing is ever as simple as it seems.

One gave rise to Two, which necessitated Three, and then Four through Nine naturally followed.

Nine of course is three times three and the fullest of all possible single digits. Thus the primary gods were completed first. These are the gods you most commonly know as Zeus, son of Cronos and Rhea, Prometheus, the defiant one, Thanatos, god of death, Aphrodite, Hades, Eros and Hermes.

But, also among the primary nine gods, before the creation of any mortal being, were the immortal couple known as Isis and Osiris.

All of them and each of them enjoy their existence with a relish befitting only the gods, using myriad names and multiple manifestations, to show every person, culture, and time exactly what is required.

Then, everything else comes in a simple cyclical flow.

And, mortals were naturally created next.

But, most important to us, the gods imagined humans, among others, as having imaginations of our own.

We humans can create new worlds too.

We can create other living beings in all dimensions.

* * *

You don't need to hear any more than what you've just been told.

On the contrary, we have all heard too much already, and we have wasted too much time trying to align all the new words with all the old, nearly forgotten ones.

We shuffle old ideas rather than generate new ones, fearing to express something we have not first heard before from others.

Words are the buttons people push to get us to work for them, to get us to buy something from them, to get our money, to live off our energy.

We need words to help us feel good about ourselves, to feel intelligent, or powerful, or loved and accepted.

Many of us fancy more intelligent words reflecting a higher level of education. We favor verbal sequences we cannot understand without at least four years of university study, and preferably, an advanced degree.

Many of us use words as our weapons and our shields, like a politician or an investment banker.

It's embarrassing. But, we behave like addicts, requiring more and more words to reach the same comforting high of whatever validity and authority we crave.

No matter what, we simply cannot live without the words. Our language has in fact infected us like an alien virus from outer space and we don't even know it.

Though it has been explained before, we still ignore it.

You are all infected. And perhaps I am too.

And maybe you experts know my linguistic predilections and psychological profile better than I know yours right now... but still, I have to tell you:

GO FUCK YOURSELF.

The Tower of Babel was not about people who can't understand each other because they speak foreign languages. No, God's curse at the Tower of Babel is that we cannot understand each other even when we speak the *same* language.

* * *

I HEREBY PROCLAIM, at this time, and for as long as I shall so desire, my own authority is The Who, circa 1969. We've all been told many times before but no one has had the guts to leave the temple.

* * *

The cross is the oldest symbol in African religion. The cross is where the natural meets the supernatural.

The Haitian Voodoo priestess, called Mambo, says, "You White people go to church and talk about God, but we Black people dance and *become* God."

I see a dancing Nubian goddess whirl around and stop suddenly, facing me, posed like a naked yogi, in dim light, one leg up, knee even with waist, calf and foot straight down. Smooth, clean, rich dark skin everywhere.

Two harmonious pear shapes, capacious, with soft smooth surfaces and seductive lines and curves, designed to delicately balance on a firm and powerful body.

Her skin is more than rich, more than royal, it is, in fact, *divine.* My eyes struggle with the magic of her living texture and the features illuminated therein. I have to listen to what her skin is telling me as I look at it.

LISTEN!

"The DNA-centric view that sex is just DNA's way of enticing us, as biological vehicles, to make more DNA, is a neat and compelling theory, but it is too dense. It ignores the subtleties.

"The reality of sex is more dependent on the imagination than we imagine it to really be.

"Knowledge of our own mortality and frailty is what drives humans to sexual excess and complications unknown among other life forms. We are the ones the gods have chosen to give them better orgasms.

"Wouldn't you if you were a god?

"Well, wouldn't you?"

* * *

"Whether we are symmetric or deformed, in body or mind, if our passion is equally deep and our pleasure equally great, the gods love us all the same.

"There is nothing the gods won't do."

* * *

Then, finally, I see the goddess has a long flaccid penis, hanging over and between two hefty testicles loosely held in a big sack. She is rotating slightly now, and elevating, so I see the space behind her testicles, the patch of skin leading to her rectum.

I tingle, literally tingle, at the shape and deep color of her buttocks. Mountainous twins supporting a spine that is the surest Stairway to Heaven I have ever seen. Each vertebrae radiant in a line of visible energy, snaking up from the small of her back to the base of her skull.

But this is no ordinary skull. There is, balanced on top of her spine, centered in the middle of a sleek and sinuous back, with arms and shoulders facing front, *there is another face.*

Yet, it does not surprise me.

Somehow, it belongs there.

She looks at me looking at her back.

The most delicate arms and hands with long slender fingers are growing in pairs, two, and four, and six, and facing me now, reaching out to me now.

Then, breasts also are growing before my eyes, two, and four, and six. Curvilinear spheroids tipped with meaty burgundy blood-filled protrusions like little penises, pointing at me now, all pointing at me.

She smiles, I think, inviting me to come and explore her unknown, and elsewhere or otherwise, unknowable, pleasures.

Her thick tongue protrudes longer and longer. She could choke me with it. She could impale me.

I'm ready to die, eager to sacrifice myself to this goddess. I'd be happy to be devoured and inside her, somehow, someway, become part of her, enrich her if I could, or just help sustain her. I would surely die before I let her leave or disappear.

But no, she *is* smiling; I am sure, *daring me to become her.* Yes, *become her*, not *like* her, but *actually become her.* Take her being, not just her body. Take her entire being for and as my own.

The tip of her penis is now pointing back this way, climbing up the space between her bottom cheeks. There is a piquant pubic patch around a receptive sexual organ of a kind I can't even comprehend yet. I don't know if it is a mouth, an anus, a vagina, or something altogether different.

Take her existence as my very own.

She is penetrating herself.

She is disappearing inside herself.

Take her karma, past, present, and future, as my own.

She is telling me, "There is still more here, still more you haven't seen yet. Do with it whatever you will, but take it all before it is too late."

So, I've got to go now, gentlemen.

She is *my* gypsy, *my* acid queen, and she is *here now* to take me for *my* ride.

Who and where is *yours* Mr. President, El Capitano, Spy Man, and Doctor of Psychiatry?

Where is *your* gypsy?

Where is *your* acid queen?

29. TRYING TO SURVIVE MAYA

Survival is the name of the game. It is the first rule of every conflict regardless of time, place, or participants.

According to Psytron, no threat is greater than the immediate wrath of Psytron itself (the imminent attack of the Holy Conman notwithstanding).

So they all went berserk obeying the Originator's last orders. Amongst themselves, it was much wiser to be seen fanatically fighting real or imagined enemies than to possibly be seen as an anti-Psytronic spy or sympathizer oneself. That would be the absolute worst.

The Secret Security Contingent had run amok. Elizabeth had been arrested for masterminding conspiracies to infiltrate the White House, the Secret Service, and the CIA. She had audaciously placed sleeper agents on the White House staff. She had actively recruited and successfully placed double agents to work for her in offices of the Secret Service and the CIA. The Psytron SSC was able to monitor and sabotage all governmental and police activities for more than twenty years, while the private sectors were secured through the usual lawsuits, public relations work, and neutralization programs.

However, once the Originator announced the final battle against the Holy Conman, the undercover agents had been pressured to the point where overzealous recklessness led them to blow their covers.

Government authority was not a significant or valid factor anymore. Or so they thought.

* * *

Elizabeth never saw the Originator after that night in his office. He left her on the desk, face-down in a small puddle of saliva, sweat, and tears, without any words of farewell.

By the time she could lift her head, he was gone.

And she could never confide in anyone the terror she felt that night, because she believed, even with her heart full of all the love and devotion she felt for this extraordinary man, that he went insane that night. Something cold and callous possessed him and used his body to take her with a viciousness that had never been in his soul before.

Then he was gone.

It was well within his power to leave his body while traveling in other dimensions. But she could find no physical body this time. Nothing. Not a clue anywhere.

And to this day, no one else has either seen or heard from the Originator again.

* * *

Everyone seemed to be disappearing contemporaneously. Timothy Leary, William Burroughs, Alan Ginsberg, even Eldridge Cleaver. Where were they all going? And why now?

Coincidence could not explain it. It was positively mysterious, like when John Kennedy and Aldous Huxley died the same day.

All of Psytron, especially the SSC, had wanted to see the Originator live to gloat in his old age over the demise of his ridiculous psychedelic nemesis. Now Leary had his head shooting through space, and his ashes in an urn, or his body in the freezer, or whatever. His vacuous ideas were left on-line for posterity, thereby proclaiming his own electronic immortality as an Internet data structure. What a joke.

The whole beat-hip-psychedelic bedrock has crumbled to dust but their chemically induced hallucinations linger on and on, refusing to either die or fade away.

And what about Psytron? How could they survive?

They can't admit or accept it, but they fear the unimaginable has happened: The Originator engaged the Holy Conman, and was defeated.

Now there is nothing to do but wait for the apocalypse and fill the time speculating whose fault it was.

Clearly, the good times were gone. Enemies were on the loose everywhere. Even the news media were slowly regaining confidence and coming back into the fray. Of course, although they were less intimidated, they still wanted to avoid a Psytron legal onslaught, so the press carefully stuck to the facts.

* * *

> Psytron Terrorist Rational
>
> New York (UPI) A machine-gun totting terrorist sent to a mental hospital after a shooting and arson rampage at the Manhattan Academy of Psytron has improved sufficiently to aid in his own defense, doctors said Wednesday.
>
> Jose Moleno, 36, is charged with killing 42 people and holding dozens more hostage while he doused the Academy with gasoline and set it on fire.
>
> Police finally persuaded him to surrender.
>
> Moleno blamed the Psytron Secret Security Contingent for hypnotizing him, ruining his marriage, destroying his business, and causing him to attempt a suicide mission with a snake-like biological weapon inserted into his rectum.

The initial psychiatric report said Moleno provided only 'paranoid, essentially nonsensical information' in preparation for his own defense.

Defense attorney, Joel Flieschman, says he plans an insanity defense for Moleno.

* * *

But the SSC was still functioning, trying their best to protect their unique passage to immortality and ensure the Originator's legacy of Psytron on Earth.

* * *

Japanese Spy Arrested in Hollywood

Los Angeles (UPI) Officials of the current Japanese administration bailed a governmental security agent out of a Los Angeles prison Tuesday, apologizing for his apparent attempt to spy on the International Academies of Psytron.

The agent is accused of soliciting help from several ex-Psytron members to help collect information – through theft, bribery, and blackmail – on the whereabouts of the Originator, seventy-two year old Reginald Johnston, who is rumored to be deceased.

The Japanese tax authorities are claiming estate taxes due in an amount exceeding U.S. $185 million dollars.

French and Swiss authorities have made similar claims.

Other countries seem to be waiting to see what actions the U.S. authorities take before beginning official proceedings of their own to deal with this mysterious organization.

A representative of the Psytron Secret Security Contingent has announced that it will take legal action against all those involved.

Psytron officials in the U.S. and Japan have issued a statement that they would soon file a complaint with the U.N. High Commissioner for Human Rights.

Johnston's wife, who is awaiting trial on unrelated criminal charges, issued a statement through her attorney. "The last time I saw him, he was stronger than ever before. I think he is getting younger, and you are all looking for an old man, so you will never find him."

Mr. Johnston himself could not be reached for comment.

30. TRYING TO SURVIVE KARMA

The Japanese government was eventually provoked to action by the accumulation of missing person reports, random terrorist attacks, and the brutal assassination of public officials. The information from the U.S. Embassy that an escaping American abductee may have critically wounded the Dreamer was exactly the opportunity the authorities had been waiting for.

Iam Asiam had had too much time to accumulate their weapons of mass destruction in a chain of *satians* around the country, mostly in and around the heavily populated areas of Tokyo. It was not going to be easy to enter their compounds without endangering the lives of unknown numbers of civilians.

Although the American information was rather questionable, this was surely the best chance the local authorities would ever get.

The Tokyo Metropolitan Police were organized to invade the Iam Asiam *satians* with search warrants based on a long list of criminal charges. There were kidnappings; abductions; manufacture and possession of illegal drugs; manufacture and possession of illegal weapons including chemical and other means and materials used in terroristic mass destruction; practicing medicine without a license; blackmail; murder; mayhem; and too many other felonies to mention, each meticulously detailed in typical Japanese style.

The operation commenced at exactly thirty minutes before sunrise, three days after the reported injury had occurred.

The press and the television networks were outraged they had not been informed of the scheduled raid on the Iam Asiam compounds.

However, one lucky American was across the street testing his new night-vision video camera when the police arrived.

And the camera worked just fine.

* * *

The American reports proved accurate. The Dreamer had in fact had his penis severed. He was in wretched straits indeed. He was far too preoccupied with his own condition to defend himself from the massive police force mobilized against him. To everyone's relief, he was caught unprepared to launch a sufficiently quick counter attack.

And thankfully, there was little organized resistance by his leaderless Iam Asiam followers.

Of course, it was reported that some fanatics and zealots were still holed up in bunkers hidden in remote areas of vast Iam Asiam owned properties, with food, medical provisions, and weapons of mass destruction. But the authorities have never been able to verify those rumors.

The officially accepted police report stressed that they had effectively disabled the Dreamer's fledgling atomic weapons program and confiscated the bulk of his chemical arsenal.

* * *

The Dreamer had had his medical team try to sew his penis back on just like James Bobbit had done in the U.S. many years earlier, but the chewing and ripping action done on the Dreamer was more damaging and much nastier than Mrs. Bobbit's clean cut with a sharp knife had been.

No one at Iam Asiam had the nerve to tell the Dreamer it wasn't going to work, so he was taken into custody with his penis pieces wrapped in white gauze and secured to his crotch like a Frankenstein cocktail weenie.

And that is just the way it looks in the video too. With the Dreamer staring right at the camera, seeming to follow every request as the American screamed out at him, "Look at me! Look at me!"

* * *

Later that morning, after filming the Dreamer's arrest, Genetic Freeman selected the most promising breakfast invitation, to a private suite at the Imperial Hotel. And as he sipped the bittersweet chocolate-powdered foam out of his second cup of French Roast Cappuccino, he concluded negotiations to sell his tape for over ten million U.S. dollars.

Then, following the advice of his newly acquired International Financial and Tax Advisors, two clever American guys named Millard and Slack, he arranged to collect payment through a series of offshore companies while he himself was on a plane flying back over the International Date Line to Honolulu.

He was going to take a vacation.

* * *

Iam Asiam lawyers informed the media of the Dreamer's innocence, and said they were confident he would be judged mentally incompetent to stand trial for his alleged crimes. They didn't admit it, but they also expected he would be forced to spend the rest of his life in national psychiatric facilities for the criminally insane and in constant need of medication.

Although they made no comment at all on this issue, they expected he would be waiting a long, long time for his penis to heal.

But the Dreamer himself still believed the assurance of his chief medical officer that it would heal as good as new.

31. MR. PRESIDENT

"Mr. President, we have received substantiated information that a drug-induced, virtual reality type experience has been developed in Japan beyond the auspices of governmental, academic, or any other legitimate organizations. Yakuza involvement is suspected, especially in finance, bribery, and coercion, but this suspicion has not yet been verified. And if in fact there is no current Yakuza involvement we expect a fierce battle for control to break out soon. We expect intense and immediate interest from terrorists, fringe political groups, radicals, environmental extremists, and various religious cults.

"We also fear the imminent exportation of this drug to America and Europe, one way or another.

"The problem is, events are progressing quickly, and we do not know the exact chemical composition of the drug at this time. However, we are advised from the best Japanese intelligence available that the drug, and the ritual in which it is used, incorporate no controlled substances and violate no laws."

"Ritual?"

"Yes Sir. They call it a sacrament and insist it is some kind of pre-ordained religious experience. The final Karmic dissolution of Maya.

"However, from what we can ascertain, they are ingesting a psychotropic agent thousands of times more potent than LSD, and more importantly, capable of being focused precisely within the user's brain during absorption into the bloodstream through the use of computer-directed chemical and electrical manipulation of the nervous system."

"Hummm. I wonder how that might work."

"No one seems to know exactly how that works yet, Sir."

"Is that so?"

"What happens next is apparently difficult to explain, Mr. President."

"What do you mean? Do you feel the bliss of mystic ego dissolution? Do you have an orgasm? Just tell me what happens."

"We really don't know yet. But I've been informed the user comes back, neurologically redesigned, regenerated into some kind of mutation. In just thirty to sixty minutes. A freak, I guess, but better than before, better than ordinary, they say. With a visible field of electromagnetism, an aura or something, and ahh, 'psychic powers' that no one has been able to explain or describe."

"Well, I'm beginning to feel a little *freaky* here myself fellas."

"Mr. President, all we can say for sure is, we had a double agent operative who says he saw one of the users yesterday with his own eyes, and he, the user, had a visible field around him."

"That's it? That's all you know?"

"Yes Sir. At this time, that is all we know. We are painfully aware of the scarcity of data...."

"But you want me to let you kill a man because he has a hallo? Isn't that what this boils down to? Or did you call it an aura?"

"Mr. President, Sir, due to the speed of reported developments and the clear danger to national and world security, we have begun working with Japanese authorities to isolate the manufacturers and stop all unauthorized use and production of this drug. The Japanese have assured us full access to examine one of the users as soon as they arrange for capture and confinement. They specifically assure us this will not get bogged down in legal technicalities.

"This morning one of our west coast analysts, on the Biological Warfare and Terrorism Team, speculated they might be using Andrenochrome, which can only be extracted from the adrenaline glands of a living human...."

"Gentlemen, I don't know what kind of fear and loathing your agency is working on these days, but I want an accurate and factual report as soon as possible. Tomorrow morning at the latest."

"Yes Sir, Mr. President."

32. WHAT IS IT?

It was lying back, relaxed. A little baby boy or girl? I couldn't distinguish. It looked like a slightly elongated slug, with a tiny head and tiny arms and feet. It was curled up so it fit in the Petri dish.

Bulbous little buds where fingers should grow. Thin translucent skin, tight around fragile insides.

So, I reach out with my right hand, extend my forefinger to just touch the baby's hand. I feel a fragile pink bulb stick to my hand at contact. My finger stops and pulls back slightly from the stickiness.

But it is too late.

The miniature hand is ripped off at the wrist. The flesh is stuck to my own finger.

I watch helplessly as reddish-purple blood rushes out of the hole at the end of the handless arm.

How can so much blood come from such a little thing? And why?

I can't touch it to pinch off the flow because it is too fragile. The whole thing would pull apart. The appendages would break off and leave only a slug-like body stuck to the bottom of the Petri dish. It is by far the most frightening thing I have ever seen.

Why doesn't it stop bleeding? Why does all the blood rush out like that? Why doesn't it clot? Is it dying? Or is it intentionally trying to scare me?

It looks like its entire body weight has drained out already and collected in the bottom of the glass dish. The thing is lying there, supported by the puddle of blood congealing around it.

Then I see it feeding off its own escaped fluids to stay alive. Sucking its own liquids back inside.

I watch, mesmerized.

Finally, the remaining blood congeals. I tear most of it away and throw it out, but I leave a nice blob around the arm and wrist hole to make sure the scab is not disturbed.

I think it will survive. But I fear it is horribly deformed.

33. NOTHING HAPPENS BY CHANCE

I'm back in Tokyo now on a brand new tourist visa.

I am legitimate now. It is official.

I stand straight. I walk with certainty and purpose in every step.

But, in many ways, my surroundings are as strange as ever.

There are dirty gray gum-wrappers fastidiously folded into neat silver seagulls on the train station steps under my feet as I rush onto the Yamanote line. I'm sorry I have to crush the pretty little birds. The doors woosh and whup closed behind me. The ubiquitous signs for *NEW ETIQUETTE*, *BOSS COFFEE*, and *BOUTIQUE CHELSEA* slide across my eyeballs. The English alphabet is set at a higher volume than the Japanese pictographic *kanji*.

Just a couple of stops to Ikebukuro station and maybe I can get a seat, if I'm nimble and quick.

We rumble past smooth cement walls dotted with neat rows of narrow-mouthed drainage pipes.

An elderly woman taps gently on the shoulder of a sleepy young office lady with a black briefcase balanced on her knees. The office lady slides over to make room for the *obaasan*, the honorable grandmother, to sit.

I'm here in the opposite seat with my elbow on the cool steel bar. The office lady's head is falling down below her collarbones. Then she jerks, wakes up, and jumps off before we leave her station.

I look around again and realize all of the hundred or so spaces for advertising on the interior walls and all the placards hanging from the ceiling of this train car are filled with the same advertisement. It is an almost all-black picture, just barely showing one eye of a girl's face, overwritten with the white letters J-PHONE.

That's all.

I don't know what to say. I'm not in the advertising business. I'm not even much of a consumer. But I feel like I am supposed to think about something in particular when I see that ad. And I don't know what it is I am supposed to think about.

When we stop at the world's biggest train station, in Shinjuku, I try to leave my eyes closed for a while, like many of the natives do, and trust my fate to the announcers. But it feels unnatural not to see the people around me.

I open my eyes again.

I watch one bead of sweat form under the sideburn of the beer-bellied businessman right beside me.

We reach Shibuya, and I get off the train.

Now I see the familiar signs for *FINK OFF*, *CAFFE LATTE CANNED COFFEE*, and *CASTER MILD PURE CIGARETTES*.

I walk through the automatic ticket-taker and see a Caucasian female tourist leaning on the wall outside the men's room, biting her lip, waiting for the man in her life to return.

A lone Buddhist monk sits on the dirty cement sidewalk and thumps on his drum.

I step around and through to the front of the crowd on the corner waiting for the next signal to walk. Nobody cares whether I'm in a hurry or I simply rather be in front.

What I do here doesn't bother anyone at all.

Japanese and gaijin are on opposite corners taking pictures of the same crowds crossing through the same intersection from different directions.

I feel quaint without a palm-sized phone to hold up to my ear, but as the Dreamer used to say, I've already been told all I need to hear. So I don't need a phone to my ear.

Next, I know I'll see the Arab gang, with their heavily shadowed faces, conspicuously flicking their decks of phony phone cards, as familiar and commercial as the Pirates of the Caribbean at Disneyland.

I bounce eyeballs with another gaijin, an outstanding, big-breasted Caucasian, to verify our mutual lack of recognition, as custom requires long-term residents to do.

Two policemen exchange salutes as they rotate standing guard in a doorway, in an alley, by a lamppost wrapped in bright yellow posters advertising *ANAL PLAY* for the Japanese equivalent of $400 an hour.

Across the street a giant red crab is clacking ten mechanical legs against the front wall of an old brick building.

I walk past an electric arcade called *GAME FANTASY* and see an old guy, dressed like a circus clown, walking in the street. He is sandwiched between two big boards. The boards are covered with painted caricatures of young girls in blue-and-white school uniforms carrying black book-bags; office ladies wearing blue business suits with white shirts carrying black briefcases; and properly-uniformed nurses holding whips and assorted other contraptions. He is advertising *PERFECT HEALTH, COSTUME LOVE, SOFT S/M ~~~ SLURP SLURP SLURP ~~~* at only $250 for thirty minutes.

There's my bank. Where I make my deposits. They take my bags full of cash and no one asks any questions.

I walk in just seconds before 3:00 p.m. The door locks after me. Of course they will still let me out, but no one else can come in today.

After my deposit, I stop at Tower Records, and walk past dozens of pictures of Mariah Carey wearing some kind of bellybutton bangles on her new CD cover.

I go straight to the Japanese Pop section. There it is. God's Pussy released a debut CD, *Blind People Selling Porno*.

Sayako made it to the big time.

I expected her to have a blatant shock-rock image, but she is clean-cut and cute as a newborn kitten on her own CD cover.

Her choice of English in some of her lyrics doesn't come across as particularly risqué to the Japanese public, because, well, just because the words are in English, and it looks good, no matter what the words mean. It just sounds so much more *twenty-first-century*.

I listen on the headphones while I turn over the plastic case and study the pictures.

Now, of course, I'm older than I've ever been before, and Sayako is just barely finished being a teenager. But she is in fact an adult now. And since we are both celebrities and all, and we have so much in common, I think, wouldn't it be fantastic if we could get together again sometime soon.

* * *

She comes out on stage in lingerie made of turquoise-tinted saran wrap, with triangles of purple day-glo aluminum foil crinkled-up on the tips of her tiny titties.

Her face is powder white. Her lips are painted deep burgundy.

She is wearing *geta*, the Japanese wooden sandals, with simple white cotton *tabi* two-toe socks.

She has 24-karat gold sea serpents wound around each of her calves, all the way from her ankle to her knee.

The stage is huge and filled with indiscriminate piles of live people and inanimate mannequins all over the place. Everyone and everything seems indistinguishably near-naked or partially-clothed in lingerie gratuitously supplied by Peach House, a newly formed subsidiary of Pink Blouse.

There are some fat old guys in skin-tone spandex body stockings. They push, shove, and climb all over each other trying to pay obeisance to Sayako's rear-end whenever she comes close.

There are young, hairless, oiled body builders with their groins wrapped in white *fundoshi* like sumo wrestlers. They seem to be ignoring Sayako, her music, the audience, and anything else, to constantly ogle each other and grope at each other's bodies.

The audience is filled with young adoring fans of both sexes.

The stage lighting is as precise as a medical procedure.

Nothing happens by chance.

She dances across the stage like an angel, navigating the mass of bodies at her feet. Then she squats down low, and I imagine I see the tail end of an eel forcefully flapping against the plastic wrap covering her crotch.

Then, when she is done, she throws the eel into the audience.

Fights break out, and guys are grabbing everything that wiggles trying to get the eel.

I plunge into the brawl, fighting hard and dirty to get it for myself. One final forearm smash, and I got it. Ripped it right out of a young Japanese boy's hand.

Sayako starts a new song. She says it is dedicated to a sad but sweet suburban housewife from Long Island, New York, who she talked to on the net. I can't understand any of the lyrics, except the English refrain, "There is nothing the gods won't do. There is nothing the gods won't do for you."

* * *

I know she and I can't meet just yet. It's not that simple anymore. We've both got people taking care of our affairs now. We each have our legal, PR, financial, and security teams.

The authorities are going crazy trying to find something illegal in her behavior, but they can't do it.

And I still have my own problems to take care of.

I have to go everywhere in disguise. Just like the old days.

But I'm working on something right now, and I'll be ready for Sayako as soon as I'm done.

* * *

I've been ripped free from reality. I am soaring, actually soaring, high and ahead of all others and all things. I have fantastic forward momentum. The air becomes increasingly palpable while showing the futility of its own resistance.

I become another flying woman, cut loose, and in search of myself.

I find her, lying unconscious, waiting for me. I am in love, and making love, as flying female, and lying female.

We are here now, together, she and I, with warm glowing breast and open thighs.

We float above a bed, in a room itself suspended in near-liquid air.

The windows are always open to let the outside in.

Time is measured funny on some random calculations.

My orgasm throbs for hours, from the slowly growing realization, *This is it! This is it!* To the clearest recognition of my female form in the blinding light of final formlessness.

How did I find myself, I wonder?

And how do I fly?

I am more like a warrior than a wanderer. My intentions have been tempered from mere wish into forceful purpose. I can feel my own strength now.

There is nowhere else to go, and there is nothing else to do.

So I wait here, somewhere only you can find me.

Waiting for you.

Waiting for you to come here and join me.

34. VCK VERSUS CIA

Vinney Cold Killer was speaking on videophone from the U.S. Embassy in Tokyo.

"I don't know who that guy was before he took that stuff, but I'm telling you, whoever he used to be, I know he wasn't the same guy anymore after he took it. I'm telling you also, he had a visible field, electromagnetic or something, all around him. Which, I have been informed, can be turned on and off at will. He can make it invisible if he wants to."

The CIA medical expert spoke next.

"This is beyond hallucination or any kind of intoxication. It seems to affect the mind like a psychoactive compound, but I am more inclined to think of it as invasive surgery. That is to say, a precise bio-chemical-electrical operation is being performed on the user's brain.

"Apparently someone has assembled and directed a staff of rogue Neuroanatomists, Psychogeneticists, and Molecular Biologists to use a fluorescent screening technique...."

"A what?"

"A screening technique used in Targeted Genomics, the precise study of the genetic fabric found inside the DNA of living organisms. The legitimate use is to search for a disease's biological cause, usually a mutation of some sort, but...."

"You think they could have found some new kind of genetic key that lets them get inside the brain like this?"

"The Japanese say the DNA code is unlocked by a guidance system that customizes the drug's molecular structure as it is being absorbed into the circulatory system. That analysis is not inconceivable."

VCK said, "Yes. But it is more difficult to comprehend from there. First you get total recall of our entire species-specific memory. Then you travel through time to a point that is simultaneously the beginning and end of finite time."

The current CIA Director of Operations tried to help out the retired agent, adding, "Same thing with space and energy. You are moved to a vantage point from which you can see and understand the essential underlying mechanisms of the physical universe. You understand the apparent complexities of physics, just like that, in a few hours."

He owed his job to the old guy. He had to show some loyalty.

The President encouraged the lecture despite its incredulity, prompting, "And then, the metaphysical?"

VCK said, "Yes, you meet other beings, and entities in other dimensions. You go to parallel worlds, alternate universes, things like that. I remember exactly, they said, 'We have tasted the essence of reality, which in Earth terms is most analogous to the existence of Good and Evil. Now we understand how and why all phenomena result from this essence.' "

Clearly, he crossed the line this time. He was too far gone.

The President said, "Um, you know, I don't care what people believe, but is there any criminal intent here, anything like 'we are good and everyone else is bad, so we must kill them' or something like that? You know, an agenda that will lead somebody to do something illegal in the real world?"

VCK said, "When we talk about terrorism and the occult, we are compelled to consider what paradigm best fits all the subtle and unknowable forces involved in...."

"Okay." The Director cut off VCK to reiterate the President's question. "For right now, what do these self-professed mutants actually do? Not what they think, or what they think they do, but what do they actually do?"

No one wanted to be the one to have to try to do it, but if the President made so much as a certain facial expression toward Vinney, they would have to kill VCK right where he stood.

The Director's young bespectacled assistant started reading off his prepared notes from VCK's post-op de-briefing. "Right. Of the ones we know about, over the very short term involved here, they seem to get into Egyptology, Demonology, and other occult philosophies. They say if we can travel through time, *transform ourselves*, somehow *assume other forms*, then we will be able to leave Earth and survive the apocalypse. Otherwise we will be enslaved here and doomed to mortal death. And, not only once, but...."

The Director broke in again, "Uh. Well, we're only talking about a couple of days observation, but one thing I find interesting is they don't seem eager to come back for more."

"You mean, of the drug?"

"Yes Sir, Mr. President. It seems once is enough."

VCK continued, almost to himself, "They believe in a kind of transgender masturbatory fantasy as the road to enlightenment and psychic power."

The President's face turned white. He looked away from VCK, and spoke to the Director.

"So we still cannot conclude there is any illegality in what they do?"

VCK continued to talk without a listener, "He told me one time, that he felt like a composite of insane inferences of various aspects of his true self. And God, he said, God is just one more character, one more character among many."

The Director said, "Ah, that's right Mr. President, not yet, but I am more concerned with the people who do it to them, especially this American citizen, Genetic Freeman."

"You mean like brainwashing or something?"

"Yes. Something like that, Sir."

VCK was concluding aloud only to himself, "I see it as a new kind of thinking, a truly original cosmological theory. Maybe we should call it *Transgender Occult Theology.*"

No one in the room wanted to have Vinney Cold Killer for an enemy. But someone simply had to say something. And that someone had to be the President. He could not let this remarkably odd behavior go unchecked any longer.

"Vinney, what exactly are you talking about?"

Vinney smiled, and walked out of the room.

The President dismissed the other men with a wave of his fingers and a perplexed look on his face.

No one looked directly in anyone else's eyes.

And no one wanted to give any mistaken indication that they were volunteering to be the one who would try to control VCK from now on.

35. THE BIRTH OF EVIL

Green, yellow, purple, and red
Blotches and splotches of slime,
Some more liquid, some more gel
Cover the walls and floors of Hell.

A demon-god so fearsome
Couldn't look him in the eyes.
A coward, crouching minion,
A pre-born baby's cries.

Running up the staircase,
The baby in my hands,
Ordered by the demon-god
To make this thing a man.

The mother with her emptied womb
Fights the hag to win her life.
With reddened eyes, and hands like claws,
Could this have been my wife?

No one here to talk to.
No other sign of life.

Running down the staircase
With darkness all around,
I feel the baby move now,
Face down to kiss the ground.

It’s sucking up some dark juice,
Like drying curdled blood.
Now reaching for the jellied stuff,
Some evil psychic cud.

The demon-god is happy with this
Reaching out for life.
I swallow down my sickness and
Keep running past my wife.

The eyes open.
I’m too scared.
The demon-god says,
“Congratulations, you’re a dad.”

36. THE FINAL WARNING

Genetic Freeman logs onto the God's Pussy Fan Club home page and begins typing on the priority message screen.

"For broad distribution to all psychic friends and sleeping agents, known and unknown, in past, present, and future dimensions at all stages of transformation.

"Think with what savagery you would struggle and how fiercely you would fight if your own sanity were at stake, if you or your opponent would absolutely lose your mind upon the outcome of a battle. Of course you would endure anything and use all your resources to defend yourself and destroy your enemy.

"The physical body has a well-documented and truly incredible survival instinct. And the mind is also programmed to defend itself from harm and maintain its own integrity. But the human soul, by whatever name you prefer to call it, has the highest threshold of all for any pain or adversity it has to endure. The soul, like the body, will do its utmost to extend its own survival, and assure the fidelity of its own being.

"And right there, at the deepest level of your soul, you have the greatest weapons to defeat your adversary in whatever form he, she, or it may appear.

"Now, I finally ask you to understand, *the sanity of all humanity is at stake.* And, that sanity, as questionable as it may be, determines the very nature of our reality, both subjective and objective.

"Reality for each of us.

"Reality for all of us.

"That is what we are fighting for.

"And that is why we must win.

"This war is so ancient, we can almost call it timeless, but in fact it isn't timeless. It is crucial to understand that it began at a specific point in the past, and it will end at a specific point in the future.

"There will be victors and vanquished. The wishes and purposes of the victors will determine reality for all.

"*Real reality*. Not just images. Everything from the physics of energy and time, to the perception of pleasure and pain.

"But this war will never show up as a proposition on an election ballot, or a resolution at the United Nations.

"The simple majority will not predominate because the majority does not even know what is going on. Only the most powerful will win. But the power I am talking about can only be acquired through knowledge of the ability to manipulate the unsuspecting majority through the use of their own imaginations.

"Here and now with me, you can know anything anyone else can know, and you can be one of the winners.

"You already know the nature of the struggle and the identity of the forces involved.

"You also know how to find me whenever you want me *or whenever you need to become me*.

"I learned the hard way. If you only care about yourself and the person you love, maybe you don't really care about anyone at all.

"We are all in this together. We need to get help and we need to give help. And two is not enough. Three is the magic number.

"Little people, big people, living people, dead people, in all dimensions and all times, we all have to help each other.

"The only thing in the Universe is People.

"We created the Universe, and we are the Universe.

"Now, please relay this message to everyone you know on all relevant psychic planes, by all means available.

"This is it.

"Here and now boys and girls.

"This is the final warning."

(Click. Send now.)

Hundreds of thousands of computers, smart phones, televisions, and pocket organizers made the same announcement at the same time in dozens of languages all over the globe.

VCK's trilingual hand-held was programmed to speak to him in English with the familiar greeting "You have mail."

37. THE PERFECT BUDDHA'S HEAD

It was all over now, finally, and just in time. Vinney could continue the charade no longer.

He knew his dead daughter had never talked to him of her own free will. He figured that out long ago. But he believed she could talk to him now. That is, as soon as he eliminated the interference from the Originator and settled the score with Genetic and the Holy Conman.

Vinney also knew Genetic Freeman was ripe for the taking, and as ready as he would ever be to fit into Vinney's plan. That is why he had the Perfect Buddha's Head. He didn't need the U.S. government anymore. He didn't need agency sanction or executive authorization. He didn't need his superiors to approve what they couldn't understand anyway.

He knew he was insane. But that was all right. Sanity offered him no hope, and no particular advantages anymore anyway. He had the Buddha's Head and he had done his homework on the characters and methods involved. Naturally, he chose Genetic to accompany him in his final operation. The younger man had experience, and his purpose was compatible, up to a point, of course. Genetic just needed guidance, and the presence of a steady hand to help him maintain his balance.

So, VCK donned his best and last disguise, as a bent and frail, sagging old woman. Then he went shuffling along the promenade in Shibuya, just after 3:00 p.m. It would take him nine minutes to reach

Tower Records like this, but Genetic would get out of the bank and overtake him well before that time was up.

One look in the eyes, and then one touch was all he needed. He drove away with Genetic safe and secure in the back seat of a gleaming Yellow Taxi. They were going out to the country for the same reason the Dreamer took Genetic out to the country when he used the Perfect Buddha's Head. It would be a convenient place to dispose of a dead body if there should be need to produce one.

Genetic woke well after sunset, and Vinney was all set to go. Genetic saw VCK and the Perfect Buddha's Head. So he took his position. He was more than resigned to his fate. He was eager for it. This is what he had always wanted; this is why he had been born. He knew he would bring Allison back this time, even if he died in the process.

* * *

They went to meet the Holy Conman face-to-face, in the only place he could ever be found. The deadliest and most extreme of all destinations in the entire Universe. Across the cosmic precipice into the biggest and blackest of all black holes, that no human would ever enter alive, no matter what technology was developed and employed.

First, they located the Originator, cowering deep in the bowels of the Holy Conman's composite spiritual body. VCK neutralized him by inhalation and absorption before the Originator could make any sense of the fact that VCK was just here a minute ago working at his side to incite a rebellion among the lower-level operators.

VCK could have killed the Originator anytime he wanted. And he often wondered why he didn't. But, as he suspected, there was always a reason. VCK never killed anyone without a reason. And he never let anyone live without a reason either.

The Originator knew the way in. He knew how to penetrate to the core of the Holy Conman's being. He was, of course, the first human to ever do so.

VCK followed him in.

The Originator led VCK to the right place, and showed him exactly what he was looking for. Then VCK knew, finally, he didn't need the Originator anymore.

It felt good to do the right thing at the right time, and finally be able to move on, progress to a higher level of accomplishment in this life.

* * *

And then, immediately, in one explosive and irreversible instant: all thought ceased.

There he was. The Holy Conman. All the billions and billions of beings in one omniscient and omnipresent being. Overlooking the intruders. Breathing fire. Fearing nothing at all, now or ever.

The Holy Conman was wondering, more than *how* these two had gotten here, *why* they could possibly want to be here. They were not even dead yet. What could they possibly want? He thought, as he observed the fragility of their forms, that perhaps life on Earth had become so unbearable, now was the time to start it all over again, yet one more time.

However, the Holy Conman was utterly baffled to see their forms suddenly and without premeditation, multiply into millions of fractal images of self, then combine and solidify into a raging white-hot star, brighter than any in all the black skies. The Holy Conman knew without being able to explain why or how, that they had bypassed him. These mortals had somehow tapped into the power behind all powers.

They had become able to intuit the correct weight of a neutrino, and deal with all the complexity, density and turbulence of space-time beyond human imagination.

The illusion of the Holy Conman's elaborate, infinitely complex hierarchy of beings was shattered.

The inherent fallacy of individuality that formed his identity was vanquished, and then vanished as if it had never existed in the first place. Infinite Universes were compressed into one single point of utterly incomprehensible density.

The Holy Conman tried in vain to avoid an unimaginable celestial tragedy. The white-hot star that had been Genetic Freeman and Vinney Cold Killer, dissolved into a blistering black hole, giving birth to a singularity of undifferentiated fiery liquid, which congealed for one final instant of nobody's time.

And then it was too late.

It was the perfect cosmic mirror.

The Holy Conman saw a reflection of his own being, for the first time ever, exactly as it was. A truly magnificent multi-dimensional pyramid of nothingness. Here and now, hollow and illusory as a dream.

* * *

Hasatan. Ha Satan. The Satan. The S-T-N.

Hebrew for the Enemy, the Adversary.

Ha Satan is in the Old Testament, in the Story of Job. Ha Satan challenges God to test his favorite, most faithful, loving and beloved human, Job, with mental and physical suffering.

And Job was driven to curse his own birth.

Ha Satan. He was a Son of God. But his Father cursed him, to die like a man.

Like a man, but he is not a man.

And he never died like one either.

Not yet. Not until now.

38. SOMEWHERE ONLY YOU CAN FIND ME

Now, at this instant, I am here, in undefined blackness.

I feel definition begin to form around me.

There are four walls out there somewhere, perfectly quiet, sound-proof. There is a black carpet floor, sloping down gradually to a black and shadowy stage. Overhead is a matte black ceiling with only the subtlest hint of phosphorescence around its edges coming from two red-light exit signs at the rear.

A thick curtain is rising slowly, soundlessly above the empty stage. The uniform blackness is differentiating into many shades of gray. One ill-defined lump on the stage remains lifeless and undisturbed.

The Sun begins to rise from stage right. Not stage lighting, but the Sun itself, just beginning to breach the distant horizon.

Birds begin chirping. Leaves are rustling in a gentle breeze. I feel a morning chill and smell flowers in the air.

The Sun....

This is the same Sun rising now just as I have seen it many times before, yet it is exquisitely more majestic and unadulterated.

"This is the real thing," I whisper, "the rhythmic source of life on Earth. Listen to our universal pulse."

Buh dum. Buh dum. Buh dum.

It happens every day, but I can't remember the last time I felt the rhythm. I can't remember the last time I saw the grandeur.

Where have I been?

Was my memory only one day old?

How could I possibly have missed yesterday's sunrise?

It is incredible!

The Sun grows bigger, brighter, and then I have to turn away.

I see an expansive blue ocean meet an even vaster blue sky.

Clouds, how funny they seem. Unpredictable shapes, there in the middle of everything, and moving, changing their forms capriciously.

* * *

"Genetic, are you here?" I call, and feel a rain of playful electric tingles pulsing through my being in a meaningful sequence I can only translate as, "Yes Allison, we are here, together forever."

But there is so much more significance to it than that, so many more questions are answered. So much fatigue is lifted. So much energy is set free.

"Good God!" I had to ask, "How did you end up here?"

"I needed to be somewhere only you could find me."

* * *

Beautifully complex rhythms of infinitely varied pulses, each one identifiable only for an instant, then and always, part of an ocean of light, no, bigger, a milky way, an unlimited cosmic flow, a....

And there I am.

I myself am pulsing for one infinite instant.

39. BORN AGAIN AND AGAIN
Honolulu, December 31, 1999

"Begin at the end," the demon whispers, as if someone else could hear.

If it were only that easy, I think, telling my wife, Sayako, "Push, push harder. His head is already out. Push. Push."

His slick silver shoulders pop right out.

Then, in another quick motion his long arched back slurps all the way out. It is half-again as long as I had imagined it would be.

I lean forward and hold my breath.

As the blood rushes to fill the spaces behind his silver skin, his hips and legs are pulled along by his own momentum.

I am pushed back by a force I cannot see.

My breath is sucked out of my lungs before I even realize it.

I hear my own voice as it echoes in the antiseptic air: "What is at the end of death?"

"Birth, of course," is the demon's instant reply.

I cut the baby's umbilical cord, as it is presented to me, with the scissors a nurse has placed in my hand.

I wait a long minute as the medical team busily checks and cleans my son on top of a stainless steel cart built and equipped for that purpose.

A nurse wraps the newborn baby inside a white cotton-soft blanket and hands him to me.

I remember being told by the Lizard Lady, "You can look into your true lover's eyes and see anything you want."

My son's eyes are squeezed shut, just as they'd been throughout his time in his mother's amniotic sac, but the lashes are already long and beautiful. The eyebrows are smooth and shiny.

The left eye remains still as the right eye begins to flutter. It takes a few more seconds for the right eye to open fully.

Then, there is one open eye. Luscious. Liquid. Luminescent.

There is a fleeting incongruity of having one eye opened with the other yet unused.

Then, the left eye too flutters itself open.

"Here," I say, handing him to Sayako. "Look at his eyes."

* * *

"Good God! How did you end up here?" I hear a voice on a frequency to which only I have access.

And I hear another voice answer on that same mysterious frequency, "I needed to be somewhere only you could find me."

The End

About the author:

Anthony Lojac, JD, CFP® has worked as a lawyer and Financial Advisor in New York, Los Angeles, Honolulu, and Tokyo.

He has also been a life-long student of occult philosophies, comparative religion, literature, technology, and art.

Anthony has produced experimental literature and various other creative projects on and off the Internet. He has done live performances including poetry and spoken word.

His hobbies include sailing, cooking, exercise, and travel.

He writes fiction and nonfiction.

Please visit www.lojac.net for more information.

other titles by
Anthony Lojac, JD, CFP®
may also be purchased from:
amazon.com
other major book sellers
&
directly from the publisher

Business & Investing Keywords
in English & Japanese
Essential Vocabulary for
International Investors & Entrepreneurs
(published 2009)

Internet & New Media
in English & Japanese
(coming soon)

THINK MORE BOOKS
269 S. Beverly Drive #1400
Beverly Hills, CA 90212 USA
www.thinkmorebooks.com
editor@thinkmorebooks.com

www.ingramcontent.com/pod-product-compliance
Lightning Source LLC
Chambersburg PA
CBHW071255170626
46809CB00001B/235